all we know of heaven

NATIONAL BESTSELLING AUTHOR

# JACQUELYN MITCHARD

## *all we know of heaven*

A NOVEL

**HARPER**TEEN
*An Imprint of* HarperCollins*Publishers*

HarperTeen is an imprint of HarperCollins Publishers.

www.harperteen.com

Library of Congress Cataloging-in-Publication Data is available.
ISBN 978-0-06-134578-4 (trade bdg.) — ISBN 978-0-06-134579-1 (lib. bdg.)

Typography by Jennifer Heuer
1 2 3 4 5 6 7 8 9 10
❖
First Edition

for melanie donovan

My life closed twice before its close;
    It yet remains to see
If Immortality unveil
    A third event to me,

So huge, so hopeless to conceive,
    As these that twice befell.
Parting is all we know of heaven,
    And all we need of hell.

*—Emily Dickinson*

PART I

# bridget and maureen

# the first valentine's day

Once she understood that she was dead, her first thought was that heaven was overrated.

Perhaps she wasn't in heaven but in purgatory, sort of heaven's mudroom. Either way, everything her grandmother and Father Genovese had taught her was a lie.

There were no streets of gold or a cappella singing, no elderly ancestors like little apple dolls gathered to welcome her, no mountain sunsets—not even Disney World without lines.

But it took such a long time to think of this that it made her wonder if she was alive—or if maybe being dead took getting used to, like cold

3

water or the dentist.

At first she could only think of the place where she was as PUH.

And even for that she had to sort of scale her way up her thoughts, as if thinking was a climbing rope in the gym.

Pee.

Pie.

Please.

Tree.

See.

Seats.

Store.

NO! Nononono. NO. START OVER.

Story.

Pie story.

Pug hug.

Piggy hug.

Pug.

It took her many times, as long as a carpet unrolling forever, to think of the word for . . . purgatory. Trying to wiggle into her own mind wore her out. She couldn't even find the door.

And being an angel was supposed to be easy compared with life. But did angels think? Maybe she wasn't an angel.

Maybe what she'd done with Danny had disqualified her.

*Maybe only ghosts had these kinds of issues.*

*How was it possible that she could think of words such as "disqualified" and "issues" but not ordinary words—and she knew that there were words—for the "lights" and "darks"? How could she remember Danny but not, half the time, her own name?*

*Her mind was like her grandmother's refrigerator: a jumble of little things, some moldy beyond recognition but still frugally saved—two brown coins of banana, a few spoonfuls of rice— all in little plastic-wrapped squares. And she couldn't open the stuck-together little squares. She couldn't get them unstuck any more than she could open her eyes. She couldn't get her eyes to open, not even for a second.*

*She wasn't sad.*

*You weren't supposed to be sad at your death. But she wasn't joyous either.*

*Where was the bliss?*


When they were tiny, adults called them the Pigtail Pals, as if they were a brand of doll. When they were bigger, they called them the Dyno Mites, as if they were a stomp team. Always together—two elfin blond things, tiny but shockingly strong (Bridget could walk up thirteen stairs on her hands by the time she was eight). They took Tumbleweeds together at the Y and after that headed off to cheerleading classes and camp, even though at their school it was the pom girls who had been revered as sex goddesses and the cheerleaders treated basically like scum. But now that they were sophomores there were cheerleading movies (and no pom-pom movies!); plus, the cheerleaders had the best bodies of anyone, thighs with strips of long, lean muscle that amazed even the girls themselves when they stood in front of a mirror in underpants.

Sometimes it seemed worth it.

As they had grown older—at least according to Maureen's older brother Jack—they resembled each other even more. Sometimes they bought the same clothes in different colors, if Maureen could afford them. If Maureen couldn't, sometimes Bridget bought the clothes for both of them. On sale, but still.

They loved being seen as a pair.

Bridget and Maureen took pride in the marks on the Flannery garage door that showed, year after year, that they were exactly the same height—not one half inch taller or shorter. They had the same huge, almond-slanted gold-flecked green eyes; and they could charm anyone—usually out of anything. Well, Bridget was the one who did the charming, which was what Maureen both loved and feared about her.

"My older sister was a Girl Scout," Bridget once told the lady who sold Girl Scout cookies outside the Shop-and-Save. "She's in the . . . in an insane hospital now, and she can't be a Girl Scout anymore. She still wears her outfit and her badges and pretends she is. She used to sell cookies."

Bridget didn't even *have* an older sister.

But her earnest sweetness as she lied was always good for a free box of Thin Mints. Somehow the lady at the Shop-and-Save never compared notes with the ladies at the Bigelow Bank or the Coffee Clutch.

"Where did you get all those cookies?" Maureen's mother had asked, when Maureen came home with a box stuffed nonchalantly inside her hoodie.

"Ladies gave us boxes of them," Maury had told her honestly.

"You're not supposed to take things from strangers!" her mother snapped, examining the boxes as if they might contain razor blades or arsenic.

"They weren't strangers," Maury said. "It was Mrs. Hotchkiss and the lunch lady at Henry's school, Miss Bliss. They were sitting inside the bank."

"Why'd they give them to you for free?"

"They like us," Maury said.

That was a fact.

It was only one of the privileges of being Bridget's friend, as Bridget explained solemnly. By the time she was six she had understood the meaning of "privilege." She knew it was good to be her. She understood her own charisma.

You didn't dare to say no to Bridget—not if you wanted to stay friends with her.

And you *did* want to stay her friend.

Everyone did.

She picked up friendships the way tape picked up lint from a sweater—effortlessly, easily, and with about as much passion. Friends were a delight to Bridget but—with the exception of Maury—readily interchangeable. Maureen was proud to be the first friend Bridget collected when she came to Bigelow and the one she had kept. Aside from Maury, Bridget took you as a BFF for two weeks, gave you the whole Bridget treatment—the pool, gymnastics on the huge tramp, b-ball and tennis on the sport courts—but most of her best friends didn't last a semester, let alone forever.

But then people at school were always recycling friendships and stealing boyfriends, putting nasty things into one another's backpacks and then telling the principal so that the innocent person got suspended. Maureen thought people treated betrayal and cruelty like a party game, though she did it, too. Still, it made her sick to hear someone say, "Here comes Em-ILL-EE. Must be Skanky Girl Day . . ." She made it a point to be sure that Bridget never had cause to put her down.

Maury treated Bridget's house like an addition built onto her own. She didn't even have to knock to go in.

Maury couldn't imagine how she would live without Bridget.

Even when Bridget had fallen in love, if she was with Danny on a date, Bridget came to Maureen's to sleep over afterward or Maureen would be waiting at Bridget's for her when she got home.

The O'Malleys, with their many children, had lived in Bigelow forever. There was a trophy case where Bill O'Malley's wrestling trophy (second in state, 1974) was still displayed. He had carved his name in a heart with the name of Jeannie Forbes on the workbench in shop class—two years before she became Jean Marie O'Malley.

But Bridget's family came to Bigelow the summer that Maureen was five.

From Chicago.

Mr. and Mrs. Flannery opened a business called Occasions that planned weddings and graduations, anniversaries and card parties. People only had to make one call, and Bridget's parents would handle everything from the food to the flowers to the tent to the deejay. The slogan was "Flannery's Occasions: We Bring Everything Except the Memories." Everyone said a business like that would last in Bigelow about as long as a French hairstylist, or a French restaurant. People were pretty set in their ways there.

Bigelow summers were short and brutally hot. People got married in the Lutheran church—even if they were Catholics—because the Lutherans had central air. Kids spent summer vacation underwater in Slipper Lake; they didn't mind pulling the leeches off their legs or having everything they touched smell permanently of bug repellant. Unless they were wacko-committed backpackers or runners, adults spent most days and nights inside with the air on after about the first two weeks of June. If they could bear the heat, they sat on screened porches because the mosquitoes got as big and hairy as Shih Tzus.

Winters lasted nine months, and the same rule held true: stay inside.

"Bigelow," Bridget said. "The town where living human beings are sighted only during the month of October."

Privately, she thought people in Minnesota were wimps. She only dimly remembered her life in Chicago, but there you were out no matter what the weather.

The Flannerys' business didn't fail (and neither did Euro-Cuts, which opened two years later).

Bridget was like her parents. She believed absolutely that there was nothing truly impossible for her. The bike jump at the end of the cul-de-sac was sort of for the boys; but Bridget, in her silver helmet, routinely sailed off it, and landed safely.

"I'm self-relying," she told Maureen when they were nine or ten. "My parents let me stay home alone since I was seven. With the baby."

The Flannerys bought the Stoddard house, on the same block as the O'Malleys but, for practical purposes, on another planet. Wynn Stoddard had owned four banks before his death from a stroke, after which Annika Stoddard just couldn't keep the place up. Although none of the O'Malley kids had ever really seen the inside of the Stoddard house, they imagined it was like a house where movie stars lived. The room Bridget's parents would sleep in was as big as the whole downstairs at the O'Malleys'. There was a pool with a slide behind black iron gates in the back. In the tile at the bottom of the pool was a mosaic of a dolphin.

Naturally, everybody expected the Flannerys to be stuck up.

They weren't at all. They were friendly and thoughtful and had big block parties.

Stuck up or not, Maury saw early on that Bridget would always get away with murder. She took money from the family's Christmas charity jar and bought twenty kids soft-serve from the Big Dipper truck. She climbed so high into the poplar tree in her yard that when a storm approached, her mother had to call the fire department to rescue her while the tree swayed back and forth and Bridget, unafraid, waved to the other kids on the block—whose parents kept yelling at them to come inside.

The tree incident had happened the summer that the Flannerys moved to Bigelow. Maureen was only one of the crowd of kids from Bigelow Court who watched in awe. She didn't know Bridget to speak to, only to admire.

But on the first day of kindergarten, Bridget asked Maureen, "Do you want to be my friend?"

When Bridget asked her if she wanted to be friends, Maury didn't know what to say. She didn't have friends yet; she only played with her mother and her brothers and her cousins.

"Don't you want to be my friend?" Bridget asked again, stepping a pace closer.

Maureen shrugged, unsure of what to say. The new girl's pigtails looked exactly like her own pigtails, her greenish eyes duplicates of hers. But Bridget wore Top Shelf jean shorts and a shirt that spelled out ANGEL DOLL in rhinestones. Maureen wore a terry cloth top with a kitty on the shoulder that her mother bought at Koberly's for seven dollars and ninety-nine cents. All the O'Malley kids only had clothes that "went" with all their other clothes.

"If you want to be my friend," Bridget went on, "you have to do what I tell you."

This was the test. What Bridget told Maury to do was to help lock the door and push all the little desks against it when Teacher left the room to get her new attendance book. Terrified, Maury found herself shoving desks over to the door as they listened to the teacher's outraged pounding. She did pee her pants a little and start to cry. But she did what Bridget told her.

"Don't be a baby!" Bridget told her sharply. "If you're a scaredy-baby, we can't have any fun."

A maintenance guy ended up having to climb in the window and let Miss Hoskins back into her own room.

This set the pattern for Bridget's and Maureen's life for the next eleven years.

When six girls went to RollerAmerica with Mrs. Flannery for Bridget's ninth birthday, Bridget told Maureen that only babies held on at the top of the roller coaster. It wasn't until the second time around that Maureen noticed that she and Bridget were the only ones with their hands up.

The dares never stopped.

They stole glitter eye shadow from the sale bins at Koberly's. Maureen—who probably looked as helplessly guilty as if she'd stolen diamonds instead of a tiny plastic case containing a cake of blue and a cake of gold—was the one who got caught.

But Bridget stuck by her.

"It was all my idea!" Bridget insisted to the mean lady store detective who saw this only as evidence of Bridget's virtue. Bridget was relieved, but horrified that Maury had to take the punch.

"You're lucky to have a friend who tries to protect you!" the mean lady lectured Maureen. And as a punishment, she made Maureen put on *all kinds* of makeup and then called her parents so they could see her looking that way.

Mrs. O'Malley grounded Maureen for three weeks; but Bridget, who was truly sorry, rigged a basket-and-string system outside Maureen's window so that she could send up more stolen makeup and a box of gourmet brownies left over from an "Occasion."

She gave Maureen things that her own family would never be able to afford—and for keeps, no take backs: fuzzy sweaters, stuffed animals, bubble bath, an MP3 player with FLANNERY'S OCCASIONS etched into the case. When they both had a crush on Brandon Hillier, they called him from pay phones so he'd never be able to trace their number. After he started going out with Becca Donahue, they scraped the filling out of Oreos and replaced it with toothpaste, leaving the cookies in a red bag covered with hearts and tied with a bow outside Brandon's locker, signing it with a forgery of Becca's big, babyish scrawl.

Bridget loved Maureen. Even after she fell in love forever

with Danny Carmody, Bridget pledged to see Danny only on Saturday nights—both so that she wouldn't get the reputation of being a "wifey girl" and so that Maureen, who didn't have a guy, wouldn't feel left out.

Maureen managed to keep Bridget's sweet sixteen party from her for six weeks—even though Bridget's parents and half of the class were in on it.

Nothing fazed Bridget.

But when she complained about having to help her siblings take down the tent in the giant heated display shed that cold night, only to have three hundred colored lanterns burst to life and a hundred kids yell "Surprise!" Bridget melted into tears. Maury was as happy as if Bridget had given her a sweet sixteen party back last spring. She had given Maureen a locket, real gold, with the pictures they'd had taken together at the mall, the black-and-white ones when they wore men's hats and black slip dresses. And that was really special.

Bridget's birthday was December 10.

Winter break started December 23, but Maury and Bridget had practice because there was a cheering competition on Christmas Eve. ("It's sacrilege!" Mrs. O'Malley insisted.)

Maureen didn't mind—but then she pulled a groin muscle and knew she would have to stuff herself with ibuprofen and wrap her thigh in the morning and even then she might not be in any shape to compete.

"Like we care about this competition! There are like four

schools in it! It's not even a real regional," said Bridget. "You want me to drive, Maury, so you can rest your leg?"

"That would be great, Bug."

And they slapped palms and threw their gym bags into the back of Maureen's Toyota.

# county highway g, december 23 7 p.m.

From a branch of one of the trees hung a little letter jacket. From another hung a sock. One of them pointed that out right away. They could see the jacket, the sock, and the glittery little megaphone that hung from the zipper—like grotesque ornaments on a Christmas tree—despite the sheltering wing of pine bough draped in heavy snow.

They could see other things, too.

"Is there blood on the trunk of the tree?" Leland Holtzer asked. She was glad that she and Caitlin Smith were there. No one else could say that they actually had been *there* before Maureen was even taken away. The cell phone tree—and Cody Halavay's police band radio—had alerted everyone, news racing through the air like blood through an artery. She asked again, "Is there blood on that tree?"

"It could be just sap or something," said Eric Kroger, the guy Leland was sort of with, though so far all they'd done was have one heavy makeout session in Britney Broussard's rec room. She wondered if they would be going out now because this was one of those things that, if you went through it with another person, bonded you forever.

A thing that changed you forever. And she was only sixteen. Leland shivered with horror and excitement.

*Forever*, Leland thought.

The snow kept falling as the police worked for hours past sundown. It fell so hard that Bob Haackstad, who was mighty religious, said it was like a vengeance. But the chief, Henry Colette, spoke up and asked Bob: A vengeance for what? No one did wrong here. Just two kids and a poor, tired, long-haul driver trying to get home for Christmas.

The skid marks told it all.

The little white Toyota had crossed the line.

The poor truck driver was not hurt, but no one could say he hadn't suffered.

He was there, working right alongside them, his cigar shredded by the snow, his stubbled chin trembling. He tried to collect the debris from his rig—the headlights and the big, ornate hood ornament.

The driver scared them at first, to be honest.

The minute they showed up, when the gasoline was still pouring and the motors were whining and smoking, he came running up out of the ditch in the woods carrying Bridget in his arms, blood all over him. The paramedics wanted to kill him on the spot for moving her.

Not until later did they find out that at least some the blood was from his mouth, which he'd knocked on the steering wheel jumping down from his cab. He ran down into the ditch in the woods after Bridget. She had been thrown that far from the vehicle, thirty feet or better.

He shouldn't have moved her.

But after they got her on the board and assessed her, all of them were thinking the same thing, though no one was saying it, that it probably wouldn't matter. Except for the bruises and the smears of dirty snow, the skin on Bridget's legs was as white as her sweater was red, her lips the color of a storm cloud—dark blue. You couldn't tell if she was blond or brunette, or a white or a black girl, or even a girl. Everything was pushed out of shape. Hat Carney, the veteran medic on call that afternoon, thought of a broken egg, or a watermelon thrown against a tree. There were no words for how awful it was. But they got a tube down her windpipe and got it working right away anyhow. They couldn't bear not to. They started a line running Ringer's and administered epi while they screamed through the small towns and onto the highway—talking to the docs at Anne Morrow Lindbergh Children's Hospital and Clinics in Minneapolis all the way.

About five minutes away, they got a thready pulse. The ambulance driver kicked the pedal and two-wheeled it into the bay.

Back at the scene, Maureen was a sodden, broken thing being extracted by the Jaws of Life.

The trucker watched. He asked if he was being charged with a crime.

"Of course not," said Henry Colette. The trucker then shocked Henry by grabbing his arms and leaning on him like he was his long-lost brother.

He babbled out, "They crossed right in front of me, on my mother's grave if I'm lying! They didn't see me none! I wouldn't ever hurt anyone. I wasn't going but forty! All I had to get to was the Days Inn up there a mile! The snow 'n' all! One more mile!"

To Patrolman Denny Folly, only a few years older than the girls and about to puke, the trucker said, "I saw the blond one's little face!"

"They were both blond," said Henry Colette.

Denny Folly pointed to the tree. "That has to be hair and skin," he said. The kid was gray. Who would clean that up, Colette thought? Not the coroner. He couldn't just leave it there. Colette grabbed an evidence bag out of his inside pocket and packed the matter from the tree into a zipped bag with a little snow. He handed it to Denny Folly, who did disappear for a moment then into the trees.

If Colette had a best friend apart from his wife, Margo, it was certainly Bill O'Malley. They had wrestled together at Bigelow and UM, roomed together all four years, stood up in each other's weddings. They didn't see each other as much now, but their four-day catfishing trip to Kentucky each spring was a sacred tradition; and Henry Colette stood godfather to one of Bill's twin boys, the one called William Henry, who went by Colette's own first name. Henry and Jack O'Malley were sophomores at Gustavus Adophus now, which must cost Bill a pretty penny, although Henry expected the twins had good scholarships. When the children were younger, they all went to the Boundary Waters together for a few summers. Henry Colette thought of Maury's sweet soprano last Christmas in the pageant given by the kids making their confirmation at Holy Mother of Sorrows. She sang one of four solos: "Some children see Him dark as they. . . ."

Now Colette's own voice sounded like a shovel driven through a crust of icy mud. He barked instructions to the officers: Pick that up; call this service or that. They watched as he looked over the trucker for signs that he was drunk or drugged up. The truck driver was no local: He drove for Memphis Mercury Cartage, a long way from home. He smelled of nothing but vinegar chips and blood. On some impulse, Colette took out his cell phone and called his Margo to ask if the man could stay over with them until inquiries were made, have a hot shower and a sleep in the guest room. He couldn't bear the thought of the guy alone with his thoughts in some cheesy motel—Colette happened to know that the Days Inn was filled with Christmas travelers and there were rooms only at the Wood Haven, a low-rent, rendezvous sort of joint. He even asked Margo if she would make some doughnuts and hot coffee. Margo already had the fryer out for making the cinnamon doughnut holes the grandkids loved for late breakfast on Christmas morning.

Colette told Denny Folly to drive the trucker, whose name was Lawrence Cooper, to his house, though he had no idea why he didn't simply go himself. There was no point standing out in this weather after the Jaws were used to pry Maureen free from the driver's side.

From what Colette could see, this was going to be as bad as that night, twenty years ago, when he worked as a Berry County deputy under old Sheriff Corcoran. It was a night as tender and warm as this one was bitter. The driver of the car carrying the Cleary girls (both of them, Diane and Deborah) and their dates, who were coming home from the Teke formal at Bright Wing Country Club, hit the Fortenses' oldest boy in his new, big, black pickup. A Dodge, if Henry Colette remembered. Not one of those kids lived. Diane was three months pregnant—secretly engaged, the way kids were twenty years ago even when they were just seniors in high school, planning to get married in a month. The top of Deborah Cleary's head . . .

Henry Colette, thirty years on the job, ten as chief, thought that maybe he was getting too old to do this anymore. Getting old.

Or maybe no one was young enough for this kind of sight.

21

Six officers tried to shield Maureen from the eyes of all those kids—fifty or more of them by then—while the medics moved her. Her face so swollen it looked like a Halloween mask, blood black as syrup all over her, her arms limp as if connected with string. Somehow she was still talking when the medics reached her, answering their questions about where she had been—cheerleading practice for the holiday competition. Then suddenly she went quiet. The medics ramped up to crazy then.

The second ambulance went screaming past the line of kids standing there shivering—their big eyes wide as deer eyes—the girls crying openly, the boys rubbing their faces on the sleeves of their Carhartts.

Colette stood, the snow frosting his beard, and watched as a big pushing vehicle from the Cities came to move the vehicles off the road. They would wait for the snow to let up to load the wrecked truck and car and haul them away.

*The kids should go,* Henry thought. "Go on now. It's bad out," Colette called softly to them. "There's nothing to see here."

But the kids stayed.

Finally, Colette shrugged and jammed his hat on his head and got into his car. He passed the single squad with two deputies hunkered down half a mile away at the roadblock. They would be there until morning, keeping any traffic off G at this stretch. "Merry Christmas now if I don't see you," he told Mary Folly (Denny's older sister and, to be honest, a better cop than Denny) and her partner, Kemper, a veteran who managed to make waiting to collect his pension look

22

like hard duty. Kemper needed to go on a diet, and after the first of the year Collette would get Kemper running off some of that gut at the Y.

Colette sighed, u-ey'ed his squad car and headed for home. He wouldn't stay longer than it took to explain all of this in detail to Margo; then he would head for the hospital. His place was with Bill and Jeannie now. God, he dreaded it. If he got home that night at all he'd be lucky. Or unlucky, depending on how it went.

It was possible, just possible, that Maureen would make it. He had heard her speak.

Or maybe it was only because it was Christmas and he couldn't bear to believe anything else.

*She was thirsty. Her lips were sore and swollen. She could hear them scratching against each other, taste the blood. Somehow her mouth moved without her telling it to.*

*She picked away at the word for . . . that shiny thing. The thing on the flat beside her. What was it called?*

*Flash.*

*Flashy.*

*Watts.*

*What.*

*Gulls.*

*Grease.*

*Gus.*

GUH-LUS.

And then she had to remember how you used a thing that was called, for no reason, a GUH-LUS and shaped like a permanent bubble.

What was it for?

To put over things. You would put it over things. A little thing that ran. Quicky. Flicky. With long . . . wavy things . . . long legs . . . no, no long hairs . . . no whiskers! Over a mouse! You would put it over a mouse.

No.

You would look through things it at . . . things covered with leather, beautiful red leather. Fleather. Flowing things, flowing past the window of her bedroom. Flowing into the trees.

Boards.

Bees.

Birds.

They lived in bird huts.

Birdhuts.

Danny made them little birdhuts. In his ship, shop, his shipshape shop, at his own hut.

He learned how in ship class.

There.

No!

It was for water! A glass was for water. For drinking water. And she was thirsty. It went together.

As soon as she'd finished with one thought she had to figure out another thought. The whole decoding thing began all over again! Every thought—every little thought—was like making a building with LEGOs, matching red to red and yellow to yellow and green to green, long to long and short to short. She wanted to scream, but it wasn't an option. Her mouth wouldn't let her scream. She felt as if her lips were sealed in plastic wrap.

She heard someone soaking . . . spiking— SPEAKING clearly. "You didn't see her then. Mary Helen! She was forty pounds heavier with the fluids! Like a bag of water! Since two days before Christmas Eve. No, it's GOOD how she looks now! It's GOOD, Mary Helen!"

Wibbledibblewibblewhisperwhisper.

"Not just her spleen. Her skull had hairline fractures. It's amazing that they weren't worse fractures. People who get thrown from a car, it's the worst thing! They usually just die. She looks good. Yes, this is what they call GOOD."

Shushwshiperwhisperwhisper.

"I know you wouldn't believe it was her. WE couldn't recognize her."

Those Mary Helen sentences were the first sentences that she heard all in one piece.

The rest was cheesy music in this weird

heaven that went up and down and around like a Ferris wheel, broken up by different voices saying, ". . . so young . . ." ". . . just asleep . . ." ". . . when she was little, do you remember the two of them with sand cupcakes?" and ". . . never one of them without the other . . ." ". . . at least she's at peace."

Last winter?

When was winter?

What was winter?

Go.

Fight.

Winter!

Winner.

Who was she?

She was she, was she, herself. Was she Mary Helen? Mary in hell? No. She was someone else. Who was the someone she was?

She was lying on a bed. Her feet were bare, a lumpy pillow under her neck. Maybe she was at her own funeral.

Her own funeral. That was where she was.

This was an excessively creepy thought, that her eyes might be not-just-shut-but-glued-shut and stuffed with gauze to look still-alive and natural (her great-uncle was a priest and went into way too much detail about these things). But if she were dead she should be an angel able to . . . flow? . . . around above everyone else in the room, to see if aunts and uncles and brothers and . . . other people were there crying over her.

One of the only benefits of being dead was finding out for sure who were really your . . . other people . . . and were staying for the whole thing, including the rosary, not just showing up to sob a little and then be carried out of the room by her boyfriend as she stumbled and cried out your name. If it was Leland Holtzer, she would stop crying right away in the parking lot and say, "Can you believe they didn't close the coffin?"

Maybe it was dark because they had closed the coffin.

But what would that matter to an angel? And the truth was, maybe they didn't need to close the coffin. Actually, she didn't even know how she had died. Maybe she looked great. If she had to be dead, she hoped she looked great. Maybe she broke her neck cheering. It happened. She tried so hard to listen for funeral music, she exhausted herself and fell asleep.

# the cross

The kids crept out onto the road after the chief left. No one spoke.

Tall, slender, elegant Leland spotted a tennis shoe strung with miniature gold-and-black pom-poms and dropped to her knees in the road. She thought if she hadn't been wearing jeans, she would have scraped her legs, she fell that hard. She wondered if anyone else noticed how hard she fell. If the road hadn't been blocked at both ends, she'd have been a target for oncoming traffic. She was glad she didn't care about that. It would have been too, too selfish.

"I'm going to put up a cross right here," she said.

"Lee-Lee, they aren't even dead!" Eric whispered, loud and shocked.

"No one could survive that!" Leland shrieked, pointing to Maureen's Toyota, which looked as if it had been wrung out like a wet towel. The hood was smashed sideways, the wheels up off the ground. Leland knelt down again and picked up the shoe. She thought maybe she would keep it, like, for years and show her daughters someday.

Then she thought she really better put it up with the cross.

She stared at the tennis shoe, still as polished and pristine as Coach Eddington—Eddy—insisted their tennies be. Every inch of their uniforms had to be like an ad for detergent. *You are a representative of Bigelow right down to the tips of your toes,* she said more times than Lee-Lee or the others could count. *You're all Eddy's Angels, better than Charlie's.*

They rolled their eyes when she said it, but it was true.

Unlike other schools that had dance teams of twenty girls in kick lines, Bigelow was so small they had only the cheerleaders. The girls saw the way people gawked at the pom-pom girls from other schools who came for away games. They acted like they were the Dallas Cowboys Cheerleaders.

But Coach Eddington had been part of a national prize-winning team at Oklahoma State. So Eddy's Angels won prizes. Bigelow was first or second in state every year. And so Leland and Sabrina Holtzer, sisters Caitlin and Quinn Smith, Britney Broussard and Brittany Wolner and Brittany Scott, Molly Schottman, Taylor Cuddahy, and, of course, Bridget and Maureen never understood why no one respected them.

29

Why?

They worked hard. They were so much stronger even than the jock girls, never mind the wasties who stayed thin by gobbling handfuls of Dexi-Slim. And even though cheerleading was fairly yesterday in high school, it was coming on in college and on the tube. Didn't anyone know that? But after this, even the big, ugly, fifth-year seniors who liked to get drunk and boo them from the stands would have to be respectful, Leland thought, and she immediately felt guilty. Maybe people would see them as sort of heroes now. This tragedy might make all that went with being one of them halfway worth it.

"Lee-Lee, should we try to get the coat down?" Caitlin Smith asked.

It was Brandon Hillier who climbed the tree—*that* tree, with the stuff on the trunk—to shake the jacket loose. No one could tell if it was Bridget's or Maureen's because they both wore an XS. The pockets were empty except for a stick of Juicy Fruit. Leland searched for a laundry mark, or anything. But there was nothing. Just a white wool jacket with black sleeves and gold lettering. Caitlin held it close, after first checking for blood.

Caitlin Smith wondered how Danny would go on living. Bridget and Danny had been together since seventh grade. Bridget was like his world. And Maureen was like Bridget's sister, so they were almost like three people in a family—if you didn't count your real family, and nobody did. Caitlin knew she would never see her own sister, Quinn, if Quinn wasn't a cheerleader, too, because Quinn was so annoying with her French camp and her guitar, like some weird hippie. Caitlin could not believe it when Sabrina texted them from the hospital: M IS DOA. It was impossible. They were totally messed up, but doctors could put you back together now. They had machines that worked for your heart if they had to fix your heart, even.

It was midnight, and they had a competition in the morning at seven AM in Ludding. Caitlin had no idea how they were going to do it with only one flyer.

"We'll probably drop out," she said.

"But Eddy will want us to do it for them—Maury and Bridget," Leland answered.

"Call her," Caitlin said. "I don't know if it would look right."

Caitlin stabbed in the numbers to call Sabrina instead. Her minutes were already used up, but this was an emergency. When Sabrina picked up, Caitlin totally babbled. They were operating on Bridget. Bridget was going to make it. Nobody said anything about Maureen. Sabrina just assumed she was dead, but she didn't know for sure. Coach Eddington was at the hospital with lots of parents, and she had told Sabrina she had not yet made up her mind if they would compete tomorrow.

Leland swore a streak when Caitlin told her.

"We don't care how things look," Leland said. "We're not in mourning. Eddy should want us to win for them."

Caitlin wondered if Leland wanted to win for *Leland*,

because it would be in the newspaper if the squad went on to victory in spite of tragedy. It was true that lots of teams had only one flyer, and they still had Taylor.

Taylor saw the accident on TV. It was nearly one AM when she showed up, crashing breathless through the woods with her older sister, Rae.

By then they'd found everything they could locate in the dark and snow: three identical size-seven shoes, both girls' gym bags with their cheering practice clothes and bodysuits inside, one brown Ugg boot, the jacket, and Maureen's CD case. Brandon Hillier's father had showed up with some lumber; Brandon must have called him. Mr. Hillier came off-roading through the woods in his big-wheeled truck. Brandon took out one of Maureen's CDs and put it in his dad's player while some of the boys made a cross with the lumber and nails and wrapped it in reflective duct tape. The voice on the CD sang, "My life is brilliant. / My love is pure. / I saw an angel. / Of that I'm sure." It was as lonely as the moaning of the wind.

# early next morning

Amber Kresky, RN, twenty-four years old, whose little sister Britney was also a cheerleader, decided to help the aides clean up the rooms.

Strictly speaking, it wasn't her job.

But she wanted to do it out of respect; and only about half the ED beds were filled, and not with people truly in danger. They were like the guy in three, who'd decided to stop taking his blood thinners and had spent the money on ice-fishing gear.

There were two thousand people in Bigelow, and it was fair to say that almost all of them knew the O'Malleys or the Flannerys from church or the school, where Mr. O'Malley had been the wrestling coach for twenty years.

The Bulldogs were a wrestling dynasty, Division Three state champions four times in the past ten years. Amber's new husband, Mitchell, had wrestled for him. People sent Coach O'Malley so many cookies and six-packs at Christmas that Coach said if he kept it all, he'd be a four-hundred-pound drunk.

Amber smiled softly, as she pulled on a fresh pair of gloves.

Please God, bless Coach O'Malley and Mrs. O'Malley.

Maureen, she heard, was out of surgery. Bridget Flannery was up in the OR. The surgeons were still fighting for her. It was bad, but it was anyone's guess what would happen. The poor little things. No one could say for sure. It was like Dr. Krill and Dr. Collins always said: The first twelve hours told the tale. But Amber knew that kids that sick, even if they lived . . . This might not turn out to be a tale anyone wanted to hear the end of.

Like, not a fairy tale.

She needed to get her mind off it. Get to work.

The parents of Bigelow would be commandeering car keys at the first snowflake for weeks at least, and maybe all winter long.

She hoped so.

If it were up to Amber, her sister Britney would never drive a car again.

She started cleaning the room where Coach's little girl had been. She had coded twice, but they brought her back and sent her up to surgery.

Amber had to catch herself. Not "Coach's little girl."

Maureen was sixteen.

Although she *was* little, only a hair over five feet tall, just exactly the same as Bridget Flannery. The Dyno Mites, everybody called them.

Almost everyone in ED had stood hushed in a silent homage as they passed—running, first with Bridget, then with Maureen—for the elevator, headed up to surgery. *As if the doctors and nurses might salute,* Amber thought.

She sighed and set to work.

The bay looked like a battlefield. It always did.

Amber drew the curtains.

With a nurse's aide, Maria Alvarez, beside her, she stripped away the blood-soaked sheets and pillowcases and began to bag the packages that held tubing and gauze, ripped open and thrown to the floor in the breakneck haste. There was a bloody spatter on the portable X-ray, though not so much as in the other room. Bridget's room.

They had gone in to start her heart again. The medics came thundering through the doors, IV bags aloft, one holding the mask over her mouth while another compressed the bag as they ran, snot and tears frozen on Carl Otterstad's face. Carl had been chief of the volunteer medics for as long as anyone knew. He lived just across the street from the Flannerys and two doors north of the O'Malleys. Carl would have known the worst the second he saw Bridget . . . but they had worked like madmen on her all the way from the north side of Bigelow anyway.

Carl still sat outside in the waiting room, crying. He had waited to say a word to the Flannerys and the O'Malleys after Dr. Collins spoke to them and they went upstairs, but he had missed them. Up there it could be hours. The social worker, Neely Cavendish, walked past and spoke to Carl, laying a hand on his shoulder, before heading for the elevators. Someone else would finish Carl's shift. It was late anyhow. Amber glanced out through the meshed glass at Carl's back, his big hands splayed and covering his face like a hockey helmet as he sobbed. After a little while Chief Colette showed up, too. Amber felt better knowing someone was there with Carl.

When the mops and sterile solutions had arrived for washing down the equipment and the bed, Amber moved over to the other bay.

How could it be just an hour ago that Bridget had been here? The mess was so much worse, actually, because Bridget was better off than Maureen. Bridget had been actively bleeding.

"One, two, three . . ." and lift; Bridget was so tiny that she felt like nothing and so broken that she looked like something built on the set of a horror movie, blood pouring from her nose and her mouth, one leg rag-doll crooked. A broken shoulder and greenstick fracture of the radius were the least of her problems. Marie Kimmer had the IV in her poor groin, with the sucs and pentobarbital that would calm and immobilize Bridget, making it easier for her body to rest

36

and respond. The charting nurse took her place at the portable desk. Tom Katz, the senior resident (who was cute, and who took a lot of teasing from the nurses because of his name) took his place at the foot of the table and called out, "GS three," meaning that Bridget was low on the Glasgow Coma Scale, which was bad. He glanced at his students: the tall, bone-skinny guy who was new and blond Amy Daater, a first-year resident. Joe Deever, the anesthesiologist, did the ABC—airway, breathing, and circulation. Katz's boss, Dr. Collins, the chief, roved around, taking it all in, gently pointing out the tiny details anyone but a twenty-year guy would miss.

Amber stood at Bridget's right shoulder, closest to the monitor, efficiently starting a fresh IV in on the first stick— not that Bridget would have noticed—and then beginning to sponge away surface blood. Dr. Katz looked doubtful about asking the first-year resident, but this was a teaching hospital and so he said quickly, "That blood. Look at the picture. Are we looking at lacerations and some teeth knocked out?"

"It's not really squirting, so I think, yes, she has a broken nose and . . . ," Dr. Daater said. "These teeth will have to be replaced with a bridge if we get that far."

"But we can't rule out . . ."

"A hemothorax . . . Blood in there, so we need an X-ray." A tech had already trundled in the portable X-ray machine.

"And would either of you . . . No, I'm going to place this

subclavian line . . . to . . ."

"Monitor blood pressure," said Dr. Daater, and then felt the idiot. A premed would have said such a thing.

"Right. Now we can see bone here at the side of her head. And I want to say there's a good chance we have a big subdural hematoma. If we have to put in a drain, well, that's another thing for the plastic surgeons. . . . We have to assume, doctors, that her neck is broken until we know otherwise. So even when we move her tongue, we want this C spine stable, " Katz said, and silently slid in the line, just below Bridget's collarbone. They all checked the monitors. Dr. Katz laid his hand on her wrist: Bridget's pulse was racing. "She's in pain, and that could be the reason for this pulse being up there; but at least it's nice and full now, not thready." Her pressure wasn't bad either, and her nail beds were pale but pink. They were going to need to order blood in any event, for fixing her cheek and arm and, if necessary, whatever else they could not see.

What they could not see was usually worse than what they could. And when the X-rays came back, even Doctor Katz cussed.

*She made her mouth move.*

*On her own.*

*She decided to make it happen, instead of just feeling it happen. She thought (it was like climbing the rope in second grade when she was fat and weak) about it for a long time.*

38

Then she tried to make the "tick tick" sound that she used to call Rag Mop, her Yorkie.

She could do it.

Why could she move her mouth?

If she was dead?

She moved her mouth wide open.

Whoa! Suddenly her head hurt. Hurt like a clock exploding inside. Exploding with wires and shards of glass and little clocker knocker chimes. Hurt? Her head hurt like a punching bag. Her chest hurt. Her leg was on fire! And her thigh muscle . . . but she had pulled it, at the last practice. Practice! She wasn't in heaven, or even in purgatory, where the souls just moped around praying and hoping for the best. She was somewhere else. The smells, metal and alcohol and some kind of reeky sweet stuff that made her want to hurl. This was bad, all very, very bad.

# what child is this?

In the following days, the hospital staff tried to limit the number of people who came to see Bridget in the pediatric intensive care unit. It was useless in the end. Somebody always took pity on someone who was family, but not immediate family, or on one of the kids from school.

And Danny. He always got in.

He was so grateful.

His parents and his brothers, and even his best friend, Evan Brock, were honestly scared for him the first night—as if he would ever kill himself. He was no pussy. And he knew that if Bridget woke up, it would be for him. With all they'd been through in four years, she would come back for him.

He knew it; the Flannerys knew it, too.

Even Coach O'Malley knew it. Coach, suffering the way he was, still came back to work after two weeks. Danny was the first one he came up to.

"You were always Maury's good friend," he said. "I want to thank you for that, son. You keep Bridget going for all of us. As long as she's alive, Danny, a little part of my girl is, too."

Danny almost started bawling right there in the weight room.

Maureen's funeral was the saddest thing he had ever seen in his life.

Over a thousand people came. Some stood outside the church in a tent with speakers and space heaters.

Grandma's funeral was sad, because seventy-six wasn't really that old; and she was in the peak of health before she got sick with flu last year. But it was nothing like Maury's.

It was a terrible moment at the funeral when all the cheerleaders came in their uniforms. They lined up beside the coffin and did the Bulldog Salute—putting one stiff arm out to the side and one overhead, then quickly slapping their arms down to their sides. Taylor Cuddahy, the captain, placed the trophy they had won at the Ludding competition the morning after the accident on top of Maury's coffin. She then sang this old song about having your friends winter, spring, summer, and fall. Coach Eddington, who was always jumping around in white shorts and a white polo with her whistle, was wearing some navy blue suit that made her look like a flight attendant who hadn't slept in six months. She began to cry loud enough for everyone to hear when she placed a brand-new varsity sweater on the coffin. Maureen was being buried in her cheering outfit, but no one could see that.

Danny hated leaving Bridget long enough even to go to Maury's funeral, but he had to say good-bye to his friend, too.

He got down on the kneeler and leaned on the pew in front of him with his head on his arms.

Evan Brock, who was sitting next to him with Danny's parents on the other side, said, "It's okay, man," and put his arm around Danny for a second. Danny rubbed his lips and nodded. He looked up, but then he could see the coffin . . . and all the pictures. It was like a freaking museum project.

The O'Malleys (Mom said they were on autopilot) had set up all these boards with pictures of Maury and her brothers and Maury-and-Bridget, Maury-and-Bridget, Maury-and-Bridget. They had pinned Maury's soccer ribbons up there, her letter jacket and about fifty letters from girls all covered with pink heart stickers and crap that said they would never, ever forget her. When his mom talked to Jeannie O'Malley, she said Jeannie staggered and slurred her words because the doctor had given her a downer of some kind. The Flannerys sat right next to Coach and Mrs. O'Malley and their four boys.

Mom saw Danny staring at the boards and said, "They're

never going to be able to give her a wedding or a graduation. They need to do something."

Danny nodded, and then Father Genovese got up. He
smoothed back his hair, something Danny had never seen
him do. It was like he didn't want to go through with this
either. The guy was a nervous wreck.

"We cannot begin to accept or ever hope to understand why this blithe spirit was taken from us," said Father
Genovese, after the traditional "The Lord is with you and
also with you too" stuff. Maury's great-uncle, Father Jim
O'Malley, was there, too, assisting; and he kept reaching
over to pat the quilt on top of the coffin—Mrs. O'Malley had
made it for Maureen's sixteenth birthday out of all her baby
dresses.

"Maureen came to this world as an unexpected gift, a
child her parents never thought they would have. I bap-
tized this sunlight child. She gave us so much light in her
short time on Earth. She sang to us like an angel, like the
angels among whom she may sing now. She was as light
as a leaf, dancing in her ballerina outfits as a little girl
and later on the cheerleading squad she loved. Maureen
showered affection on her dog, her brothers, her circle
of friends, her school . . . and she loved her best friend,
Bridget Flannery. As we pray for the repose of Maureen's
unstained soul, let us take a moment to pray for Bridget's recovery. . . ." Danny felt his face heat up then. He
didn't want to blubber. Maureen was a flower, like Father
Genovese said. If you turned her toward the sun, she was

happy. If you just gave her a smile . . .

She was a girl you could really talk to.

He would sit on the sled hill behind the O'Malleys' house and tell Maury things he would never tell Bridget—about one of his brother David's friends who'd tried to grab him coming out of the shower when he was little and about his hope to work for the FBI someday because he loved the idea of going after real bad guys. He even sang her the country song he wrote that began, "You said I'd walk away from you . . . that I'd get bored or I'd get blue. / I'd be the one to say we're through. . . ."

Bridge would have laughed at him, but Maury looked at him as if he were some kind of genius.

She couldn't understand the guitar. Pianos had keys: They were straightforward. But how did he know how to make a particular note from a combination of six strings, she would ask? Maureen could tell you all the republics in the former Soviet Union but had never even seen Chicago. She'd never been on a plane. She'd never smoked a cigarette except when she and Bridget were little. And though she tried to slam Jell-O shots like the rest of them, she just couldn't.

". . . The last time I saw Maureen, I reprimanded her for doing the Communion sneak. . . ." There was a ripple of subdued laughter at the reference to what kids who still went to church—all six of them—did after Communion at Saturday night Mass. They would walk right out the back door after they took Communion and not wait until the service officially ended. "And she told me that she was sorry and she wouldn't do it anymore but that she always felt that God was in her pocket. . . . She said she felt safe wherever she went, because her parents and God were looking out for her. She told me she didn't know what it would be like to grow up and have to do that for herself. But she will never have to know that pleasure and, yes, that pain, because God has taken her straight from her parents' arms and holds her close and safe now. . . . She never needs to be afraid."

Damn it! Danny heard Mrs. O'Malley make a noise between a scream and a sob. "My baby!"

Mrs. Flannery grabbed her, shushing her as if Mrs. O. were a baby or a puppy.

He thought of that one night when Bridget was away in the Bahamas with her parents on spring break.

He was bored out of his gourd. His parents were putting in a hot tub and so the family didn't go skiing like they usually did at spring break. His buddies were all somewhere else, either on trips or at their grandmothers' houses or something; and it was right after his grandma died.

He ended up going over to see Maureen.

When she opened the door, he busted out laughing. She had on flannel Mickey Mouse drawstrings and a gigantic UM sweatshirt that came down to her knees. But what was funny was that she had this guck on her face, as green and lumpy as guacamole; and she tried to shut the door on his foot. Once she'd let him in she said, "I made it myself, from cucumbers and yogurt. I should probably eat it. But it's supposed to make your pores all clean. . . ."

After she washed it off and tied her hair back, she looked like Bridget's little sister Eliza in her PJs and flip-flops. She brought him her brother Tom's old guitar and, after he tuned it up, asked him to play for her. He played "Dueling Banjos" because girls loved it, even though he missed a bunch of notes.

"I wish I could do that." Maury sighed when he was through.

"It's not that hard," he told her. "I wish I could do trig."

"All the musical notes look like spaghetti to me," Maureen said.

"You mean you don't read the notes in choir?"

"Perfect pitch," she'd said, pointing to her ear and blushing. "If I had to sight-read, I'd be out of it now. Play another one. Nobody's home but me. My parents are at poker club. Jack and Henry are out. And they'll probably be out all night, which will mean a great fight in the morning." The twins were in college at Gustavus Adolphus on scholarships—Jack in soccer and Henry in wrestling—so their father raised hell if they touched a beer or did anything that might get them bounced.

Danny said, "I will if you sing."

"I can't do that."

"I know you can. You sang the solo in church."

"That was church!" Maureen said. "When you're in church, you don't think that people are watching."

"Okay, forget it then," he teased her.

"Well, just once," she said. She got out a book from choir and showed him a song called "Aura Lee," which turned out to be the same as the old Elvis song "Love Me Tender" but with different words about a maid with golden hair.

Maureen's voice was like a flute, strong and pure. She seemed to forget him being there as she sang until the last notes died away, and then she sort of crumpled down on the floor and hid her face. He pulled her back up and said, "Do you take lessons? Because that was beautiful. You should."

She shook her head.

It happened then.

He could never explain it.

Maureen was his pal, his buddy. He loved Bridget totally. But that night he just leaned over and kissed Maureen, and lay down with her on the sofa in the living room; and pretty soon his shirt was off and then hers was . . . and then she was crying and saying it was all her fault and that she would never be able to face Bridget. He had to joke around with her for an hour to get her to stop, asking her if she thought he was a werewolf or something no girl would ever want to kiss or if she was some dog no guy would ever want to kiss.

He meant every word of it. They were still friends. But he got all confused after he left.

Did he spend so much time talking to Maury because he had feelings for her?

Jesus!

They never talked about it again. She seemed to forgive

him. Besides a few dates with Sam Hillier, Brandon's brother, he knew she didn't go out with anybody. It was probably the furthest she ever went with a guy. After he got over feeling lousy about it, he was actually kind of happy, because she was clearly as into it as he was.

Danny leaned his face into his mom's shoulder. He thought his face might give him away—it was sick to have sexy thoughts about a dead girl who was his friend. His mom reached up and touched his cheek.

Near the end of Mass, when everyone was beginning to get hot and the smell of the flowers was sickening, Maureen's cousin Jeremy, who was what Mom called an Irish tenor, sang this old song called "Beautiful Dreamer."

Then came Communion and, finally, Maureen's great-uncle, Father Jim.

Danny thought he was never going to get to the point. His dad frowned at him for shifting around in the pew.

Father Jim said, "That song was a favorite of my mother's. I can remember sixty years ago, her singing it to me with her Irish brogue, although it's not an Irish song. It was written right here, by Stephen Foster, I believe. But in any case, I remember thinking then that I was safe in the world so long as I could hear her voice. I think . . ." The old man stopped and took a handkerchief out from under his robes. "At Christmas, before we had our family meal, Maureen sang for us in place of a formal blessing. Of course, I did insist on a formal blessing. But last year, which would be the year before last, really, she sang 'What Child is This?'

And I think of those words now: 'What Child is this who, laid to rest / On Mary's lap is sleeping?' No one who is loved every really dies; and no one who dies in Christ is ever dead, only sleeping in hope of the resurrection to come. Beautiful dreamer, we must say good-bye to you now and tell you sleep tight, as my mother once told me. And we must pray for Bridget Flannery, that she awakens and grows well and strong, because it is not only our family who suffers tonight and questions God's will but our friends, our community."

Mrs. Flannery sat up straight in her white suit and bit her lips.

Danny did not think Bridget's mother had left the PICU, which was what they called the kids' intensive care unit, for more than eight hours since Bridget was injured.

Danny tuned out the old priest and thought about Bridget.

She would have hated the way she looked. Her lips were cracked, and her face was covered with crude rows of black stitches. Her hair was greasy and pulled back in a dirty scrunchy. They didn't want to wash her hair because parts of her head were still covered with bandages from her surgery and the swelling in her poor rebuilt cheek was fresh, purple and blue. Her shoulder was broken, although it turned out her neck wasn't, and she cried out when the nurses had to turn her. Sometimes, Danny knew, they hurt her on purpose or clapped next to her ear to try to bring her out of the coma.

When they sat her up, to keep fluid out of her lungs so

she didn't get pneumonia, they had to tie her head and chest to the chair with fabric strips.

She looked like a broken doll in a toy hospital.

She was breathing on her own now. After three days the doctors had "weaned" her off the ventilator, the machine that was breathing for her, and had cut a little hole in her windpipe where they put in a tube. Oxygen was pumped in—at first twelve puffs a minute, then four, then two, then none.

As time passed, the fluid pockets in her brain that the doctors had initially seen on the MRIs of her head went away.

The fractured bones would heal on their own, but some needed to be fixed. So once she was stable, they had taken Bridget back to the operating room and repaired the bones in her arms. At the same time a cosmetic surgeon from Chicago, Dr. Traverian—who was a big pal of the main surgeon, Dr. Fahey—had taken tiny bits of skin from places on the back of Bridget's head and had grafted them where they would, he hoped, grow on the area where the scalp had been ripped away over Bridget's ear. He opened the rough patching of the gash under Bridget's eye, replaced her broken eye socket and cheekbone with Teflon—Danny was sure he said Teflon, though that was what they put on the inside of no-stick frying pans—and closed the cut with Super Glue (really, Super Glue!) so that there would be hardly any scar at all. They worked quickly to minimize Bridget's time under anesthetic.

He did all this for free, Mrs. Flannery had told Danny.

And though Bridget had had a setback after that surgery and had to be on oxygen again, it didn't last long.

Her body got better and better; but still she slept on.

It was like she was a house fixed, patched up, and waiting for someone to move in.

With a probe stuck through a hole in her head, Dr. Zimensi, one of the neurologists, monitored the swelling of the brain, which was a huge source of concern. Bridget's brain had banged back and forth against her skull like a balloon in a jar at the time of the impact; and as the doctor explained, like any bruised part of the body, it swelled. She debated the radical step of removing a section of bone to allow the swelling to run its course. That proved to be one more bullet they could dodge. Daily, the swelling went down.

The doctors were pleased and surprised by Bridget's improvement.

But she didn't wake up.

It was more than four days now.

Finally, the team—the pediatrician, Dr. Coy; the head of the rehab, Dr. Park; another neurologist, Dr. Zimensi; and the surgeon, Dr. Fahey, all women—sat down with the Flannerys and explained that they "needed to see" Bridget make signs of conscious movement, recognition, sight, and responses to speech that were more than reflexes. Sometimes she squeezed their hands and her eyes moved under the closed lids. Sometimes her lashes fluttered.

But that was about it. The brain scans showed what some doctors called "shallow" damage, mostly in the area that controlled motor function, like walking and stuff. Dr. Park said mild to medium brain injury was a good result, relatively speaking.

Then she told them what she meant by "mild to medium brain injury."

She said that eventually Bridget might be able to learn to walk and feed herself and that "special" schooling might be possible in time.

Finally, Mrs. Flannery asked, "Isn't there any chance at all that she'll be like she was and be able to go back to school in the same way she did?"

"Well, there is always some chance, but it is a small chance. Still, with kids, we can be surprised," said Dr. Park, tracing the line of an invisible necklace with one finger.

And that night, a neurologist intern told them that the real truth was, the longer Bridget was in the coma, the more likely she would be "gorked."

That was the actual word he used.

He got in trouble for it and apologized. But they all knew what he meant. He meant that Bridget would be a veggie. So on the one hand the Flannerys and Danny were completely grateful Bridget was alive. And on the other hand, sometimes Mr. Flannery said that maybe the O'Malleys were luckier than they realized. Maury was at peace. She would never be "gorked."

As the service ended, Danny didn't want to think about

Maury; and he couldn't bear to look at Coach and Mrs. O. as they put their arms around the coffin—as though they were trying to pick up Maury and take her home. The O'Malley boys finally had to gently pull them away.

After the Mass came the burial.

The short line of cars took less than a half hour to get from the church to the cemetery.

Danny fell asleep on the way.

He just couldn't take any more depressing stuff. He was depressed enough to last until he was forty.

In a line at the grave, the cheerleaders wrapped their trophy in Maury's quilt. They stepped back, sobbing and holding one another up. And the priests each did a quick, quiet blessing. The wind was sharp edged and probing, so Danny turned up his coat collar and let his mom hold on to his arm. Though there were only twenty or thirty of them alongside the grave, he later heard that about five hundred people came to the funeral.

He just wanted it over.

The priest said that because of the nature of the O'Malleys' tragedy, the tradition of a reception was going to be suspended. The O'Malleys would forever be grateful for the outpouring of love from their friends and neighbors—all the food and flowers, and the donations that would eventually go to a scholarship fund in Maureen's name—but now they needed quiet time alone to try to heal.

As they all walked away except for Coach, who stood there slumped by the grave in his camel-colored coat and green fedora, Danny told his mother that he had to see Bridget.

He thought about the big board in Bridget's room with ranks of cards and letters pinned to it, such as the one that said "Spirit!" in Leland's big, loopy writing. Danny would tidy up the pictures of him and Bridget and Bridget with her sisters and Bridget with Maureen. He would read the card on the newest delivery of baby pink roses, Bridget's favorite. There would be the nurses and therapists to joke with, warmth, a Coke, and a chair to sit on.

And Maureen . . . They had to leave her there all alone, with a stray corner of her quilt flapping in the hard wind under an iron-colored sky. Danny couldn't hold it together. He thought that most of all he would miss her voice—as sweet and high-pitched as her singing. He would never hear it again. Her flower-open face, always with a big grin for him. He would never see it again.

He thought of her back there. All alone.

# a slow turning

"Do you think she'll ever come out of it?" Leland asked Molly. It was two weeks after the funeral and just before lunch. They were in the first-floor bathroom. As if on command, they both threw their long hair forward, brushed it ruthlessly, and then pulled it back into ponytails, carefully tugging strands out at the back. They stared into the mirror and regarded the just-out-of-bed effect with satisfaction. "I have ten thousand zits," Leland added.

"I don't," Molly admitted. "I don't mean I don't have zits; I mean I don't think she'll wake up."

Molly didn't have zits, however. She was physically perfect in every way, with a tight little butt and cute boobs. Guys all thought Molly was sexy, although she didn't date anyone because her mother was so strict. She liked the attention, though. She made Leland feel like a stork. Molly wasn't always loved on the squad because she was such a hardnose, always pushing them to do the next thing, to point their toes and really stretch so they could all do splits—she said it was a disgrace that there were four varsity cheerleaders who couldn't do real splits, since she herself could do both kinds. She wasn't the captain, but she acted like it. She nagged them to smile and put some life into their kicks. Molly never did anything halfway, and she didn't expect other people to. She missed Bridget for that reason. Bridget had been sloppy but so enthusiastic and naturally athletic that no one ever noticed. Molly frowned now. Underneath her attitude of perpetual criticism, she was a tender person. "My uncle is a doctor, and he says it's been way too long."

"What happens, then?" Leland asked. "Do they take her off life supports?"

"She's not on life supports, you idiot," said Molly. "Life supports are breathing machines."

"There's that thing in her neck."

"That's only if they have to give her oxygen all of a sudden. It's taped over. She can breathe."

"And she has a food tube."

"I don't think they can take that out. You have to get a judge to do that or something," Molly said. "I'm not really sure."

"Because she could just go on living if they don't stop

the food," Leland said. "I heard Mrs. Flannery say that they gave her four thousand calories a day or something."

"Well, I really think you can't just starve somebody. You have to give them food. It's a law," Molly said.

"So do they bring her home now?"

"My uncle said they could bring her home as soon as she gets her casts off and stuff. You can feed a person at home with that tube if they teach you how," Molly said. "She could just lay there."

"That's sickening," Leland told her, as they grabbed their books and ran for the commons. "Really, could you imagine just laying there with people looking at you and your mother putting ground-up food into your stomach? Just laying in your room? I'd rather be dead."

"We have to pray she wakes up," said Molly, embarrassed. "There's not much time left, my uncle said. I pray every night. I miss Bridget so much more than I thought."

"More than Maureen?"

"No. But it feels like if Bridge wakes up, we'll have a part of Maury back, too. I have weird dreams that Maureen is alive. And, Lee-Lee, they don't grind up food and put it in the tube. It's like diet shakes."

"Are you going to go see her today?"

"She doesn't know we're there. I mean, I'll still go sometimes. It's a long drive, Lee-Lee. My dad is getting pissed about how much I spend on gas going back and forth. It's an hour drive with traffic. You know Coach gives Danny some gas money to go see her. . . . Isn't that sweet?"

"It is. It's almost like he feels the way you do, that Maury is a part of Bridget. I wish somebody loved me that much," Leland said. She and Eric had split up right after Christmas break. Despite being together at the accident scene. Eric was a pervert. He wanted to go too far and she was only a junior. She wasn't going to do it until she was a senior. She and Caitlin had decided that a long time ago. Besides, he was a swimmer and did farmer blows with his nose after he got out of the pool. He was cute; but when she saw that, it made her want to puke. She wasn't going out with anyone now. She might as well get behind the Bridget effort. She said, "We should just designate people to go on certain days."

"That's good," Molly said. "I'll make a chart. I'll do it in computer lab. But only once a week. I can't keep up if I go more than that. I'm too tired. I have a paper to write in, like, fifteen minutes on Edna St. Vincent Millay, so I have to run."

"Oh, I did that last semester. Just talk about how it was all about suicide."

"Did she commit suicide?" Molly asked.

"No, she fell down the stairs," said Leland. "But she was always writing poems about it."

"That so creeps me out," Molly said, shaking her head. "Another accident. If it can happen to Edna St. Vincent Millay and Maury, it can happen to anybody."

"Yeah. Bridget was always a crazy driver. But Maureen?"

"Don't say that. I know what you mean," Molly whispered. "But it's like you're blaming them."

"Well . . ."

"It was snowing and slippery. And Maureen's leg was sore. And that curve has had a hundred accidents on it. My brother said they used to call it Dead Man's Curve."

"I'm just saying," Leland went on.

"Well, don't. Think how she'll feel if she does wake up and finds out Maureen is dead."

"It's not like she killed her. That would have been worse."

"Yeah, but still. I think about that all the time," Molly said, and ran up the stairs two at a time. "Do you know they used part of Maureen's bone to fix Bridget's arm? Britney told me. Her sister Amber is a nurse there."

"That is so gross," said Leland, leaning against the railing.

"Now it's like she's always with her," said Molly, and disappeared.

Danny had heard all the stories: The O'Malleys had donated one of Maureen's kidneys to Bridget. Bridget would have one of Maureen's eyes, or part of her bone. None of it was true.

But as the days grew longer, people just had to have something to talk about, he guessed.

He even knew some people talked about whether or not the Flannerys should let Bridget die, although the nurses said that was ridiculous, that they would only start talking about stuff like that if someone was really brain-dead, not just brain-*injured*.

Danny tried not to admit he was beginning to give up. He loved her, but it was hard to see past the ugliness and the smell. Even he didn't go every single day anymore.

At first people semicompeted in line to go in and see her.

The paramedics came, and Chief Colette. Coach Eddy came.

The cheerleaders came as a team every day at first. They played Bridget's music and did the Bigelow Bulldog Stomp until the nurses made them shut up, although Danny didn't know why.

Then it was just Britney and Leland and Molly.

Then just Britney and Molly. They came every week.

Danny didn't get mad at the others.

It was like talking to the wall.

But he read his books for honors English out loud to Bridget, and he watched her soap opera: *Days of Our Lives*. Bridge and Maureen never missed it. Danny couldn't see how a single thing had changed on the show in, like, fifty years. Half the time he missed most of school. But no one cared. Except Coach. Obviously he counted on Danny to cadet in freshman PE. But the other teachers just let him show up for tests mainly. He passed trig, but only with a C. His father didn't even ream him the way he normally would.

The nurses finally washed Bridget's hair and pinned it back with Hello Kitty barrettes. She looked about ten years old. But she smelled good and they cut her nails. Somehow it was almost more awful. You could see how she might look forever.

The social worker said that it was fine to keep hoping and praying—the Flannerys were Catholic but not *Catholic* like the O'Malleys—but they had to prepare themselves for the fact that the Bridget they knew was gone forever.

"Even if she wakes up today, it's going to be a long, hard road," said the social worker, who had a smiley face name tag that read NEELY!.

"But she's such a fighter," Mr. Flannery told Neely.

"It's her brain, though, and you have to understand that it doesn't heal the way other parts of the body do. Sometimes, with people as young as Bridget, her youth is on her side and there are ways that the unbroken parts of the brain can take over some things for the broken parts. But if she wakes up, this will be just the beginning. There will be differences. Speech. Personality. Learning. Even when she seems to know who you are . . ."

"Know who we are?" Mrs. Flannery gasped. "She'll know who we are!"

"Not necessarily, not at first," said Neely.

"I know it will be different with Bridget," said Mr. Flannery. "You don't know my daughter. She never gives up."

One of their clients knew a woman who said that what Bridget needed was acupuncture and toning. A woman they knew did it. Toning used these little tuning forks in specific ways to stimulate the brain. Acupuncture used little needles as thin as hairs.

The hospital staff didn't see anything wrong with it, so the Flannerys brought this woman in with a little case of bells and needles. The nurses drew the line at burning some black stuff in the room, but they were okay with the rest.

But after three weeks, the woman said she wasn't "hearing" Bridget respond, and back she went to St. Paul.

Danny was alone in Bridget's room, watching Kentucky play Wisconsin for a play-off berth, when it happened.

He felt particularly down that night, and the game did nothing to cheer him up. He was about to pick up his junk and leave when he noticed something out of the corner of one eye.

He jumped up. Bridget was trying to say something.

Her eyes were open.

*"Oh, Bridge," said the boy-voice. "Oh honey, did you say something? Please say it again. Just one thing. Just a noise. Blink if you understand me. Please move your hand for me. Anything! Bridge, it's been two months. I can't eat. I can't sleep. If you don't wake up now . . . Please, Bridge. Come on. What if Maury was here? You'd . . . You'd tell her to gut down. Think of Maury. Fight harder for Maury. You have to fight!"*

*Mo-ry.*

*She did what she knew as thinking for her, the rope climb.*

*Moor—eee.*

*Mo-ruh. Mo-ruh-un.*

*She was . . .*

*So she fought. She fought with every atom of her being, every pound of muscle, every electrical watt of brain cell. She wrestled like a wild animal to rip apart the smog and coils and wires and layers of plastic wrap that held her, and finally, in a voice so tiny and hoarse it didn't sound human, she croaked, "Mo-ruh."*

*He screamed.*

*The scream slammed against the back of her head and echoed over and over as if he had pulled it out of his mouth and dropped it down the quarry.*

*He screamed again, and a gallop of feet came slapping and tapping. "She talked!" he shouted. "I heard her! She said 'Mother!' I swear she did! Mrs. Flannery! She said 'Mother!'"*

*She had said nothing of the kind.*

# *wonderland*

Danny was not the type to brag; but he was sure it was he, not the lady with the little bells and pipes, who brought Bridget around. Why else would it be on their fourth anniversary, February 23? The twenty-third, and not the fourteenth of February, because he'd been too shy to ask her to the Valentine's dance.

She had to know that, somehow. It couldn't be a coincidence.

It was just a matter of time now. He would have her back. He could almost feel her, the tiny cup of her bare stomach; the soft, downy place at the base of her back; the taste of raspberries when he kissed her.

Three days later, on Saturday they bagged all the pictures and cards, threw out the flowers, and moved Bridget to rehab.

She was officially "awake."

The cell phone artery spread the news: Bridget is out of the coma. She tried to talk! Molly called Danny at six AM on Thursday.

"Is it true?"

"It's true . . . and what the hell time is it?" Danny asked.

"Could you make sense of it?"

"I thought she said 'Mother.' Now I wonder if she said 'Maureen.'"

There was a gap in the conversation. Molly was crying. Danny's annoyance melted. "I prayed and prayed. I heard her saying 'Maureen' in my dreams. I'm not lying," Molly told him.

"I'm going there in a few hours to see her. I'll tell her you said hey."

"Oh, Danny, that's something I never expected to hear again!"

"Me either, Mol."

On Saturday he didn't have to be at the hospital until nine, but Mrs. Flannery called him at seven. Not that he minded that much; he just wanted to sleep. It was as though his whole body dropped its guard when Bridget spoke. He could feel the ache in his neck and shoulders from how tight he had held them for these long weeks. Even lifting weights didn't tire him enough so that he could relax. That first night after she spoke, he slept with no twitches or dreams.

They got to Anne Morrow Lindbergh, entering at a different door, and the desk clerk told them to wait. Dr. Park and Neely, the social worker, wanted to talk with them for a little while, as the nurses were still "getting Bridget settled."

The talk was so viciously depressing that Danny had no idea why they even bothered. It was like they were SAD that Bridget was awake, not excited.

Dr. Park said some nice things first, as if to get them out of the way. She said, "This is so wonderful. And you must be incredibly happy. This is just proof of everything we know about kids. They can turn around and surprise you. But, Mrs. Flannery, you can't expect her to be the girl she was before the accident. Not now. Maybe not ever. And certainly not all at once. It's a long, long road."

"I know that," Kitt Flannery said, and glanced at the doctor, perturbed. What was all this gloom and doom about? "I'd like to see Bridget now," she said.

The social worker sighed and lead them into the rehab unit.

As they went through the oversized doors into the bright blue-and-yellow striped ward, they passed a plaque on the door that read: THIS UNIT IS ENDOWED IN THE MEMORY OF ALISON LEE CHRISTIANSON, WITH GRATEFUL HEARTS, FROM HER GRANDPARENTS, LEE AND CHARLES COMPTON. Danny shivered.

"You have to remember," Neely told them. "This isn't like a medical show on TV. It's not like a movie even. In a movie, they make months seem like overnight. You see one moment when they're trying to stand the person up, and a minute later the person is walking along with a cane. What they leave out is months and months of frustration and hard work. And they leave out how pissed off the kids get."

"I get it," said Kitt Flannery.

But as they passed the doorways, she got quieter and quieter.

She tried to avoid looking in; but it was impossible. *They're like monsters,* she thought as she glimpsed kids—some tiny, some already with hair under their armpits—with grotesquely, painfully twisted-in limbs and long strings of silver drool dripping from chafed and gaping mouths. *Dear God,* Kitt thought, *if she's going to be like this, please take her.* Then, quickly, she mentally slapped herself across the face.

It was just three days since Bridget had awakened, but Mr. Flannery had to host an "Occasion." It was a wedding with three hundred guests at the Bright Wing Country Club, which was why Mrs. Flannery had asked Danny to come with her. Mr. Flannery kept calling Mrs. Flannery on her cell every fifteen minutes until she finally turned it off.

"We're running out of money," Mrs. Flannery had told Danny as she got into the car. Danny couldn't imagine that the Flannerys—the Flannerys, who had *shrimp* every Sunday—could ever run out of money. "I mean, we have to accept these dates. Winter is slow anyhow, and all this . . ."

Kitt had begun having terror dreams about the piles of un-opened medical bills that lay on the computer table. They might have to sell the house. Mike should never have bought a BMW, even used. Their insurance had eighty percent of this covered and seventy-five percent of that. But just the PICU costs were already more than a hundred thousand dollars, a third of their yearly income.

It didn't matter; but it had to be faced.

And so did this.

Kitt tried to be cheerful and nonchalant, shoving her hands into the pockets of her jeans and tugging on her red sweater; but Danny saw the horror on her face as they made their way toward Bridget's room.

A teenaged boy with tiny, swizzled-in legs who was strapped into a wheelchair with leather supports on either side of his shaved head tried to grab Mrs. Flannery's hand as they passed him in the hall.

A big, pretty, red-haired nurse pushing the wheelchair said, "Rob, quit flirting!" The kid made a goofy face Danny supposed was a smile. Mrs. Flannery swallowed hard.

There were more kids with a teacher in what looked like a schoolroom. Some of them had shaved heads with stitches still visible on them. Only small portions of Bridget's head had been shaved. When she'd called last night, Britney told Danny they would just tell Bridget she had a faux-hawk when patches of her hair started to grow and stick straight up. Before the accident, Bridget's hair had only been trimmed at the ends—never cut. Not since she was seven and had demanded a short haircut like the one she'd seen on a German figure skater.

Were those kids in the schoolroom boys or girls? Danny wondered. It had to be a school. There were books and a blackboard. One kid's head was swiveling around and his arm was working up and down. How could anyone think they could pay attention to the teacher? How could the teacher stay sane?

The gray-looking mothers in baggy denim jumpers sat knitting in rockers beside the kids' beds or wheelchairs or pushed the kids around so they could look up at the TV. There was a nice, big-screen TV in every room, and Neely said the kids also had a theater where groups came to sing and football players and race car drivers came to visit them. The mothers were completely into staring at the kids. Every few seconds they reached out and wiped away the spit. The kids' faces were all raw from the spit and shiny with Vaseline. Some of them were babies, in cribs with gigantic high sides. *Are they really babies?* Danny thought. *Or something worse?*

Neely led them to a nursing station, and a rehab nurse, who introduced herself as Lorelei, handed Kitt some forms to sign.

*She has to face this work every day*, Danny thought.

"What can we do to make Bridget get better faster?" asked Kitt, as she bent to the forms.

"There really isn't any way. It happens on nature's clock," said Lorelei. "The best thing you can do is keep her stimulated. Music. Books on tape. Get the home movies put on DVD and bring 'em in."

"Won't that just make her sad?" Kitt asked, thinking of the scads of discs they had of Bridget's competitions, made at her request so that she could study where she went wrong and correct it.

The nurse shrugged.

"Kids sometimes do better at accepting things than we do," she said.

"But is there ever any real . . . Does anyone get better?"

"Of course!" said Lorelei. "We've had kids so much worse off than your girl walk back in here a year later to show us their navel rings! I mean it! I have the best job in the world."

"What happened to them?" asked Kitt. "The ones here. I mean, to make them that way?"

"Some motor vehicle accidents, like your daughter. Some drownings. A couple of interrupted SIDS cases. Some diving accidents. You name it. The boy we just passed? He fell off a stool in his kitchen onto a tile floor. That's all. He was horsing around with his younger brother when he was six. . . ."

"But he's big now. . . ."

"Well, he's sixteen, Mrs. Flannery. And he's an outpatient. He has to come every week to keep those muscles worked and stretched out, or they're going to wither up."

Was this what was in store for her daughter? What would the children, Sarah and Eliza, think? They'd barely seen

70

their sister since the accident. They'd never seen her in the PICU. Mike forbade it. The doctors advised against it, in case it was to be their last memory of Bridget—and even if it was not, a traumatic picture that would last for the rest of their lives. Sarah was only thirteen. Eliza was eleven. How would they adjust . . . to the worst? Come to think of it, what would Kitt . . . how would Kitt learn . . . what these mothers knew? They were all mothers. It seemed that fathers were banned from the rehab floor. How many careers had been relinquished, friendships lost, social lives erased? Kitt had expected to be getting ready to take Bridget on her first round of college tours now. Bridget in her microskirt over her leggings. Bridget casually doing a back walkover and landing just inches short of the bench at the kitchen table, supple as Catwoman. Bridget, her face shining with sweat, proudly on top of the pyramid at the homecoming game. Bridget in her first strapless dress—a creation that seemed to be made of sugar glaze that fell down her sweet, beautiful little body like icing . . . *Oh please, dear God,* Kitt prayed. *She would never want to live this way. I would never want to see her. . . . I couldn't* . . . And then she mentally slapped herself across the face again.

How could she be such a fool?

How could she forget that first terrible revelation about Maureen? How? *Kitt Kelliher,* she said, using her maiden name as she did when she was angry, *Get over yourself*.

As they entered Bridget's bright pink room, with its border of daisies stenciled around the top, Kitt said, "Danny,

71

you don't have to stay. I'll be here all day anyhow."

"I can stay," Danny answered.

*What a darling boy*, Kitt thought. She fought against Bridget and Danny being so serious so young—she knew they were sleeping together already—but now she thought, *If Bridget comes out of this at all and looks anything like herself, Danny will probably be one who would stick by her.* Kitt hoped that would happen. Danny was as steady as the stars.

"You go home now. Your own mother hasn't seen you in weeks."

"She does say that," Danny admitted. "I'm sorry. It probably sounds rude."

"Go ahead. I'll call you if she wakes up anymore."

And after he left, somehow Kitt fell asleep in one of the chairs that were so much more comfortable than the ones in the PICU, probably because people were here for the long haul.

Dr. Park, the compact Asian woman who headed the department, popped in to check on Bridget; and though she clattered around a bit, Kitt didn't wake. The little girl did, though, her eyes blazing. She shook her head violently. *No! No!*

"What's up, peanut?" Dr. Park asked.

"No-oot!" Bridget said, obviously furious that it took so long. "No-oooot!"

"New?" asked Dr. Park.

"NO!" Bridget snapped, obviously meaning what she said.

"We'll get it out in time, honey. Don't worry. Let me take a look at your eyes, please. Can you blink for me, Bridget?" Bridget shut her eyes tightly. Dr. Park was pleased at the show of spirit.

She glanced at the girl's mom, crumpled in the chair like a fashion doll thrown down by a child. She thought it best to let her sleep while she could.

# *a slow storm turning*

Slap. Slap. Bump. Bump.

She was conscious, but what did that mean?

She didn't want to look at this woman. This woman didn't smell Mom-smell.

Nothing seemed to have a name; and then, up would pop a name, like a message appearing in the window of the little 8-Ball they had when they were little. *My sources say yes.*

She knew that the sounds and smells meant people like the people before: people-there-all-the-time with soft shoes and people-who-came-and-went with hard shoes. These were the sounds-from-before, from the lights-and-darks. But this was a different place that didn't stink. It smelled a little like a house.

"My baby," the not-Mom-voice said softly. "Oh, I thank God. And Saint Anne. And Saint Catherine. I prayed more than I ever prayed in my life."

"Mor-un . . . ," she said again, helplessly.

The mom-but-not-Mom-voice coughed and a bell rang. A little-radio-voice said, "I'll be right there!"

"She's asking over and over . . ."

"She's very confused now, and you have to expect that." It was a nice voice, a pancake-voice, she thought. Like summer pancakes.

"I . . . I . . . mu . . . Mor . . . un . . . ," she said again, louder. Her tongue was moist.

"Ahhhh," said the sweet-voice.

Impatient, she wiggled her hands and made a fist.

"Well!" the same voice said. "We've got a feisty one on our hands." She clapped and the clapping clanged in her head. She could see the nurse wavering, as if underwater, her hair like a cloud of flame. Why did the nurse applaud? It banged her head like a broken banjo. She cringed away into sleep.

"What do you think she was saying?" Lorelei asked.

"Her best friend, the girl who . . ."

"Oh. Of course. That was Maureen."

"Yes. Maureen O'Malley."

"She was asking about Maureen?"

"Yes. I can't tell her Maureen is . . . you know. Not now." Kitt crawled back into the chair. Lorelei thought Kitt looked as whipped as a wet dog.

"She's going to sleep for a while now. And I think you should, too, Mrs. Flannery," Lorelei said. "I promise I'll watch over her like she was my little sister. Scout's honor."

"I can't."

"Go ahead. Go home and get a good night's sleep. She'll be here in the morning. Call us ten times if you want to. That's what we're here for."

And so Kitt let Mike pick her up on his way home from Bright Wing. He looked in on Bridget and kissed Kitt's hair. "It's a miracle."

Mike had not seen the open doors that morning—the lolling, twisted children. Now the ward looked like a twilight nursery, like the girls' bedrooms when they were tiny.

"It is," Kitt sighed and agreed. "I don't want to leave her."

"Just for a few hours."

The next day, at six AM, the dental surgeon showed up on his rounds.

Chris Styles was tall, dark, and oh-so-handsome. He

had played basketball at Stanford, and half of the nurses on the floor had a crush on him. Lorelei wasn't immune. She didn't know how Dr. Styles stayed single with all those hormones coming at him all day. He must go home exhausted. She usually worked Saturday nights; and Dr. Styles, who was Jewish, made a point of working Sundays. It was always a little pleasure in her morning to see him when their paths crossed.

Gently, after asking her permission, he examined Bridget's mouth.

Then he sat down in the rocker and studied the open file of Bridget's dental chart.

Lorelei had one of her odd feelings. Those weird hunches were the thing that made her decide she would become a nurse when her parents both thought she would make a wonderful teacher. And they had served her well. She could tell when a kid was going to go south, the way dogs can sense hurricanes. She flipped through the girl's chart, one eye on Dr. Styles, as the tech did the routine blood draw, on the prowl for infections—the danger to any body, however young, when there was injury and prolonged inactivity.

Dr. Styles looked up at her. "I've seen teeth that were chipped after accidents, but I never saw a chipped tooth get better," he said.

"What?"

"The kid in the chart has a big chip in her left lower bicuspid. This kid doesn't. This kid has had four canines removed for alignment. The kid in the chart has her canines."

"Maybe you got the wrong records."

"You know I didn't."

Dr. Styles and Lorelei exchanged a level look.

"You already thought this," he said.

"Yeah, I did."

"Why didn't you say anything?"

"She just got here a few days ago. I thought I was nuts at first. But I had these funny impressions."

"Well, I'll do impressions when she's a little further along. But the doo-doo is going to hit the fan," said Dr. Styles. "Call me if you need me."

*I need you*, Lorelei thought, and laughed at herself.

She called her sister. They had plans to go shop the sales at the Mall of America. "Let's just say I won't be able to come today and watch the news tonight," she teased Eudora.

"Tell me!" said her sister.

"Can't!" Lorelei said, and turned off the phone before she did say something. Eudora could convince sea turtles to give up their eggs.

She helped the day nurse, a nice guy named Ben Kipness, hold the girl in a standing position for a moment.

"Look," Ben said. "She's reaching for the floor with her toes. Both sides."

"She's trying to balance. Well, she was a cheerleader. Glad she wasn't a little couch potato."

"Why are you still here?" Ben asked.

"Waiting for some orders. I'll go soon," Lorelei said casually. In fact, she would not go home until late that afternoon. They lowered the girl into a chair. Her eyes opened and she felt for the armrests.

When Ben left, Lorelei spoke sharply into the girl's ear. "Talk to me, honey! Tell me what the deal is!"

*There was time. She was uncomfortable. She back her. Her toys, tins, tops tingled.*

*Light. She said, "Hey!"*

*They heard her! She lifted her arm and waved it.*

*A boomy voice shouted, "Look! Her finger moved! Call Dr. Park!"*

*Her finger? It was her whole left side that moved!*

*Time.*

*Time.*

*Light.*

*Then a singsong but very teacher-y voice said, "That's definitely intentional."*

*"Here," she said clearly.*

*"Hear what, sweetie?" asked the girl-voice, as gentle as a violin. "Dr. Park, you heard that."*

*"Mmmm. She's coming along very quickly. Did you, ah, hear what Dr. Styles . . . ?"*

*"Yes, I was here."*

*Time rolled over her like a wave, dragging her down. And then she rose up again.*

*"Here Mor-uh . . ."*

*"I'm here," said the sweet-violin-voice. "Are you awake, honey?"*

Lights came on, big lights. Flashlights in her face.

"It's not possible," said the voice-she-remembered-from-what-seemed-like-years-ago.

"Dr. Collins, this girl has had braces. Bridget didn't. This girl has a different pattern of dentition and an intact tooth where Bridget had a chip."

"It's not possible. This is going to be a firestorm. Run through it again."

"We ran it twice," said a low, musical man's voice. She would call his voice the kettledrum.

"Damn," said the doctor-voice. "Kathy Fahey knows this girl. Kathy did three surgeries on this kid. She'd have noticed something. Traverian came from Chicago and fixed her cheek and scalp because we didn't have a good enough cosmetic surgeon. He would have noticed something was off. Someone would have. Damn."

She decided to say clearly, "Damn."

"She hears you," said the violin-voice.

They all fell silent.

She opened her eyes and looked around at them. The sweet-voice had a soft cloud of red hair.

Finally, the sweet-voice said, "Well, I'll stay here while we call . . . while you call . . ."

"Fine, good, thank you, Lorelei. Dr. Park. Dr. Daater, do you think you could stay, too? Someone page Dr. Fahey. I guess. And the counsel."

"Legal counsel?"

"I guess. Ask Whitby."

She had seen the nurse. She had seen Danny. She had seen the skinny lady in the red sweatshirt, sweeter, sweater. She knew her from someday, someway. She had made her voice say on its own real words. Hey and damn and no and . . .

She was not dead.

She was not in heaven.

And she was not Bridget.

PART II

*maureen*

# beginning with the end

On Monday, Neely Cavendish came in early. She went up to see the girl before she made the first call. Before that, she started a fresh clipboard with stacks of forms and plain paper, and drank a full cup of black coffee. Although Janie's cough was better, her daughter hadn't let her sleep much last night. And Neely needed all her wits about her.

In the wavering March sunlight that leaked in through the closed drapes in the pink room, she asked the girl, "Are you Maureen?"

*Oh, thank you, thank you,* Maureen thought. She nodded so hard her head began to hammer again with the pain.

"Take it easy," said the tall, pretty black woman with the clipboard. "We're going to make this okay. I have to go and call some folks now. Don't worry."

She slept. She dreamed of Danny, sitting in the chair, his blond hair falling in a tangle over his forehead, his sleeves rolled up deliberately to reveal his powerful forearms. She dreamed of Danny kissing her every night and saying, "That's my girl." His smell, of some peppery shaving junk and the bubble gum he was never without. She felt her stomach lurch in her sleep.

Back in her office, Neely looked at the clock and wrote down "8:20 AM." A random thought from grade school drifted through her mind. Some dimwit teacher had told them that clocks on display for sale were set at that time not just to show off the hands to best advantage but because, in legend, this was the time of day when Abraham Lincoln died.

It must have seemed bizarre to Dr. Styles. How could he understand that people didn't examine the dental patterns of someone whose life they were trying to save every minute of every day? Someone who wouldn't wake up from a coma? They'd barely been able to clean her teeth because of the damage to her mouth.

Now, in addition to Dr. Styles's report they had some close observation and questioning of the girl by Dr. Park, and the blood tests. It was pretty conclusive.

She knew that the O'Malleys wouldn't hear a word she said after she told them that there was a very good chance that Maureen was still alive—that she, not Bridget, had survived the crash.

They wouldn't hear her when she talked about the long road Maureen faced, or the real likelihood that she would never be the girl they had raised. They wouldn't believe that a brain-injured kid might be rude. She might sexually misbehave. She would probably ask for the same thing ten times in sequence, forgetting that she'd asked five minutes earlier. She might burst out in displays of rage and might require classes for the mentally challenged.

And that was if things went well.

But they wouldn't hear or accept anything like that for weeks. That burst of absolute, blinding, unexpected elation would carry them through the first shocking moments of disillusionment they would certainly experience. Neely had seen it over and over, although never with this set of circumstances.

She dialed the O'Malleys' phone number.

Answering machine.

*Damn it!*

Okay. Mrs. O'Malley worked . . . where? She worked at the church, at Holy Mother of Sorrows. Part-time. Okay. Neely would call her there. But how would she get her to come to the hospital? How would she . . . Should she call Mrs. Flannery before the Flannerys got to the hospital? No. The O'Malleys were the principals here. Should she call the coach first?

Neely looked up the number for the rectory.

Jeannie O'Malley answered on the first ring. Neely crashed.

"Hello?" Jeannie said. Neely said nothing. "Hello? Is anyone there?"

"I need to speak to Father Genovese, urgently," she said.

"Is this the hospital? Aren't you the social worker?" Jeannie asked.

"Yes, I . . . just really have to talk to the father. I do."

"Well, Neely, I can have him call you in . . . about five minutes. Mass is just ending."

Of course. Mass was every day, not just Sunday. Neely bit the bullet.

"Mrs. O'Malley, you have to trust me on this. I really need to ask you, the father, and your husband to come to my office now. I know this is unexpected, and I really cannot give you details over the phone. There's been a misunderstanding regarding your daughter Maureen's care. . . ."

"Oh, Neely. Is this about the organ donations? We signed off on that. It gave us some measure of peace. We know everything was done that could be done. We never even thought about a lawsuit or any of those terrible things. Of course, we're still . . . I don't think we'll ever be the same. The parent group has helped me. Bill has gone with me a couple of times. It's at least something to know you're not alone, even in a town as small as ours. But no, we'll never be the same."

*You bet you won't*, Neely thought. She said, "Well, I'm glad. But, well. It's not that. It's something more personal."

"Something we left? Something of Maury's? Something

we forgot to take care of?" Jeannie asked, puzzled. She had only this week cleaned Maury's room, then let herself lie on her daughter's bed and cry until she was exhausted and fell asleep.

"Yes, yes. Something we all forgot to take care of. And it's truly urgent. Please. If you can . . ."

"The father is here now. Do you still need to talk to him?"

"I'd like to speak to him if I can," Neely said, sighing with relief.

"Anthony Genovese here."

"Father, this is Neely Cavendish. . . ."

"Of course. Hello."

"Father, I really need you to come to my office at Anne Morrow Lindbergh with the O'Malleys as soon as you possibly can."

"I understand," the priest said evenly. "Of course I want to know the reason."

"Father, what I'm going to say is going to either sound to you like a lie or a miracle or a hoax or just plain crazy. But it's absolutely true. The medical staff here believes that the girl upstairs in the rehab unit is actually Maureen O'Malley. They believe she is not Bridget Flannery. The girl you buried was Bridget Flannery."

"Well," said Father Genovese. "Well, and how was this, ah, discovered?"

"Yesterday morning the dental surgeon on call compared her teeth to the records of Bridget's teeth. And they did not match. The hospital did blood tests. And now she's doing other things, making a clicking noise with her tongue. . . . Amber Kresky, a nurse—"

"I know Amber. I married Amber and Mitchell."

"I gather, from what Amber says, that this is how Maureen called her dog. . . ."

"Yes. That's true. I'll go into my office now. Thank you, Jeannie. Yes, you may hang up now. Great." Neely heard the priest's voice drop to a harsh whisper. "How could this have happened? How can you be sure? This is so traumatic. Of course, for the O'Malleys it will be the answered prayer. But there are so many complications. The Flannerys will be completely devastated. I don't know how to minister to them. This is a unique situation. So how can you be sure?"

"We have the proof. We . . . well, the doctors have already determined that she has type A-negative blood, like Maureen. Bridget was type O. We have Maureen's dental records. They match this girl's teeth."

"Jeannie was in agony when she was pregnant with Maureen, thinking Maureen would die because of the Rh factor," said Father Genovese. "The danger grows with every pregnancy. Especially seventeen years ago. But she took the shots so that Maury wouldn't have to be fully transfused at her birth. I was the assistant pastor then."

Neely went on. "Father, this mistake isn't as outrageous as it seems. It's happened before. It shouldn't have happened, but I have found at least two other cases within the past ten years where it did happen in the United States.

There was so much injury to both girls. So much swelling from the injuries and the fluids the doctors administered. And it was Maureen's car. We assumed she was the girl in the driver's seat. But we believe now that Bridget may have been driving, for some reason. They were so similar in every way. Height. Weight. Hair color. Eye color."

"But how can we determine if she really is Maureen?"

"It's an easy test. A DNA swab from the inside of Bill O'Malley's cheek will determine the paternity within twenty-four hours." Neely paused. "Obviously, the doctors here fought to the greatest extent of their ability to save Maureen and Bridget. And there was never any negligence."

"No one thinks that. Well, in any case, I've seen no evidence of that."

"In a trauma situation like that, where two kids are so very, very sick, decisions have to be made in seconds. The doctors try everything. It was only a matter of five or six minutes before both of them were in surgery and, from what the paramedics said at the scene, the doctors made the best determination they could of who was who. Neither one had any ID. It was all over the road. They were both given a great deal of blood during surgery, but none of it was A-negative; it was type O in the ER because they can transfuse that for any blood type usually," Neely explained.

"And no one looked back over the records."

Neely hesitated. "No."

Neely heard a rustling sound.

The priest told her, "This is going to have lasting consequences in this parish, and in Bigelow. This town is never going to be the same. Now, I have just been informed that Mr. O'Malley is on his way to pick us up here, so we should be there in less than an hour, Mrs. Cavendish."

"Thank you. Please come straight to my office on the first floor, right outside the emergency department."

"And . . ."

"Father?"

"God bless you, Mrs. Cavendish."

*Red sweater lady in the hall.*

*Boy-crying in the hall.*

*I see them hear them hear the violin-voice tell them, "Right now, we have to make you wait justafewminutes. . . ."*

*"But why?"*

*"Justafewminutes. We are doing some tests on her."*

*"Is something wrong? Did she have an infection? That . . . care center was a hellhole."*

*"No, it's not that. Please, just . . . oh listen. That's Neely Cavendish. The social worker. She would like me to bring you to her office. She would like me to bring you to her office now. Actually, our nurse supervisor, Mrs. Gressley, will take you."*

*Mumble, dribble, mumble mumble.*

*Stillness.*

*Her lips moistened, lemony. Then a cold toaster. Cold knife. She tasted. "Honey, this is a little spoonful of pudding. Try to swallow."*

*She didn't have to try to swallow. It was easy.*

*"Good girl!" a guy-voice said. She opened her eyes. It wasn't Danny, but a guy in a nurse coat with sailboats on it, holding a pudding cup. "Is that good?"*

*"Go-yes," she said.*

*Then it was cloud-red-hair again. "I don't know if you can understand me, Maureen. I know it's you, Maureen. Your mom and dad are coming, Maureen. We know now."*

*"Mo-reen," she said gratefully. "Yes." The tears that rolled down her face hurt. She tried to raise her arm.*

*"Go ahead," someone said.*

*She did. It was so hard to raise her arm and touch her own cheek that she fell asleep with pudding still in her mouth.*

*Someone was running in the hall. Hard-shoes. Outside-people. Someone came in through the door. She opened her eyes. The flame-nurse turned.*

*The lady was small and plump. The man with her was bigger, wearing just a blocker, breaker, jacker. The lady had on a long, gray*

*winter coat and a hat with a tassel. Hat with a*
*tassel. Hat with a tassel. Striped gray-and-blue*
*hat. Tassel.*

Jeannie knelt at the side of the bed.

"That my hat," Maureen said.

"Oh, dear God in heaven. Dear God in heaven. Merciful Jesus. Blessed Saint Anne, we are so unworthy. Maury, it's Mama. Do you know me, Maury?"

"It siz my hat," Maureen said. "Fits. Bits."

"This kid's freaking me out," said Lorelei. "She's talking in sentences. At the end, she was trying to say it fits you."

"She's very intelligent," said Jeannie. "I wore it every day because it smells like you. My darling baby. My Maury. Your room is clean and waiting for you, Maury. Maury, I almost gave your clothes away. I almost boxed them all up and gave them away. Father, how can this be? We lost her. This is truly a miracle. We lost our only daughter."

"Jeannie. I'm overcome. I have never seen anything like this."

"Maureen, it's Daddy," Bill said.

Maureen tried to smile at the guy, but it hurt her mouth. She made the signal to the nurse that she needed pain stuff. The signal was wrinkling up her nose. And then she clucked her tongue twice.

Dady-dad? He looked like a niceman, bigman. Scary hands. She had seen these scary hands. They were so big they could hurt. Did they hurt.

"Hi?" she asked. "Where?"

"It's Daddy, Maury," Bill said.

Maureen clucked her tongue again. It seemed to be what her tongue wanted to do.

"She's calling Rag Mop," said the chunky man, the old guy Maureen had never seen before. She had never seen the younger guy in the black coat either. "She's calling our dog."

"Mop, come," said Maureen. Jeannie took her hand. Maureen pulled the hand closer to her nose. She sniffed at it. Mom's cologne. Flowers of the Valley. She could think it right away.

"Hi, Mom," said Maureen.

Jeannie put her head down on Maureen's leg and cried so violently that her tears soaked through two blankets.


In Neely's office, Dr. Collins thought it would be necessary to administer some kind of sedation to Kitt Flannery. He didn't blame her. *Bastard situation*, he thought. *Incomprehensible*. He squirmed with guilt and pity.

Mike sat in the straight chair like the statue of Abraham Lincoln in Washington, D.C., his face utterly immobile except for the occasional blink.

Kitt literally tried to crawl the walls.

Steve Collins had never seen a physical demonstration of the phrase before. If only Kathy Fahey would come. Not once in fifteen years of practice had he felt so totally inadequate.

"It's my fault! I was afraid she wouldn't be perfect!" Kitt

screamed. "I was afraid she'd be like those kids up there, all in diapers and drooling and wailing and groaning. I asked God to take her if she was going to be like that. God took her. It was my fault!"

"No," Neely said. "No! Nothing you thought about Bridget had anything to do with this, Mrs. Flannery. Kitt. Nothing! This is not your fault or anyone's fault. It was normal to think that. Any mom who had a beautiful, smart daughter would think that."

"I want to die!" Kitt screamed. "I had a beautiful daughter! Had!"

"Sit down, Kitt, please. Just for a moment. Let's have a drink of water," Neely said.

Dr. Collins thought, *This woman needs help*. He would ask the dad for the name of Kitt's primary physician. *Oh hell. Foolish to wait.* He said, "Let's find Dr. Sasuko. Is she out there? Five milligrams of Valium IM stat . . ."

"We should talk to our lawyer?" Mike finally asked. The emphasis on each word was the same as on the previous word.

"You can do that," Dr. Collins said gently. Kathy Fahey knocked and then slipped into the room.

"Lawyer? For what? To sue? Sue for what, Mike?" Kitt screamed.

"We were led to believe that this was our daughter. That our little girl was alive. I don't know," Mike said. His hands fell uselessly at his sides. "I don't know."

"We all want someone to blame when something like

96

this happens. But no one intentionally misled you," said Dr. Fahey. "There was no bad practice. We fought to save both girls equally."

"I . . . know," said Mike. The room was outlined, for him, in its every element, in black marker, sharp as sunlight behind trees in the fall. He would never, never step entirely outside this moment. It played over and over in his mind already, like a song on constant repeat. *Bridget!* His mind screamed. *Bridget!*

But Bridget lay out under a walnut tree in Forest Home Cemetery, marked by a brand-new headstone that read MAUREEN ANN O'MALLEY. BEAUTIFUL DREAMER, WAKE UNTO ME.

He watched as Kitt drooped slowly into a chair as the Valium took effect. It was like seeing a woman go into hypnosis. Finally, blessedly, she began to cry. She dropped onto her knees and laid her head in Mike's lap.

The doctors left, Dr. Fahey to return to surgery and Dr. Collins to send someone with a swab to take Mr. Flannery's DNA.

"Please stay as long as you need to," Neely told them. "I have to check on one patient, but I'll come right back and will be here to answer any questions you have after the swab is done. There are some phone numbers I want to write down for you. Some parents who can talk to you when you're ready, and for your daughters there's a group for kids who have experienced the loss of a sibling that meets at the Y in Henderson Falls, just a few minutes north of you. And some online resources, too. You won't want these now, but you will someday."

"We'll go in just a minute," said Mike Flannery. He had left the car running in front of the building.

"I think it's best that we have someone come and drive you home," Neely said. "Who should I call?"

"I don't know. My brother lives in Wisconsin. Kitt's sisters do, too. I guess Father Genovese."

*Oh no,* Neely thought. "It's better if it's immediate family, really."

"Okay. Uh. My brother in Madison, then."

A technician appeared and collected the skin cells from inside Mike's mouth. "That has to be done stat," Neely said.

"No kidding," said the lab tech.

"Mr. Flannery," Neely said then. "I will drive you. Let me call the chaplain to watch out for my territory for a while."

This was unprecedented, but all of this was unprecedented.

"Thank you," said Mike. He was a big man, at least six-three or six-four, and as trustful as a little boy. He got up and rummaged in his pockets for his keys. "Oh," he said. "I lost them."

"It's okay," Neely said, taking her coat off the hook and pulling on her gloves. The ED sounded as loud and raucous as a train station when she opened the door; but as each person saw the Flannerys, he or she fell silent, in the middle of a sentence, a laugh, a bite of food.

"I won't be back. Tell them," Neely whispered when she

passed Amber Kresky, who nodded. Amber's phone rang—the ring tone was a giggle. Kitt looked sharply at Amber.

"My sister," she said.

"Don't tell her now," Neely said firmly.

"Uh, okay," Amber replied, a blush spreading up from her throat.

*Great*, Neely thought, *Amber has already told her sister!* Why was Amber even on staff today? She worked PMs. Was she just hanging around for the drama? Well.

Neely had contacted Sarah and Eliza Flannery's schools and asked that the girls be brought to the office. The principals were told that their parents would be coming for them. Sarah had asked if Bridget was in a coma again. *Oh God*, Neely thought, *those kids are never going to get past this.*

The Flannerys' sleek, glass green BMW looked comical in the circular drive, running, with both doors open.

"Oh, help me. Please help me die," said Kitt as she crawled into the backseat and lay down. Mike got in the passenger side in front.

Neely wanted her to fasten her seat belt, but Kitt would not move. Neely started the car and drove.

Danny Carmody was sitting in his truck in the parking lot after the first real workout he'd had in weeks, feeling every muscle and delighting in the pain in some perverse way; and it was only chance that made him flip on the radio.

He could have driven off and not paused to turn on any

tunes until he was on the road; he often did. But because his dad had used the truck to pick up a computer desk the night before, it was set to one of Dave Carmody's wallpaper news stations. BORU-FM, Bridget called them. And so he sat with the motor running as people called out to him and waved good-bye and listened to the report: ". . . of mistaken identity involving two sixteen-year-old girls who grew up together in Bigelow, just north of the twin cities of Minneapolis–Saint Paul, and were involved in a head-on collision with a semi just before Christmas. When she awoke from her coma, the girl presumed dead, for whom services were held three days after the accident, turned out in fact to be her look-alike best friend. While DNA tests are needed to determine for certain that the deceased girl and the living girl were somehow mistaken for each other, Grady Carmichael, a spokesman for Anne Morrow Lindbergh Children's Hospital and Clinics, said that the regrettable and entirely inadvertent error was made because of the extent of the trauma injuries to both girls as well as their striking physical similarity. It was only when the surviving girl began to come out of a coma that suspicions were aroused that she was not who she was believed to be. Carmichael said, 'I would plead with the press and others to understand that both of these families are in a state of extreme crisis right now, and we would ask that you give them their privacy at this time.' DNA testing had as yet not revealed . . ."

Danny's phone trilled "Good Vibrations."

He stared at it. Lee-Lee.

He didn't answer. It rang again. Home. He didn't answer. It rang again. Evan. Mom. Finally, after his mother's sixth attempt, Danny picked up but said nothing.

"Danny?"

"I'm here. What?"

"Do you know?"

"Yeah."

"There's a LAK13 news truck in front of the house," said Mom. "What do I tell them?"

"Whatever you want."

"Danny, you should come home."

"No. They'll take a picture of me or . . ."

"Now there's another truck. ABC from Minneapolis. Danny! And a car from the *Star-Tribune* . . ."

"I'm going to David's," he said. "I'll stay at David's tonight." His brother, a junior executive at a bank, lived in Hamilton, about ten miles from Bigelow.

"What about your toothbrush and things?" his mother asked.

"I'll pick some up at the Walgreens, Mom. For Christ's sake."

"Are you okay, Danny?"

"Not so much."

"But honey, you know she would never have been all right in the head, Danny. She might have to wear diapers or be fed all her life."

"So I'm better off. That's what you're saying."

"No, but . . ."

"Just screw that, Mom! Screw it!"

"Danny!"

"Just don't bring it up with me now! Don't!"

"You're my son, and I have to think of you, too. It's all been about them. . . ."

"Because it is all about them."

"You've done enough," his mother said wearily. "That's all I'm saying. Dad and I have talked about this. Bridget . . . well, now we know it wasn't Bridget. But Dad has done a lot of internet research on brain damage and that much damage . . ."

"So you thought I would just leave her because she was hurt?"

"No, but, Danny. You couldn't expect a girl with severe brain damage. Work. College. Even motherhood. All that. You're only sixteen, Danny. You have your whole life ahead of you."

"And you didn't say this until now because . . ." He stared at the phone and snapped it closed. It must have gone off twenty times before he pulled into the driveway of David's two-flat, where he lived with his beautilicious girlfriend, Dee Dee Stetser, a pharmacy student.

Danny didn't wake until four PM the following day.

His brother had left about ten newspapers on the kitchen table, along with a shaver and a toothbrush and some B.O. juice.

As a goof, Bridget and Maureen had had best-friend pictures taken at Thanksgiving. The two of them had posed in short black slip dresses and men's black top hats they got online. That was the picture the Minneapolis paper used. It took up half the front page.

It was just a joke. They had wanted to look, Bridget said, like sexpots from Paris. But they looked like hookers or something, not kids fooling around.

Who gave the newspaper that picture? Even Mrs. O. didn't have one. Danny did. Bridget had left one in his locker as a joke gift. Who else had one except Maury and Bridget?

The other newspapers showed the two of them sitting on the shoulders of one of the big fullbacks last year, when the football team went to state in Division Three. The night they'd won the game.

They could have been sisters.

They were sisters.

Danny wondered if it were mentally possible to climb out of your own skin. He thought he would like to get in the truck and drive until he ran out of gas and not call home until he was a sophomore in college. But instead he took a shower, slipped into the clean sweats David or Dee had laundered for him while he was asleep and went home. He left a note: "Thanks, David and Double-D," in answer to theirs: "Hang in there, Danno."


Jeannie tried to do first things first.

She helped Bill calm himself when it became clear that Maury didn't recognize him.

And an hour later, when the boys came, Maury seemed to know Tom and his wife, Mary—she smiled at them—but not the twins or Patrick. Dr. Park had told them there was an outside possibility that Maureen would have to reacquaint herself with her own family, though it also was possible that, as time passed, memories would be triggered by smells, music, photos of them together, and particularly, in her experience, family videos.

"Why is that?" Bill asked, anguished. "My girl came back from the dead. She might never know I'm her dad!"

"No, no. That's not true. It's just that the realization might take a long time to come. We don't know what triggers it."

"Why pictures?"

"We don't know," said Dr. Park, calm and kind. "And, of course, the people who do know the most, the ones who suffer the worst damage, can never really tell us what they experience. We know more about the deepest hole in the ocean than the engine every one of us has that powers our every breath and our every dream."

Jeannie comforted Pat, who couldn't understand how it was possible that his little sister could come back from the dead and not remember the brother she loved best.

Each of her brothers thought that Maureen loved him best. That was Maury's gift.

Could Jeannie have borne it if Maury didn't know her? She thought that, now, with her girl back, she could bear anything.

. . .

On the morning after they'd learned about the mistake, after they had received the DNA test results that showed a likelihood of less than one half of one percent that Bill was not the biological father of the girl lying in the bed, Jeannie found her way to the hospital's tiny reflection room, which was what they called a hospital chapel these days; and when she was sure no one could see, she dropped to her knees on the carpeted concrete and prayed for Mike and Kitt Flannery.

That she was half mad with joy was a given to God, Jeannie believed. But she knew—truly knew, perhaps as no one else knew—the icy pit in which Kitt and Mike floundered now. She knew they would find themselves standing in the middle of a room, not knowing why they were there, what they were wearing, what they held in their hands. She knew, truly knew, how it was to hope your own life would be brief; to shun the sunrise because it dared, with its beauty, to provoke your welcome; to want to enfold yourself in the coats at the back of a closet, shut out all light and sound, and breathe only long enough for your breathing to stop on its own.

In her own first days, she had tried so hard to act normal for the boys. She had dressed and brushed her teeth. She had even gone with them to Bill's mother's on Christmas Day, though the funeral would be the next morning. She remembered all of them sitting at the table and how someone, Bill's father or Mary, her daughter-in-law, would try to start a conversation of some kind and how each time it would sputter out, like a candle. Jeannie didn't even try to join in. Finally they stopped speaking to her at all.

The morning of the funeral Jeannie had overheard Jack say on the phone, "We're all a mess, but our mother is gutted. I don't know if she'll make it."

Reawakened to life from her own grief, she asked God for guidance down the new path opening before her. She prayed that Kitt and Mike could somehow scrape away the layers of outrage and hatred to find some measure of acceptance, for Eliza's and Sarah's sake. And she asked God to bless the Flannerys for their constant vigilance over Maureen.

Then she headed back up to the unit.

Supported by two nurses, Maureen was standing in her bare feet.

Standing?

When Maureen was back in the reclining chair, a physical therapist came, asking Maureen to push as hard as she could against the woman's palm with one foot, then the other, over and over again. The therapist sounded like Bill with his wrestlers: "Come on, Maureen. Gut it out. Kiddo, we're going to get you out of that bed as fast as we can. At least you still have your flexibility. You must have been a rubber band!"

And Maury, whose every gesture and expression now was a shrine to Jeannie, nodded because she understood.

She understood!

And though the hair around Maureen's reddened face exploded in tendrils from the sweat of exertion, it seemed to Jeannie that the leg barely moved, that the therapist was doing most of the work. But the therapist said she was pleased.

"No excuses," said the PT, Shannon Stride. "This is where we'll start. She clearly hears me. She clearly sees. We'll work on speech. Identifying objects. Aphasia could be a problem."

"And that's?"

"Trouble retrieving the names of things. It's all in there. We have to tease it out. I'm impressed with her leg muscles. Did she run track?"

"She's a cheerleader," said Jeannie.

"Huh," said the therapist, almost as though disgusted. Jeannie saw Maureen shake her head as if to say, It figures. What she always said was true. Cheerleaders got no respect.

When Shannon left the room, Jeannie brushed out Maureen's hair to plait it into a neat braid. Though it was clean, no one seemed to have brushed her hair in days. Together, she and Lorelei, the red-haired nurse who came on at three o'clock, secured Maureen's hair out of her face, avoiding the slight surgical swelling, keeping the area where the skin grafts were growing clear.

"Just touching her hair is like seeing the sun again for me," said Jeannie. "I'll never stop crying."

"No one expects you to," Lorelei said.

She got some nail polish from one of the nurses and they painted Maureen's stubby nails one by one. Maureen smiled her poor, half-toothed smile.

"Than, Mom," she said. "Is it snowing?"

"No, honey," Jeannie said.

"Than," Maureen said again.

"Do you want to sit up or lie down."

"Sit," she said. "Rag Mop, sit."

Her thoughts would come to her now if she called them. They weren't instantaneous or always exactly the ones she wanted, but they would come. Nail polish. Earlier, the pleasure of hand cream. She was happy to be alive and with her mother. It was like being born again, only born knowing you were born. Sometimes an image—of the cheerleading squad, of her nest of pillows with their Irish lace slips hand-crocheted by Grandma—would slip across her mind like a hummingbird, so clear and so quick that Maury was not sure she'd really seen it. Childhood, she could remember all of that. Christmases, her first bike, riding on Tommy's shoulders and touching the ceiling, the smell of leaves burning. But the past year . . .

"Do you have a Bible I can use?" Jeannie asked Lorelei. She did, but it wasn't the one Jeannie wanted. She preferred her grandmother's old King James with its "thees" and "thous"—at least outside of church.

She found Psalm 30: 2–5, her favorite since school days, on a computer Lorelei let her use: *O Lord my God, I cried unto thee, and thou hast healed me. O Lord, thou hast brought up my soul from the grave. . . . Weeping may endure for a night, but joy cometh in the morning.*

The few lines she chose seemed to say it all.

While Maureen slept, Jeannie went to the little computer room that the ward provided to email her sisters, Rose and

Grace, who still lived in her hometown, Verona, Wisconsin, to tell them what they had probably already heard on the news.

She sent another message to Bill's sister, Sandy. At the top she typed in the lines from Psalm 30. She added, "I think that I have loved this passage all my life because it led us to this moment. For we were cast down into the pit, Sandy. We were in the grave. And I cried out only for the strength to go on, but instead I received this magnificent gift, truly a new morning in our lives."

When she returned to Maury's room, Jeannie wrapped herself in a blanket and slept in the chair.

The following morning Lorelei, shrugging on her coat and about to leave, woke her gently by saying, "Mrs. O'Malley, I think you might want to look at the TV."

Lorelei pressed the button, and the wide screen revealed Molly, Britney, and Leland! They were being interviewed by Matt Lauer!

"Oh my goodness!" Jeannie said.

"Yeah," Lorelei said.

"They were so completely messed up that it was impossible to see what they really looked like," said Leland. "I saw when the ambulance took Maureen away from the accident. She was totally covered in blood. Her own mother wouldn't have known her."

"We were just starting to get used to missing Maureen a little when we found out," said Molly.

"It's like we have to change our grief now. A totally different person died. I don't know how we can feel happy and sad at the same time," Britney said.

"And you have started a website where people can send their thoughts and prayers and offers of help for the families?" asked Matt Lauer. "I heard about this. Someone said this website has gotten more than four thousand messages already—from Israel, Australia, Italy. . . ."

"People are totally supportive of it," said Leland. "We haven't seen Maury yet, because she's in rehab. But we have been sending the checks that come to us to the bank in a special fund for her that Mr. Vonnenburg created. There are actually two funds, one for her and one that was already set up for a scholarship in Maureen's memory for a cheerleader. Now it will be in Bridget's memory. But it's getting to be a lot, just in a few days. We were going to send someone to a cheerleading camp, but now it might be a college scholarship."

"Wouldn't that be great? Here is the address, folks, if you want to send a donation, or you can write to the blognet address called 'These Two Girls,' all one word and all caps . . . ," Matt said.

A line crept across the screen with the address of the Bigelow Bank.

"You were all cheerleaders together?"

"Since eighth grade. It's not like anything else. You get to be each other's best friends. It's like a family," said Molly.

"A dysfunctional family," Leland added. Everyone laughed.

A few seconds of the girls, videotaped in state competition, flashed across the screen next.

"I thought our names weren't released to the media," said Jeannie, watching anxiously as she saw Maureen begin to follow the images on the screen.

"Hmm," said Lorelei. "Not by us they weren't."

Watching Bridget drop from her stand on the others' shoulders into the basket of the others' arms was an eerie moment.

"If you're just joining us, that was Bridget Flannery, a champion cheerleader, who was killed just before Christmas. Bridget was in an auto accident with her best friend, Maureen O'Malley. Until just three days ago, her family believed Bridget was alive. But it turned out that the girl they were caring for was really Maureen. This terrible mix-up has caused great joy for the O'Malleys and, understandably, stunning grief for the Flannerys.

"We are talking now to Bridget's and Maureen's best friends, fellow cheerleaders from Bigelow, Minnesota. How is the school reacting? It's a very small school, isn't it?"

"Just four hundred kids. We don't know how to feel. They'll be bringing counselors to talk to any of us who want next week," Britney said. "We're happy, of course, but we're sad. The whole town is, like, torn apart. We were destroyed that Maureen was dead. But now that it's really Bridget who is dead, we have to live through this all over again. It's not just their families. It's all of us. This is a tragedy and a miracle for a whole town."

"In a moment we'll hear from one of the paramedics

who was on the scene that night, in this strange and heart-breaking case of two young Minnesota girls. Friends and families mourned at Christmas for Maureen O'Malley, only to learn after eight weeks that the girl who died was not Maureen but her best friend, Bridget Flannery. We'll be back after the break."

"Bug," said Maureen.

"Oh, Maury," said her mother. "Oh, sweetheart. Of course you didn't know."

But she had known.

Some part of her had known Bridget was dead.

Some part of her had reached out, and Bridget was not there. To hear them say it, though, that was different. She didn't want to die—already did that. But live without Bridget? Never hear Bridget call her and say, "I have the most disgustingly exciting news." Bridget, her other self, who knew things about Maury no one would ever know, who she needed now more than ever. Maureen began to breathe harder. It was as though she couldn't grab enough air.

She heard a murmur, felt a silvery shot of fluid slide into her arm, and fell asleep.

# blog fight

Leland, Molly, and Britney had their pictures taken with Matt and one of the female anchors, Meredith. The other one, Ann, was busy talking with an author. They got autographs and zippered carry bags. "Will you come back and give us an update?" a producer asked.

"Totally!" said Leland.

The girls went outside, into the bright sunshine. People behind the barricades in front of the studio's big plate glass windows were waving to them. A boy on a bike stopped and said, "I just saw you on TV!"

When they finished taking pictures in front of the building with its rainbow logo, they were taken back to their hotel in a Lincoln Town Car. It was one of those fancy

Japanese hotels. Mrs. Broussard took advantage of the night they would be spending here to get them tickets to a musical. They ate dinner at Joe Allen's and saw the guy who was in *Honey, I Shrunk the Kids* and a famous old lady Mrs. Broussard said had the most beautiful voice of any singer on Broadway, and who had been the original Griswolda or someone in *Cats,* whatever that was.

They went shopping at Sephora and Henri Bendel, where Molly lost it and spent everything she had saved from two birthdays and two Christmases on a purse. They took a horse carriage ride through Central Park.

"I've been in Chicago, and how much bigger this city is just blows me away," said Britney. They ran up and down the stairs in the Nike store. They bought CDs at a huge record store with five floors. Afterward they saw the show, a musical based on the Little House books, with Laura as an older woman singing, "My father built this house of logs, now trees have moved inside. The child I was comes running, her arms flung open wide. Oh Laura, barefoot girl, take me back with you. . . ."

It was the best time they ever had.

They were totally exhausted.

They fell into bed at midnight and got up to hear more about themselves on TV as they dressed to fly home.

Molly got a hundred text messages on her cell phone from friends who saw her on TV. When Lee-Lee called home, her mother told her that somebody from *England* had called. A magazine, *Your Own UK*, wanted to interview the girls. Somebody from Australia called in the middle of the night, too! And *People* magazine was coming next week. They wanted to try to get pictures of Maureen, and would Leland help? Britney's dad told her a lady had called and asked him about a *movie*. But when Britney told Molly, Molly's mouth turned down and she boringly said, "You know, maybe we should have asked the O'Malleys before we did this."

"Didn't I leave them, like, a hundred messages about our blog?" Leland asked.

"You can imagine why they're not returning calls," said Britney.

Leland flopped back in her seat.

"You know, you are so small-town. This is a national thing. This is a miracle and a huge tragedy all wrapped up in one. What were we supposed to do, refuse to talk to Matt Lauer? People care about this. And it was your idea to start the blog, smarty-pants!"

"I know it was," Molly said. "But that was different. It was to help the O'Malleys and the Flannerys pay off their bills and stuff. Can you imagine having to pay bills for a girl who died? And I really think there should be something in Maur—I mean Bridge's memory. And cheerleaders from all over were calling us and texting us and emailing Eddy to find out what they could do so people would hear. It was natural."

"And you were very professional, with your little pictures and everything. . . ." Lee-Lee egged her on.

"I didn't do it for the attention!"

"So you did not like being on this show! It's something you regret!"

"I liked it! I just think we have to go to the hospital as soon as we get home and tell the O'Malleys. We should have asked them."

"Hmm?" said Leland. Eric had texted her. He wanted to see if she could hang out Friday night. But then so had Shane Baker and Matt Wright.

To Jeannie's alarm the appearance of the trio on *Today* was only the first salvo of the media army that descended on Bigelow and camped outside the hospital.

"I can't imagine how they all found out about us," Jeannie told Ben, the nurse.

"Mrs. O'Malley, I'm sorry, but this is a really big deal. I know that no one from the hospital was supposed to say a word, but there are two thousand people working here, and every single one of them knows about this. You could hardly expect them to keep their mouths shut."

"I guess. Do you think it will stop now?"

Privately, Ben was surprised that somebody hadn't used a phone to take a picture of Maureen in her pigtails and flowered pajamas. That didn't happen for another week. But there were already photos in *Ours* and *The One* of the cheerleaders and of workmen replacing Maureen's headstone with a temporary cross for Bridget Flannery, and of the Flannery house and Danny Carmody jogging across the parking lot of the school to his truck. Ben thought, *No way is this going to end.* He looked at Jeannie with pity. People loved their miracles! They were in short supply in the real world. It came with the territory.

When Jeannie finally could no longer bear to wash with little foil packets of Castile soap and wear hospital scrubs, she dodged reporters successfully by leaving through the staff exit. But once she was home, she found the answering machine clogged with forty-five messages that she dutifully copied down—from a distant school friend who now worked for *Nancy Cassidy Live,* from two different *Today* show producers, from the BBC and *Stars and Stripes,* from Leland Holtzer and Molly Schottmann. The last was from Danny Carmody.

Jeannie called Danny back.

"You probably don't want to hear from me," he said.

"Why ever not?" asked Jeannie. "You're Maureen's pal, Danny."

"I was honestly broken up that it was Maury and not Bridget. I fell apart for a while. A few of us did. Bridget . . . no one on earth is as sweet as Maury, but Bridget . . ." Jeannie waited, not wanting to intrude. "I . . . can't say what I mean," Danny concluded.

"Bridget was like a comet, Danny. Everyone loved Bridget. Why should I blame you?"

"Does Coach?"

"Danny! For goodness sake!" Jeannie scolded him.

"I can't believe Bridget is gone," he said.

"Neither can I," Jeannie said honestly.

"You must be totally happy."

"Not really. Of course I'm overjoyed for us. I'm sick for the Flannerys," Jeannie said. "Have you seen them?"

"I went over once. I talked to Mr. Flannery and to Sarah. They're trying to plan a memorial service. But Mrs. Flannery is like, out of it."

"I should have gone to see her by now."

"They're pretty out of it."

"Danny, I'm so sorry," Jeannie said.

"Yeah, it's rough. I don't think it's really hit me yet. It's just days. . . ."

"This will be with you for years, Danny."

"Would you mind if I came to see her?"

"No, of course not," Jeannie answered, slightly shocked. We . . . actually, we want to encourage her friends to come to see her. The last few days have been a blur for me. Maury is starting to talk, and she saw Lee-Lee and the others . . ."

"On TV, yeah. Bridget's memorial fund at the bank has thousands and thousands of dollars in it already, Mrs. O."

"Well, I certainly don't know about that."

"People wonder why . . ."

"What, Danny?"

He thought he couldn't say it now, though going to see Maureen and saying this was the real reason he had decided to call. People were saying Coach and Mrs. O. didn't seem grateful. Nobody understood why they refused to talk to anybody. It was like Maury belonged only to them and not to anyone else who loved her.

"What?" Jeannie asked again.

And so he did tell her, and Jeannie went silent for a moment before she replied, "That makes sense."

"So, I thought I'd come to the hospital maybe Sunday."

"That's good," said Jeannie.

She put down the phone and called her son, Henry, at school to ask for his help. Henry agreed to drop all but one class and come back to Bigelow to become the O'Malley family spokesman.

Bill had to be coaxed into letting his son make such a sacrifice. He had to confer with Henry's coach to see if a semester off would mean cutting off Henry's scholarship. The coach was adamant: Henry would be welcomed back in the fall.

So with easy grace, Henry appeared on the Nancy Cassidy show and provided a home video of Bridget and Maureen for *Today*. He held a press conference in front of the hospital and spoke of his sister gradually growing more responsive by the day, answering questions, asking for her dog.

Henry told Larry King, "She's my sister, and so it's private to us, the family. You can't blame my folks for not wanting to leave her bedside. But we also understand how people can really genuinely care so much about a stranger. These people have become our friends even though we'll never meet them."

Jeannie was proud of him.

Henry started his own blog. He asked Jeannie to contribute a daily Bible verse, knowing that she would like that. The first was from Psalm 121.

*March 10*

Psalm 121:1   I will lift up mine eyes unto the hills, from whence cometh my help.

*There was great relief when my sister recognized my brother Pat today. Pat came home from school for the weekend because our family is having a sort of celebration at church, a Mass of thanks and then a small get-together. He went to the hospital and right away Maureen, who was sitting up in her chair, said "Fat!" And we know it wasn't a mistake, the kind she makes when she says "gulls" but means "glass" or "slider" when she means "window." When he was in about sixth grade, Pat was chubby, and Maury would tease him and call him "Fatty Patty." It was a great moment, because my brother was very depressed that Maury didn't know him at first.*

*Maureen's therapy is going well. Her right leg is still very weak, but her left leg is getting strong and stronger. Her arms were injured very badly in the crash, so the therapists are encour-*

*aged that she can do some small things like lift a glass—actually that's a pretty big thing!—and put together a simple puzzle.*

*The hospital let us bring our Yorkshire terrier, Rag Mop, to visit. He was Maury's twelfth-birthday present. I thought she was going to jump out of the bed when she saw him. All the kids on the rehab unit loved petting Rag, and Maury was so proud that Rag would lie down on her lap while our mom was wheeling her around the unit. She still has trouble with ordinary words, but she startles us sometimes with more complicated ones. For example, Mom said she looked into the big playroom and right away said, "Chimpanzee," because there was a chimpanzee family painted on the wall.*

*My mom asks all of you who read this to please pray for our dear friends, the Flannerys, who are in the first stages of grief for their daughter Bridget.*

Jeannie spent one whole night reading Henry's blog and the answers to it, which came in by the dozens.

Then she read the blog begun by Molly. There were hundreds of posts from people who signed themselves "CheerleaderMom" or "BlessingBabe" or "SurferDude" or "FrancaisFrancis," all of them wanting to share their puzzlement and grief for the Flannerys and their joy for the O'Malleys.

She was particularly touched by one of them, from a woman in Utah who wrote: *"We understand now in part but will understand all in time. We aren't given to understand what happened, but we need to rejoice for both of these girls, for one has gone home to God and the other has come home, like the lost lamb, to her family."*

Jeannie thought all of it was good. But the cheerleaders' blog annoyed Henry.

One of them had changed the name to THESETWO-GIRLS: The Original Bridget-and-Maureen Blog.

Henry changed theirs to The Official O'Malley Family Blog.

Then Leland wrote: *"Of course we love Coach and Mrs. O. to the sky, but it's hard to not be invited to see your best friend if you thought she was dead. They keep her to themselves like they think we're these intruders with germs or something. I haven't been to see Maureen one time and they haven't returned my phone calls."*

Henry looked up the Holtzers' number and called.

"Leland," he said, "it's Henry O'Malley."

"Oh," she said. "Hi."

"I called to ask you to come and see Maureen. You didn't need an engraved invitation, Leland."

"You don't have to be such a jerk, Henry," she said.

"I'm not the one being a jerk. You're making us sound like we don't want people around Maury, but we actually would love it if she could see some of you."

"Just some of us. Not me?"

"I didn't say that."

"Well, you act like it," Leland said. "I know the Flannerys are really offended that you didn't talk to them, too, which I personally would have done myself."

"Have you been over to see them?"

"No, but I know that's how they feel."

"I didn't call to fight with a seventeen-year-old kid, Leland," said Henry, pulling the college card.

"And what are you, twenty? Please."

"This is ridiculous. You guys act like this is all about you going on the *Today* show and getting quoted in magazines. My sister was dead. We thought my sister was dead," Henry said.

"We did, too, Henry. And we love Maureen, too. We probably know her better than you do. We spent every day with her for the past three years. You've been in college since she was in eighth grade. Give me a break!"

"Well, then come and see her. Come a few at a time. But don't be surprised if she doesn't recognize you at first. She's still getting better, and she doesn't even recognize my dad."

Leland gasped. "No way!"

"It's very common."

And it was in the *Star-Telegram*, on the front page below the fold, in the morning. The fact that Maureen didn't know her own father was there with an anonymous quote from someone "at the scene" saying that Maureen had not been wearing her seat belt.

But the O'Malleys decided to ignore it.

Jeannie offered Father Genovese a hundred dollars to rent the church gathering room for an hour after Saturday night services so that she and Bill and the boys could throw an open house to thank everyone who had been so kind to them.

Seeing people again, Jeannie felt as though it were she who was awakening from a long sleep.

She realized that it had become a custom for her to go for days without taking a bath or washing her hair, simply stumbling out of bed and shrugging on Maury's old UM sweatshirt over whatever she'd had on the day before—leggings or sweatpants or pajama bottoms—and heading to the hospital. If it were up to her, she would have eaten nothing but chocolate because it gave her a sensory moment of being alive—not pleasure, simply a short reentry into the realm of human comfort. Jeannie hadn't cooked a meal in months.

Every day since the accident, though, there was a casserole and a dessert outside the door. No notes, no bids for gratitude. Jeannie had enough Corning Ware to open an aisle at Sears! All the offers of support and kindness, the benefactor who would not give his or her name who paid off the emergency treatment balance—and it was huge, despite what the hospital deferred, more than ten thousand dollars. She couldn't believe she had been so lost and so, honestly, demented that she couldn't respond to these gestures. How could she not have been aware of such love?

Father Genovese, of course, refused any payment for renting the room. The Altar Guild decorated it in gold and black—in tribute to Bill as well as to both girls. And when Jeannie saw all the older ladies down there before Mass, all of them just itching to hug her and tell her that their prayers were answered, she almost felt guilty.

It was a beautiful occasion.

Bill got choked up thanking everyone, and Jeannie had to take over. "We're just so happy and so blessed," she said.

After an hour or so people drifted away, happy.

Dr. Park said that the comfort of familiar things in a hospital setting was important to any child, no matter how old she was. So parents were encouraged to bring everything they could find that wasn't too big or cumbersome.

The O'Malleys filled a duffel bag with Maury's things— her favorite Mickey Mouse flannel PJ bottoms; her CDs and a boom box; photos of her brothers and Rag Mop, and of Bridget.

Jeannie wished she had the quilt she had pieced from Maury's baby clothes and middle-school cheerleading uniform, but it gave her comfort knowing it lay over little Bridget, like a touch from Maureen's hand. Instead she took out the precious old quilt her grandmother had brought from Ireland—these many years in the cedar closet.

Bill was strangely quiet on the drive toward the hospital;

Jeannie had known this man for thirty years. She finally asked, "What's eating you, darling?"

"Well, you know we should go see them."

He didn't have to add who "they" were.

"We could send them a letter," Jeannie offered.

"Jean, you know we can't do that."

"How can I face them?

"We have to," Bill said simply.

And so they backtracked and knocked for several minutes on the Flannerys' door before Sarah answered.

Dark haired and broad shouldered, she looked nothing like her older sister Bridget. She and Eliza were both more like Mike.

"I'll get Daddy," she said.

Mike came down the hall to meet them. Impossibly, he seemed to have lost ten pounds in two weeks. His thick, dark hair stuck up in spikes, and the sweats he wore were stained with something, coffee or syrup.

"Bill," Mike said. "Jean."

"Mike," Bill said. "I'm so sorry. Jean and I and the boys are so sorry. We loved Bridget."

"I know that."

Jeannie asked, "Can I see Kitt?"

"She's, ah, asleep," said Mike. "Yeah. She is asleep. It's best for her now. She can't really handle it . . . the calls from the newspapers and people trying to take pictures of the little girls. Yeah."

"Who is down there?" a voice shrieked from somewhere

high above them.

"Yeah," said Mike distractedly. He called, "It's Bill and Jean, honey. They came to talk to us."

They heard the quick slap of running feet.

"NOW!" Kitt screamed, leaning over the railing of the vaulted foyer twenty feet above their heads. "Where were they when we found out it was our daughter who died?"

"Kitt," Jeannie said, beginning to climb the stairs.

"It's probably not the best time," Mike said.

Jeannie kept climbing. Kitt ran at her, swinging her right arm out perpendicular to Jean's face; but before she could strike, Jean wrapped her arms around the taller woman and together they sank to the carpet, Kitt sobbing and clinging to Jeannie. "Why couldn't we keep both of them? Why would God play such a cruel joke on us?"

"Oh, Kitt, I don't know. I only know you helped keep our girl alive."

"I can't go on living," Kitt whispered, sitting back on the carpet.

"You don't have to, for a while. Just keep breathing. I didn't ever want to see another living soul. But I had to. I had to because I had four sons, like you have those two little girls."

"A part of me hates you," Kitt said. "Can you believe that?"

"Completely," said Jeannie. "We felt the same way."

"No, you're a good person. You're naturally good," Kitt replied.

"No one is that good," Jeannie told her. "We had awful thoughts."

They sat together on the floor for ninety minutes. Finally Kitt nodded off in Jeannie's arms.

# the pipeline

After she finally visited Maureen, Leland showed everyone the photo she had taken with her phone. Maureen had tried to put her hands up to block the picture, but her hands were too slow.

"She looks like Frankenstein," said Elly Mazur. "I don't mean that in a bad way."

"And she talks in one word. 'Hi. Mom.' And she can't remember the easiest things, like the word for 'window,'" Leland said.

"Lee-Lee, shut up!" Molly said. "That's not fair!"

"I am only telling the truth," Leland said.

"You are only doing your favorite thing, causing trouble," said Molly. "We have practice in ten minutes. The

NBC crew is coming to film us."

"Ohmigod," said Leland. "I look like dung!"

"Well, if you weren't so busy running off your mouth!"

"I heard Danny went to see her yesterday," Elly said. "Is that true?"

"I have no idea," Molly said.

"Yes, it is," said Leland.

Molly grabbed Leland by the arm and let her fingers dig in.

By the next day, Leland had sold the photo of Maureen to the British magazine. When it finally worked its way over the Internet back to Minneapolis, her parents grounded her for two weeks and made her apologize to the O'Malleys.

Henry was furious.

Jeannie was hurt.

Danny Carmody told Lee-Lee she had gone nuts and she was no friend of his anymore.

Danny hated the attention and couldn't understand why anyone would feel otherwise. Reporters followed him to and from school in cars. People took pictures of him bringing pink roses to lay against the temporary marker on Bridget's grave. It seemed that whenever he said something, it showed up on a blog or in the newspaper. It got so that Ev was the only other human being outside his family he spoke to.

Ev and Coach.

And then he went to see Maureen, and it was all so familiar. Danny felt as though he had crept into a refuge. The hospital was more real to him than school.

The first thing that happened had terrified him.

When he got to her room, Maureen wasn't there. He stood just inside the door, hoping someone would come along and tell him what was going on. The person turned out to be Maureen, returning to her room in a wheelchair pushed by Mrs. O.

She had changed so much in just over a couple of weeks that he had had to sit down.

There was also the painful knowledge that she wasn't his Bridget. The last time he had seen her, he had thought she was a different girl. It was too much information to organize on the spot.

So Danny simply looked at her.

The bruises on Maureen's face were fading. She had teeth instead of the caved-in place at her cheek. Her hair was French-braided loosely, and she had on her Mickey Mouse pajamas and her big UM sweatshirt. When she smiled at him, she looked almost like a regular girl.

Danny couldn't help but think of that spring night last year.

Maureen had probably forgotten it ever happened.

But she did know him.

"Danny!" she said clearly, and held out her hands. He got up and hugged her while Mrs. O. watched. "Danny! Bug . . . not here," Maury said. "Danny, so sad. Danny, it's so sad. Danny, I gush the try. I gush . . ." She wanted to pummel herself. She thought, *I sound like a retard, and I probably am.*

"The confusion gets worse when she's upset," said Mrs.

O. She and the nurse maneuvered Maureen from the chair to the bed. Then Mrs. O sat down in the rocker. Danny sat in the big, overstuffed chair.

No one said anything.

Jeannie took out her knitting bag.

Maureen finally said, "Mom. Go. Banana. Split."

"Oh, I'm so sorry! Maureen, I'm so sorry! Of course you don't want your mother sitting here! I'll go get a bite to eat! I like the ice cream downstairs. She's not being random."

"It's okay," Danny assured Mrs. O. "You can stay."

"Nuh!" Maureen said, louder. She rapped on the arm of her chair with her knuckles. "Splits. Bigelow. Go. Go!" She blushed. "Sorry. I thought of cheering. In the brain, out the mouth. That is what Shannon says. Shannon is the physical therapy person."

How could she say some things so plainly but stumble over the word "no"? Danny was dumbfounded.

"Maury's right, Danny," said Mrs. O. "She would have killed me for sitting here watching her talk to her friends before the accident, and I don't blame her for feeling the same way now!"

Alone, Danny took Maureen's hand and kissed it. "You know, you're probably thinking I'm sad that it's you. How I really feel is sad it's not Bridge. I'm happy it's you. I missed you. I couldn't stand that I would never see you again."

Maureen nodded and pointed to her chest. Danny took this to mean that she felt the same way.

"I loose," she said. "Let loose. No. no. I have loose."

"You lost your best friend. I lost my girlfriend—the girl I really thought I would marry someday," Danny said, frightened he would cry.

He did begin to cry.

"Okay, Danny. Okay, Danny," said Maury. Of course it was okay. They had both loved Bridget so. Anything you said was safe with Maury.

Maureen had felt confused. The strong, square line of his jaw made her stomach tighten below her belly button. She remembered Danny had kissed her once. They had done some things. She and this person right hair. No. Here.

But she also knew that Bridget and Danny had done everything. Their first time was at homecoming—a warm October night on top of the hill at the ritzy golf course subdivision. . . . What was it called? The Covers? The Corn? Bridget had told Maureen everything: how much it hurt the first time, how good it felt the second time.

"You're probably going to wait until you're married," Bridget had told Maury.

"I'm probably going to wait until I meet someone who wants to do it with me," Maureen answered.

"Lots of guys would want to," Bridget argued.

"Yeah, sick perverts like Grant Milorry!"

"Lots of guys like you," Bridget insisted.

"They like me, but they don't like me like a girl. They like me like a sister," Maureen had told her. "Danny says I'm as good to talk to as a boy."

"That's quite a compliment," Bridget said, heading for the bathroom.

She watched now as Danny talked, and unwanted thoughts kept crowding in on her. This boy had been naked with Bridget. She felt her face get warmer and warmer. If Danny looked up now, he would see a girl who looked like a potato. No, no. A tomato.

"So, all those days I sat here and read and cried and watched TV and farted, it was you all the time," Danny said. "I guess I'm glad it was you, because you know me. But it's really weird seeing the same girl I saw for all those weeks and knowing it's not Bridget." Maureen nodded. "You look so much like yourself, which means you look so much like her. You look . . . pretty."

Maureen made a motion as if she were holding something in two hands, moving the fingers of her right hand.

"The guitar?" Danny guessed. *Oh hell. She did remember that time.* "Would you like me to bring it sometime?" Maury nodded.

"I drink. I drain. I . . ." She pounded her small fist on the railing of the bed. "I dream about Bug."

"I do, too," Danny said. "I dream about when we were younger. I dream about all of us at Memorial Pool. I dream of Bridget in her homecoming dress."

Maureen looked away, startled by her own anger. Had she always been jealous of Bridget and Danny?

"Are you tired, Maury?"

"No!" she answered, sharper than she meant to be. It

134

was her turn to talk. "Do see Kitt?" she asked.

"Yes."

"Does she know?"

"Know?"

"Know Bridget hit . . . cross . . . hit . . . truck?"

"No," Danny said. He was stunned. "Are you sure?"

"Yes," Maury said. "Yes. We. Fooling. My fool. My fault."

"No, Maureen. Just an accident," Danny said, his mind whirling.

"I want Kitt see." God! Would she always be an idiot? She sounded like an idiot with her mouth full of oatmeal. The new teeth looked pretty, but they made her talk funny—as if she didn't talk funny anyhow. But Danny understood. He looked surprised.

"Uh. You want to see Kitt? I'll tell her; but, Maury, I don't think she can handle coming to see you now. She's a basket case. May not even go to her own daughter's memorial on Monday. The cheerleaders have made up a ballet sort of thing to this song. . . ."

"You Got Friend."

"Yes, it's the same one that they played . . ." Danny realized that he had been about to say that it was the same one that they had played at *Maureen's* funeral.

"I know," Maureen said clearly. "My dead."

Her mother had told her all about it. The salute by the cheerleaders. Her beautiful quilt that now kept Bridget warm. The trophy won in her honor.

She was glad she had died young, at least once, while

135

everyone still liked her.

"Yes," Danny said. "Taylor sang that at your . . . service. She was named after the guy who wrote it, I guess. I have to speak at this service. . . ."

"Say lub, lush . . . ," said Maureen.

"Try again."

"Love. Bug," Maureen said carefully.

"I will," Danny promised. "I'll tell them you are thinking of Bridge. I don't know how to get through it. It's not real to me that she's gone."

"Home," said Maureen.

"I don't blame you," Danny said.

"Home," she said again. "Rag. You. Kiss me. Oh, God, sorry."

"You'll go home soon."

Abruptly, Maureen reached for a button and flicked on the TV.

"Sorry," she said. "*Days* is on."

Danny couldn't believe it. She was going to ignore him because of a soap opera! The first time he saw her after she literally came back from the dead. Maureen was utterly absorbed in the boring antics of Alice and Julie and Lucas and Maggie. Danny thumbed through a *Time* magazine from 2005.

"It's time for her to rest now," said Mrs. O'Malley, peeking in. "They tell us a half hour . . ."

"No!" Maureen almost yelled, snapping off the television and pushing a plastic water jug off onto the floor. Danny jumped out of the way. The floor flooded.

136

Maureen began to cry.

"She gets so emotional. It's normal," Mrs. O. told him.

"Come? Coming? Common. Mom!" Panicky, Maureen thought, *He's never going to come back. He just dropped by this one time.* And she had turned on the TV! "Don't go."

"She wants you to come back, Danny."

"Tell her . . ." That was crazy. He could tell her himself. "I will next week, Maury. I promise. Do you want me to bring Leland or Molly or Britney? It's probably easier if we come in a group because of gas."

"No!" Maury cried again.

"Okay, I'll just come."

"I think she feels you were closer to Bridget," Mrs. O. said, as Maury's eyelids blinked and drooped.

"She can't remember anything from the first few weeks after the accident. We're sure of that. But she has impressions. And she wants to see the picture of her car . . . all that. She wants to know more about the accident, Danny. We haven't felt entirely okay about telling her everything. She wants to see a picture of Bridget's grave. It's like she's obsessed with it."

"I guess I kind of get that. It's her life," Danny said.

And it was Bridget's death.

The O'Malleys were in the front row at Bridget's memorial, held in a heated tent on the Flannerys' wide lawn. Kitt did not want it at church; she said it would have reminded her too much of the first time, when they had buried Bridget without knowing it. There was hardly any room, and hundreds of people stood in their coats outside. A huge blow-up photo of Bridget's graduation picture stood on a stand, flanked by banks of pink roses. Between the news trucks and the regular people's cars, it was a mob scene. Henry Colette finally got disgusted and had his deputies block off the street so he could park his own squad car and get himself and Margo in.

The cheerleaders' "dance," which everyone thought would be incredibly stupid, was really sweet and short. It seemed to be about everyone laying down a rose or a leaf or a snowflake.

Mr. Flannery sounded like a robot.

He thanked the hospital for trying to save Bridget's life and nodded at the line of doctors seated toward the front. He thanked the hospital foundation for forgiving Bridget's expenses. He thanked his daughters, Eliza and Sarah, for giving him the will to go on. "I never was a church guy," he said. "Just on holidays. But now, I guess I want to believe that when I'm an old man, I'll see Bridget Katherine again. I guess she'll be as cute as she ever was, and not hurt; and she'll come running to me. I guess that's how I imagine heaven to be. My wife and I want to thank all of you for so much caring and love you showed us and continue to show us. We are putting together an archive of photos of Bridget, so any of you who have any . . ." He stopped and seemed to forget where he was. "Obviously, we are having a very hard time, my wife particularly. In fact, Kitt is going to stay with her sister in Wisconsin for a short while until she can face life again." Kitt's sister, Sherry, smiled and waved. He stopped again, for about five minutes. People looked around nervously. But then he started again. "The O'Malleys are our friends. They will always be our friends. Well. I just wanted to say that. Yeah."

Father Genovese got up and led them all in the Lord's Prayer.

Then Danny Carmody walked to the front of the room.

He looked down at a card, then put it into his pocket.

"I just want all of you to know that Bridget was an amazing person, more amazing than anyone I've ever met. And I know she wasn't afraid that night, because she was never afraid of anything in her life. I would imagine she would not be afraid of death, either. If she can see us, she's probably glad that the news trucks are here, because Bridget had no doubt that she was going to be famous in her life. On the red carpet. Not this way. But she probably doesn't mind." There was mild laughter. "I have a message for all of you from Maureen. She wants you to know she loves Bug—that was her name for Bridget. She misses her as much as I do, probably as much as anyone except her own mother and father and sisters do. I think it's important to remember that." In the silence, Kitt's thin, keening cry was the only sound. The news cameras pressed close. Henry Colette got up to tell them to get the hell out. "I wish this didn't happen. I wish we were all together again. I will always love Bridget Flannery. But we have to love Maury, too. We all lost something out there on County G that night. The Flannerys lost most of all. None of us will ever be the same."

He sat down.

His mother gave him an odd look. So did other people. He felt scratchy and hot in his suit, which was a little too short in the arms. Then, just as the caterers began to open tables and lay out silver bowls and platters, Mr. Flannery tapped him on the shoulder. Danny put his hand out to be shaken, thinking Mr. Flannery was going to thank him.

But he asked, "How dare you bring up Maureen at my daughter's memorial?"

Danny felt like Mr. Flannery had punched him in the gut.

"I'm sorry. I didn't think you would mind. She asked me to."

"You didn't mean to be offensive," said Mr. Flannery. "But it was completely wrong, Danny. Maureen is getting better. Bridget can never get better. You have no idea what we're feeling."

"Actually, I think I do," Danny replied, surprising himself.

"What? A kid crush? This was our child! Listen. Just . . . I'm not saying you're a bad kid. But you remind Kitt . . . just . . ."

"Well, okay. I won't come around."

"Just for now."

"Fine."

When Mr. Flannery turned his back to tell the men where to put the food, Danny and Ev took off.

# homecoming

Over the next two months, Jeannie met other mothers on the ward—each of them clutching her own shot glass of hope the way Jeannie's grandmother used to wrap her long fingers around her hot whiskey and sugar.

"You're so brave," she told one woman whose son had been airlifted from up north. The boy had been a piano prodigy at ten but was hurt diving into a shallow pond at his cousin's birthday party. That had been a year ago last summer. Every time he was about to go home, he got a fever or bronchitis and was readmitted to a medical floor. And then he had to come back to rehab. His injury was not only to his movements but also to his mind. "I'm not brave," the mother, whose name was Denise, told Jeannie as they strolled the long corridor, Denise pushing Charles in his wheelchair toward the soft-drink vending machines. "You do for your child what you do for your child. Everyone here does that. You did it when they were babies, and they need for you to do it again now."

"Skank!" snarled Charles, snatching at the vending machine with a hand cocked sharply at the wrist.

"He doesn't mean me. It's okay, honey," said Denise. "With the brain, it's like being obese. The more you have to lose, the more you can lose, or so it seems. But it's also true that the more you have to lose, the more you know you've lost."

Jeannie was submerged again in the wave of guilt: Maury was doing so much better than most of the kids. She was recovering more words each day.

Her regimen of physical exercises was endless. Maureen came back from physical therapy sweating as though she'd been at a long cheerleading practice. They had her bending her knees and raising her arms overhead to improve her range of motion after the shoulder injury. They taught her to use exercise bands and little dumbbell weights. Jeannie sometimes watched Shannon barking out orders, "No, I said squeeze that ball! Do you want that right side at all! I said squeeze it, missy! Don't you throw it away!"

Shannon was like a mean sergeant in some bizarre army. That her daughter should have to undergo this after everything she'd already endured . . . but it was for the best. It was all for Maureen's own good.

And when Maureen went home, Jeannie would have to do the same things with her every day.

But Jeannie didn't know if she was adequate to the task of helping her child.

She thought that kids cramming for medical school exams must feel this way. There was so much to learn. They all said it would become routine once Maureen had done it a few times. Muscle memory, Shannon insisted. Dr. Park, so encouraged by Maury's progress, was beginning to talk about home, perhaps by May. Jeannie was horrified.

It was too soon.

She barely knew her way around the rehab!

But she tried to count her blessings.

Jeannie felt okay about leaving Maureen overnight now.

There was always someone from the family there. Henry came almost every day, as did Jeannie and Bill. Danny came several times a week. The cheerleaders came, too, but not with Danny. The story was slowly draining away from the front pages. There was so much to be grateful for that it seemed absurd to worry.

Jeannie remembered her vow to live life now, and tried to enjoy those moments that weren't a trial.

Molly and Taylor and Britney came to deliver a get-well CD with the most raucous dance music they could find. They did the Bigelow Stomp as they had for Bridget—well, as they had when they thought Maureen was Bridget. And as Maureen watched from her wheelchair, clapping in delight, Molly did back walkovers all the way down the hall of the ward. All the rehab kids were enchanted. One guy was so enchanted that he showed Taylor his penis. Taylor burst into tears and ran for the elevators. She never came back.

For Maureen, the visits were bittersweet.

Seeing Molly do the things she once could do—and knowing that Molly wasn't as good as she and Bridge had been—reminded her of her great hefty bag of losses. Bridget. The two of them in tumbling class. In their teeny Bulldog uniforms when they were in second grade, the two mascots for Bigelow High. Her aching, stubborn muscles could remember how it felt to throw herself confidently back and touch the floor, to jump and almost touch her outstretched toes, to slip down into a split.

Never again. Never, never again.

Part of her wanted Molly—refreshing, healthy, pretty Molly—to go away and stay away. But when they weren't there, Maureen wanted all of them to come back.

One day when Molly visited alone, Jeannie could tell that there was something on her mind. And sure enough, Molly walked out into the hall and motioned for Jeannie. She asked if they could speak privately for a moment. From her room, Maureen roared. She hated it when people talked about her outside her hearing. With a troubled face, Molly confessed, "I knew it was her all the time. I had dreams."

Jeannie nodded and admitted something she hadn't even told Bill. "I had dreams that she was talking to me. I had dreams that she was telling me she was here. I thought she was trying to tell me that heaven was wonderful. Now I think it's possible that if you're close to someone, that person can kind of hear your voice in her head. And maybe you can hear her thoughts."

"Like ESP?" Molly asked.

"Who knows?" Jeannie answered with a shrug.

"I guess I was closer to her than anyone except Bridge," Molly said. "I mean, she was closer to Bridge than I was, not that I was closer to Bridge than I was to Maureen. I don't mean that the way it sounds. . . ."

"I know," Jeannie told her.

"So I kept thinking, Why am I dreaming about Maureen? Not Bridget? And still, I'm really, really happy for you. I hope you forgive us for going on the TV. . . ."

"We do."

"It was just all so exciting and so strange. I've read about other times it happened now, before this. But then I thought it was the first time it had ever happened. It was so scary and thrilling to be part of it!"

"It was."

Maury shouted to them, "Hell-OH!!"

Laughing, Jeannie and Molly hurried back into the room.

"You might have lost some teeth, but you found a temper!" Jeannie said.

*You try living in a shell and see how polite you are*, Maureen thought. But she only said, "Yes. I did."

"Keep it up," Molly told her, and Maureen could almost feel what she was going to say next. "You need that fighting

145

spirit! By fall you'll be back on the squad."

Was Molly stupid? Or only trying to be nice? Maureen knew she would be lucky to be able to sit in the stands for a game by next fall. When she left, Molly said, "I'll come back tomorrow."

But she didn't.

When the spring days started to lengthen and the flowers bloomed, Jeannie began wheeling Maureen out onto the roof terrace to see the daffodils and trilliums budding in the big tubs and boxes out there. Visiting Maureen had become a daily grind. The drama was over.

The cheerleaders' visits dropped off.

The kids were doing term papers.

The prom committee was having meetings twice a week.

It was only natural.

It broke Jeannie's heart.

And for Maureen it was devastating. There were days when she actively fought the therapists and nurses. She cussed them with words her mother didn't realize that Maureen knew. Why not just stay in bed? This was going to be her life anyway. Why should she let people push and prod her like a baby? Put stupid stickers on a chart when she walked a step alone on the rubber mats between the railings? She grew so depressed that rehab sent a psychologist to talk to her.

"I hear you've been refusing your therapy," the man

said. He wore a jogging suit and Nikes. Probably this was supposed to make kids feel he was "one of them." Maureen put a pillow over her face. "You're only hurting yourself, Maureen. If I were you, I'd want every bit of power back that I could have."

"You not me!" Maureen spat at him. "Fat. Fat butt." The man clearly wanted to be seen as a jock type. But his gut betrayed him.

"But if I were you, I'd stop feeling sorry for myself," he continued, shrugging off the insult.

Maureen burst into tears of rage.

The psychologist handed her a tissue. Why did people always do that? Didn't they know how good an accumulation of tears felt? When you cried, you wanted to drown in your tears, let them course down your neck and into your ears. It felt real.

"I loose my face. I can not walk! Bridget die. My head hurts all day. Sorry? For me? Sorry? Yes. Why not?" She looked around for something to throw. She was getting good at throwing things.

"Yes, feel sorry. Feel sad about Bridget. Feel hurt that you got slammed. But Bridget died. You didn't. You can sit here until your legs shrivel up into wet noodles or you can fight. I think Bridget would have fought," said the man.

Later, in the hall, he told Jeannie that Maureen was grieving entirely appropriately for her situation. The happy zombies were the ones who really worried him. He also said she might need weekly counseling later, that it would be worse when she was at home. Friends would be flipped out by her blurting and her impulsiveness. They would all promise to visit every day and then stay away. Here, her astonishing progress won her superstar treatment. Back among fully abled people, she was going to seem like a freak. The dumbest baggy pants guy would be more with the program than Maureen was. It wasn't that he wanted to say these things, the psychologist told Jeannie. But she needed to know.

Jeannie thought that if there was just one more thing she "needed to know," she might lose her mind altogether.

But of course he was correct.

"We'll all come around when she gets home," Molly told Jeannie and Bill one day when they ran into her at Apple Creek Mall, where they were buying clothing without zippers for Maureen, whose newest task was learning to dress herself. "I think the hospital is just such a downer."

How could Jeannie prepare Maureen for the inevitable? No one except a mother wanted to sit for an hour and try to make sense of a few sentences scrambled like Scrabble tiles tossed randomly on a table. The OT said that Maureen's speech would improve as she learned to manage a new way of communicating. She would always have to think before she spoke. It would be excruciating at first, then only difficult, then second nature—and probably not a bad idea even for people who didn't have brain injuries.

On the THESETWOGIRLS blog, Molly had taken to referring to herself as Maureen's best friend, which prompted some nasty comments from someone who took the nickname A Forgotten Friend.

*"Who does Molly think she is?"* A Forgotten Friend wrote. *"We were there the night it happened. Caitlin Smith and Leland Holzer and Britney Broussard were at the hospital. Molly was off visiting her relatives and didn't even know about the crash until she showed up in the morning for the meet. Really! Who wants total attention here?"*

THESETWOGIRLS turned into a sort of sniper fight. *"Who sold a picture of poor Maureen to a newspaper for a thousand bucks?"* wrote someone who signed himself OneGuy. *"I think some people are jealous that they aren't getting asked to be on TV anymore. They thought they were going to be the next Katie Couric!"*

An anonymous post read, *"What do you expect from a cheerslut?"*

Molly shot back: *"Well, all you so-called friends gather around! It's pretty lonely up there in the rehab ward for Maureen! I don't see you guys when I go up there. If you were all there for the crash, how come you're not there for her now? Was it oh-so-fine being there for Bridget but not Maureen? Huh?"*

Henry's blog remained daily and steadfast.

> *April 12*
> 1 John 4:18   There is no fear in love; but perfect love casteth out fear: because fear hath torment.
>
> *A huge day! Maureen took her first walk*

alone. *Three steps! She was holding on to the railings in the PT center, but barely. And she definitely walked! She wasn't pulling herself along with her arms. My dad was there and he burst out crying. Although Maureen still doesn't completely recognize Dad, which makes him very sad, she is getting to like him—which of course she would! He's her dad, after all.*

*Most of the damage to Maureen's brain—we THINK—was in what is called the primary motor cortex, which is part of the frontal lobe; and most of that was in the part that controls the movement of her right leg. There was some damage to the part that controls the planning and the movement of the hands, too, on the left side of her brain—so that the right side was affected. But I guess that when the swelling went down, there was less damage than they thought there was at first.*

*Maury's job is really hard. Because of the trauma, she has to relearn things she could already do, like decide how to reach for a glass based on where that glass is in space. Otherwise her hand could shoot past the glass or knock it over. She might be able to touch the glass but not be able to close her fingers around it. As best as the doctors can tell, Maureen's memory loss is from the psychological trauma, not actual brain injury. It might all be in there, but she has to work to bring it out. Or some of her perception of her life may be gone for good, and she'll have to "learn" it the way a kid learns a story. She'll have to memorize events from her own life.*

*A good example is this: When we show Maureen videos of a picnic or a birthday, she can remember everyone in the pictures, even our father. But she can't remember him when he is actually in the room with her.*

*What's really, really weird is that some people who came into the hospital and appeared to be far less "hurt" than Maureen may never be able to do the things she can do already.*

*Although she may get a bunch of the strength back in her right side, especially her hand and arm, the way the brain works is that things that are controlled by the one side happen on the other side. Most of the damage was on Maureen's right side sort of in the middle. So she is using her left hand more strongly every day. She will probably come out of this as a mostly left-handed person. And she will probably never be very good at writing in journals or doing embroidery. At least not for a year or more. But she made the letters of her name, and they were legible, though very shaky. The tutor thinks that she may need a scribe to do papers in school. Eventually, she will learn to use a word processor. Relearn, that is.*

*Okay! Maury will finally get her Mac!*

*I forgot to say, Maury has gone "back to school."*

*The school at the rehab unit is a room with books and materials for all ages. The teacher was shocked when she started to show Maury the alphabet, and Maury pushed it away and began to read from a book. She couldn't say all the words, but she could follow them. Dr. Park was completely amazed. It wasn't a children's book either. It was* To Kill a Mockingbird, *which the teacher was reading aloud to the other kids.*

*Maury is eating on her own now. She eats regular food, cut up. She is getting used to her new teeth, and there are none of the problems we were afraid of with her chewing and digestion. She is even sitting in the shower, though the weakness on one side makes it hard and she needs help with some of the many "shower ops" girls have to do.*

*Her hair is growing back! That's a big plus for Maureen. The skin grafts have taken. She made it VERY CLEAR that she would rather give up her long hair than have little thickets of new hair sticking up on the one side.*

*So last week a stylist from a very upscale salon in Minneapolis (thank you, Claire!) came and gave Maureen a sassy Euro cut. She looks so different, but she says it feels like her head has its clothes off. We are praying that the doctor is right and that she can start coming on an outpatient basis in a few weeks. We really want her home. We know it will be hard, and she'll have to sleep in a hospital bed with sides so she doesn't get up at night and injure herself. We know that she is going to be short-tempered when she can't do things. But if you saw where she started from and where she is now, you would see it is all worth it.*

*Thanks again, Mrs. B., for taking over for Mom at Holy Mother of Sorrows. Thank you to A., H., L., T. M. M., and so many others for your gifts and prayers. Maureen loves the stuffed dog that looks just like Rag Mop. The other day when her friend Danny came in, she made the dog say "Bark! Bark!"*

Her friend Danny was Maureen's most steadfast visitor outside of her family.

Maureen looked forward to his visits, and Jeannie and Bill noticed. At first they worried. Jeannie thought that Maureen might be trying to replace Bridget in Danny's life. Bill didn't think that. It was normal for a girl to want to look nice for any boy.

"But, Bill, what if she never has that kind of life as a

girl again?" Jeannie asked.

"That's nonsense. People who are paraplegic get married. Maury's a long way from that," Bill insisted.

So they took special care to make sure that her hair was clean and her teeth were brushed before Danny came. That made Maureen more comfortable and less likely to get agitated. One day Maureen struggled with a question the whole day. She kept grabbing at her mother's wrist and sniffing.

"Fumes," she said. "Bubs. Bubbles. Fumes and bubbles. Calling."

Finally, Lorelei asked, "Is what you want cologne, Maury?"

"Yes! Yes! Yes!" Maureen cried.

Cologne was in short supply on the unit. The nurses weren't allowed to wear any. Lorelei called down to the gift shop. There were only herbal scents, but the pink ladies sent the whole batch up for Maureen to sniff. She picked attar of tea rose, and Jeannie bought the bottle. When Danny Carmody came, she slipped him a note that said, "Say how nice her perfume smells."

Danny hugged Maureen.

"You smell like a rose," he said. To his shock, Maureen kissed him on the mouth.

Jeannie said uncomfortably, "That's just the impulsiveness we're supposed to expect. Maury doesn't have an editor in her brain right now. She's going to say whatever she thinks and do things without thinking about them beforehand. I'm sorry!"

"Not sorry!" Maureen insisted. "I like to kiss him."

Danny was not sorry either. He realized that it had been four months since he had kissed a girl, not counting his mom.

Danny pushed Maureen in her wheelchair—now one without head supports—out onto the roof terrace.

The lights of Minneapolis were just beginning to wink on.

Now that it was spring, Danny had gone out for baseball; he felt he needed something to do. A couple of girls had asked him if he wanted to hang out, but he felt it was way too soon for that. If he got good enough at baseball, he could play American Legion in the summer. Between that and working for his dad, it would pass the time. But practice meant he was coming up to see Maureen in the Cities in the evening rather than right after school. And he didn't stay as long, because he was so tired out.

It was a beautiful night, though. Maureen opened her coat and let the breeze tickle her throat. Her short hair was like long blond feathers now; to Danny, she looked like an extremely pretty little boy.

"The whole . . . ," she said, pointing down.

"The whole world," Danny said.

"Help," said Maureen, struggling to stand. She put out her hands and struggled to get up. Then she leaned against him, so light and small, as they looked out at the river of cars flowing through the loops of the highway. "I want to home."

"Of course you do. Pretty soon," Danny told her.

"I miss Brid-get."

"So do I."

"I miss her not as much with you."

It was the same for him. Together, they almost kept Bridget alive in their minds. That was the reason he kept coming, Danny realized, not only because his life was just an empty pit. He felt closer to Bridget with Maureen than he felt at Bridget's grave, where a pink headstone had been erected reading BRIDGET KATHERINE FLANNERY: OUR WILD IRISH ROSE.

It was all so sad; but when he was with Maureen, he was reminded of the other side of the sadness—the up side, if there was one, of losing Bridget. He saw Maury's guts, how hard she struggled every day for the things that he took for granted. He saw her pump the air with her fist when she lifted a spoonful of peas to her mouth.

Danny asked her how she did it, how she put up with all the drooly kids and the constant stretching of her legs and the battering of the questions and instructions. ("Do you know what the date is, Maureen?" "Read me the time on the clock, Maureen." "What is nine times twelve, Maureen?" "What's your address, Maureen?" "Come on, Maureen. Try again. Now harder. Try again. Punch my hand. Again!")

She shrugged. "Cheerleading. This is not as bad," she said.

Danny laughed out loud. Maureen had made a joke!

"Danny. Just alive," she said. "Hate therapy, but it's the

price being alive."

"Do you remember anything about that night?"

"No."

"Anything?"

"Trying to find . . ." Danny eased Maureen back down into her chair. She made a circular design with her two hands.

"Doughnuts? The rings of Saturn?" he teased her. She didn't get mad, just shook her head and rolled her eyes. Finally he said, "CDs."

"Yes."

"So you were reaching for the CDs in the backseat."

"Yes."

"And then."

"That's all." She couldn't tell him that this might have been another time that she recalled, any one of hundreds of times they'd been in the car. She *seemed* to be able to see Bridget driving, but she knew that and couldn't be sure it was a memory or information. She could clearly visualize Bridget's face turning to her and the headlights of another car, but that had happened a hundred times, too. Maureen had worked at this. She could not remember the names of any of the cheerleaders except Molly. There was not one teacher whose name she remembered. There was not one class she could say she'd taken.

Gone.

Zip.

She could no more have done trigonometry than she

could have climbed Mount Everest.

But she knew that Bridget had been chosen for sophomore representative for the homecoming court and she hadn't. Everyone forgave Bridget for being a cheerleader. But they dissed all the others. Maury hadn't even gone to the dance—too humiliating. She just sat at Bridget's, playing poker with little Sarah for kitchen matches.

"When did you start to remember who you were?" Danny was asking.

"Lots of time before I come say something."

"So you knew for a long time. . . ." *How would that have felt? Having Kitt and Mike here with her, knowing she wasn't Bridget? It must have been a torment, like slow torture.* "That must have sucked."

"Sleep," she said, with a big smile.

"You slept a lot of the time."

"Yes. I don't like her anymore."

"Who?"

"Kitt. She will not come."

"Maury, you have to understand. If Mrs. Flannery come . . . I mean, came up here, the memory of thinking it was Bridget would just drive her wacko, I bet. She was here so long thinking it was Bridge."

"My mom come."

"But she's your mom!" Danny insisted. He hadn't really talked to the Flannerys since the memorial, but he thought Maureen was being unfair.

"No, my mom come to Brid-get."

158

"Oh, your mom came when she thought you were Bridget."

"I heard her."

It was dark, and the wind was beginning to kick up. Danny pushed her back inside. When they hugged, she clung to him. He felt her hard little spine and the softness of her breasts under the nightgown. He would have to be careful that she didn't confuse being pals with something else.

As he was leaving, Danny turned back to Mrs. O., who was sitting in her chair, knitting a baby blanket for her new granddaughter, Maura. "Maureen said a funny thing."

"What?"

"She said you came up here when . . . you thought she was Bridget."

"I did. But no one was here. She was still in a coma."

"She knows, though. She told me. She heard you."

"She did?" Jeannie put down her knitting. "I had to go to . . . well, to the doctor. I had . . . Well, it didn't turn out to be anything but a cyst. Bill drove me because my nerves were shot. And I just came in on an impulse. She was still on the other floor. I spoke to her and said we loved her."

"She knew it was you. She's mad that Kitt doesn't come to see her."

"Well, I'm sure in time . . ."

Danny wasn't so sure.

The days passed, spring racing along in the world, plowing forward like steps in wet sand in the rehab ward. Maureen began to use a walker. The physical therapist pushed her every day to keep going, just one more step, then just to the end of the counter. Once, exhausted and sweaty, Maureen slipped and fell to her knees. She wasn't hurt at all; but when the PT helped her up, Maureen tried to spit in her face. Nothing came out, but Shannon Stride said, "Don't you dare. You're fortunate, Maureen. Do you know how much harder it's going to be when you go home? Is there going to be a bathroom with a shower three steps from your bed? No. Is there going to be a button for you to call someone whenever you want to change the channel on the TV and you can't reach the remote? No. You have to win yourself back, Maureen. The prize is what you had before. Yeah, it sucks. All this work to be not quite as good as you were before. But remember. Kids here would give their eyeteeth to be able to do what you can do."

"I got no eyeteeth," Maureen snapped.

"But you have so much else. You look normal. You got so lucky. You think they want to look the way they do? You ever look at the pictures in their rooms? You think they weren't as cute as you before? You ever talk to them? Or are you too good for them?"

Maureen was ashamed. With every ounce of her strength, she pushed toward the end of the nurses' station countertop.

"Well done," said Shannon. "Well done."

That night Maureen sat next to Charles and Zoe in the hospital's little theater and watched the old version of *The*

*Parent Trap*. It was better than the new one. Zoe was funny and sweet. She was fifteen and had been a figure skater. She fractured her skull when her pairs partner dropped her. Every kid in rehab, except the little babies, seemed to have been something great. And from that day until she left, Maureen visited Zoe's room every afternoon to watch *Days*. Zoe's speech was much better than Maureen's. But Zoe's mother had told Maureen that Zoe would never be mentally more than ten or twelve years old. She would always have to live with her parents.

How did they know?

Maureen doubled her efforts.

She asked Jeannie to bring her sheet music; and when the music therapist came in, Maureen begged for fifteen minutes of piano "lessons." Within two weeks she had begun to sight-read. After two weeks she could play songs from *The Lion King*—but only with her left hand. Her right hand was still too weak. Still nobody could believe that she'd actually learned something new, and something that was traditionally linked with math.

At night, she squeezed her exercise ball until her right hand ached and sweat trickled down her breastbone. She asked Shannon for something more challenging than the ball. Shannon gave her a device that looked like a slingshot. Its rubber-tipped metal legs were so far apart that Maureen could barely grasp both of them.

"When you can squeeze that closed, you'll have most of the use of that hand again," Shannon told Maureen.

Dr. Park began to hold out the hope of home to her like a scoop of ice cream just out of her reach. When she could walk three steps without holding on to anything . . . even the walker . . . When she could read three sentences aloud with no mistakes . . . When she remembered past tenses . . .

Maureen stayed up late, unlocking, unwrapping, peeling away the plastic around the items in her brain. . . . I go to the store. I am going to the store. I went to the store. She squeezed the ball and the slingshot. Without telling anyone, and knowing it was dangerous, she walked to the bathroom alone. Once the nurse, Ben, caught her; but instead of grabbing her arm, he nodded and simply watched her carefully, closing the door so Maureen had her privacy.

The last week in April she began to have anxiety attacks: Rag Mop was dead; that was why they wouldn't let her go home. Tommy's baby had died. They didn't want her to know. That's why they wouldn't let her go home. Mary brought baby Maura to see her and asked her to stand godmother.

"Sit godmother," Maureen said. "Is Rag Mop okay?"

"He's fine. He sleeps on the foot of your bed every night," her sister-in-law said.

"Is Tommy fine?"

"He's fine."

"Where is Danny?"

"At school, I think."

"Where's Mom?"

"She should be here any minute."

"Is Rag Mop dead?"

Mary stopped for a moment before she said, "No, Maury. Rag Mop is fine. He's at home, waiting for you."

Finally, Jeannie brought the little dog to the hospital again, though, strictly speaking, there were no animals allowed on the ward except the fish in the giant aquarium and the zoo animals that educators from the Minneapolis Zoo brought to the auditorium.

Two days after Jeannie brought in the dog, Maureen asked again if Rag Mop was dead.

But Dr. Park told Jeannie not to worry. "Most kids with brain injury ask the same question every couple of minutes. You could walk out of the room and come back after getting a soda out of the machine and she'd greet you as if she hadn't seen you in weeks," Dr. Park told her. "That's how short we thought her memory would be, but instead she is on the high end of the memory curve. She's just stressed out. Her mind is whirling."

In the last week, as her ticket out, Maureen had to do the equivalent of a marathon.

She had to get up, get to a chair, pull on a sports bra and panties, get into pajama pants and a T-shirt, put on her own socks, pour her own cereal out of a box, remember to ring for the nurse and tell her that she had to go to school at exactly nine in the morning, write a full sentence, read aloud, take a vision test, sing one verse of a folk song from memory after hearing it only two times, then walk to the front door of the ward and back to her room without any help in locating it.

And Maureen did it all.

As she left the schoolroom for the last time, Maureen sang to Shannon, "If I had a hammer, I'd hit you in the knee."

Shannon laughed uproariously.

After it was all over, Maureen slept for fourteen hours.

Finally, with fistfuls of prescriptions—antibiotics for her bladder infection, pills to help her establish a regular sleep schedule, anxiety medication to use as needed—and a binder of instructions and the gear for exercise, Maureen was released. As they did each time a kid went home, the nurses lined the hall and clapped. But Maureen felt something other than the pride and sense of celebration.

In the big, echoing lobby, she was seized by a crippling fear. So many people, so many open spaces and strange faces. It was as though she'd just hatched out of an egg. She thought of the blue-and-yellow striped halls of the unit with longing. She was safe there. Everything she thought she wanted so passionately to see and be in—the smells and sounds of spring, the sights and privacy of home—now seemed huge and threatening.

"I'm not really. I'm not real. I'm . . . I'm not ready," she told Jeannie. She could see white vans with loops of wire on top and big letters on the sides. "Real. Feel. Ward. Safe. Have rehab. Have rehab."

"We can wait for a moment," Jeannie said. "Daddy is going to go around back where the ambulance is so that we can avoid those TV people out there. Here's Molly, Maury."

Molly had just run between rows of reporters and gave Maureen a hug.

Maureen was stunned to see that Molly was dressed in a couple of T-shirts, shorts, and flip-flops.

"Where is your coat?" she asked. "Cold. Coat. Cold."

Because she knew what the repetition meant now, although it still gave her the creeps, Molly said, "Maureen, it's spring! It's sixty-eight degrees outside!" She could see the reporters with their microphones gazing in at them and knew it would terrify Maureen if they began to shout questions at her. Even now a nurse was trying to see what legal issues they could use to get the trucks to move. Careful planning went into choosing Sunday afternoon for the time to release Maureen. But the reporters had their sources, and were vigilant. Finally, the reporters were told by a hospital spokesperson that they were blocking access for patients. Reluctantly, they moved to the outer parking lot, where at least they would see the O'Malley family car and be able to follow.

That was Molly's cue.

"See you at home, Maury," she said, darting back toward the emergency bay.

The news vans did follow Bill as he headed for home. But it was Molly Schottmann who had volunteered to sit in the backseat, a cap with a fake blond ponytail attached to it on her head.

Jeannie and Maureen came later in the ambulance.

So, just as he had headed the crew that drove Maureen to the ED that night four months before, Carl was at the helm when the ambulance brought her home.

Jeannie was on top of the world. Her tulips had never looked so regal. Pat and Jack had come home, although it was finals week, and Henry had cleaned the house from the top down. Mary and Tom had steaks on the grill. Although Maureen would have to return two days a week to Anne Morrow Lindbergh, there was talk of a physical therapist in Bigelow who might do some of the work on a private basis. Bill had found a music teacher who would come to give Maury private lessons and bought an old upright piano from the parents of a student.

A return to some kind of ordinary life seemed possible, and ordinary had never seemed so precious.

Across the street, the Flannery house was silent, the blinds drawn.

Bill saw Sarah peek out of her bedroom window, then slip back inside as he walked down the drive to meet the ambulance.

The medics set up her wheelchair and slid Maureen into it. Bill unloaded her walker. Maureen waved shyly at her brothers, who gradually realized she wouldn't break and rushed to kiss her and hug her. Bill began to push her up the front path.

But Maureen stopped him.

"Walk," she said. Bill pressed his lips together and helped his frail daughter stand up.

She took her last few steps down her front walk as she had taken them four months ago—on her feet, without the use of her walker, while news photographers perched in trees and lay on the sidewalk to capture the moment. Her right foot dragged like a reluctant puppy, and she had to stop twice to get her balance. But she made it.

When she got to the steps, Bill scooped her up and carried her in. While the boys unloaded Maureen's bags and bags of equipment, which filled every available inch of floor space in the laundry room, Bill settled Maureen for the moment in his own big blue leather recliner.

He watched as she ran her hands over the arms of the chair. She glanced quizzically around the room, examining the fireplace, grinning at Rag Mop's excited dance on the carpet in front of her. For a moment, Bill nearly rushed forward, thinking that Maureen was about to fall, but she was only bending down to smell the leather. She stroked it again and gazed up at him, a puzzled frown on her face.

"Daddy?" she asked, as though he had just returned from a long trip.

"Yes!" Bill said, and dropped to his knees.

"Okay, Daddy. I am now," said Maureen.

# *prom night*

After the nationwide splash of photographs for the "Risen-from-Dead Girl Comes Home," Henry wrote the final blog entry.

> *May 4*
> Luke 15: 4–6 What man of you, having an hundred sheep, if he lose one of them, doth not leave the ninety and nine in the wilderness, and go after that which is lost, until he find it? And when he hath found it, he layeth it on his shoulders, rejoicing. And when he cometh home, he calleth together his friends and neighbours, saying unto them, Rejoice

with me, for I have found my sheep which was lost.

*One day before my birthday, my sister came home from Anne Morrow Lindbergh Children's Hospital and Clinics. What a mouthful! No wonder they call it "Anne's House"!*

*She was on her way home on December 23 last year, but it turned out to be a trip that took four months and involved some of the most heartbreaking and heartwarming events of any of our lives.*

*Although we would never have asked to have something like this happen, we have learned so much from it.*

*We have a new respect for the dedication and training and care that doctors give every day. We have, maybe even more, a greater understanding of how much devotion and compassion nurses and therapists have—every hour of every day.*

*It has been nearly five months since Maureen was injured and believed dead. But not one day of that time has she complained. She has grown angry and frustrated. She has had to do things over and over. She gets tired and discouraged. But she keeps us all going; and she comes roaring back, more determined than ever, after every setback.*

*And you—all of you, here in our hometown,*

and in Minneapolis and in Turin and Barce-
lona and El Paso and Miami and Juneau—have
helped us to keep going, too.

Yeats wrote,

*Out of sight is out of mind:*
*Long have man and woman-kind*
*Heavy of will and light of mood,*
*Taken away our wheaten food,*
*Taken away our Altar stone;*
*Hail and rain and thunder alone,*
*And red hearts we turn to grey,*
*Are true till Time gutter away.*

But our hearts never turned to grey, though
they stayed true, because we were inspired by
you and by our sister's courage. Someday, I
hope I will be able to tease her again and trip
her again (yes, brothers look forward to these
things!) and jump out from behind her door and
make her scream.

For now, just seeing her sitting at the table
trying to copy every letter of the alphabet is like
watching an artist carve a statue out of a block
of marble. We just don't know how she does it. But
every day, Maureen does it because she has to.

It was the longest winter of our lives.

Now it is spring. Maureen is alive and getting
better.

Next year, she will go back to Bigelow High

*as a junior with a special tutor provided by the state's coordinator for disabilities services.*

*We will never forget the grief of this winter. As Shakespeare wrote,*

> *For being both to me, both to each friend,*
> *I guess one angel in another's hell.*

*We will never forget Bridget Flannery, who was like another little sister to us.*

*But we hope we have all learned to treasure life more fully and be better human beings.*

*With friendship,*

*William Henry O'Malley*


Henry was going to petition his college that his blog be counted as a literature course. There were more than a hundred entries. He realized that petitioning for credit was fairly slimy but figured that sympathy was on his side. He also had searched Shakespeare and Yeats for appropriate quotations for each entry, so, in a sense, it was a literary endeavor. And his mom was always good for a quote from Grandma's old Bible.


Though Maureen had only been home for a week, Molly and Danny planned a "quiet" surprise birthday party for her the following Saturday.

Inevitably, word got out. All of the cheerleaders, along with about sixty other class friends—everyone but the weirdest Goths and even some of them—came to welcome

Maureen home. They brought her music boxes and earrings and bracelets and sweaters, gift certificates for books and movies, stuffed animals, and a big straw hat for reading in the sun—all tributes for the miracle of her being restored to them. Brandon Hillier gave her a lawn chair that popped open on its own. Danny planted a rose tree where Maury could see it from her hospital bed in what used to be Coach's office (she couldn't manage stairs yet). The girls on the squad and Eddy chipped in and bought her a DishDelish jogging suit and a new letter jacket with her senior letter on it—despite the fact that she would never be a cheerleader again.

The cake that Jeannie baked read DARLING MAUREEN, WELCOME BACK HOME AND BACK TO YOUR LIFE.

Everybody clapped as she cut the first slice, and Bill videotaped her taking her first delighted bite.

But Maureen started to cry after the cake was cut and couldn't seem to stop, so finally Coach carried her inside. The kids drifted away in small groups.

"Do you think she's thinking about Bridget?" Britney asked Molly.

"Maybe," Molly answered. She had her own ideas but wasn't about to toss them into the gossip hole. She believed Maureen was overcome knowing that she was so much less than what she had been before—a tiny, pale thing, like a baby bird fallen from its nest. She wore new jeans, but a size 4 hung limp on her. Her arms were as thin as chopsticks, her wrists bigger than her biceps. "I think she's just

172

emotional." And then there was the future. Sure, she was way past other brain-injured kids, but what did that mean in the real world? Would she ever be able to live on her own? Danny had said she was still confused sometimes, that she didn't recognize ordinary things, like stop signs. It would be more than a year, he'd told Molly, before Maury could even try to drive.

But Danny had his own notions, too, about Maureen's sudden tears.

Seeing everyone—over half the class—must have reminded Maureen how much she had missed and would miss. They would be juniors next fall, thinking about college. She would spend the summer swimming in a therapy pool to build up her muscles and coordination, making tapes of herself speaking and playing them back, keeping a notebook of questions she asked over and over so she didn't drive people nuts. She didn't have a child's mind in a woman's body. She had a young woman's mind in a young woman's body. But all of it was barricaded.

He went back to the O'Malleys' alone on Sunday morning with a plan.

Maureen was sitting up in bed goofing around with the new laptop that someone from somewhere had sent to her. Danny sat down beside her and helped her program a Face Place page, picking out a pink-rose background, helping her tap out a profile that told people she was Maureen O'Malley, age sixteen if you counted from birth or three months if you counted from her coming out of the coma.

He took pictures of her posing in the big leather chair and uploaded them to the site.

When Maury typed, he saw for the first time how clumsy her fingers really were, how she had to stare at a letter before making the decision to use it.

Mrs. O. had been planning to go to Mass; but Mary, who was going to stay with Maureen, called to say the baby was sick.

Danny offered to stay with Maureen. What he wanted to say was private anyhow.

Once Mrs. O. was on her way, Danny put the laptop to sleep and took Maureen's hand.

"I don't want you to take this wrong," he said. "But I don't think you should miss the prom. I know we're sophomores, but everybody goes. Do you want to go with me?"

Maureen threw her arms around his neck like a child at Christmas.

"I would love this!" she said.

"I don't mean a date. I don't want to upset you," he said.

"Of course. We're friends," Maureen said. "But a dress and everything!"

"It's prom," he said. "I don't want you to think that I'm doing this because I feel sorry for you, though, Maury. I don't feel sorry for you. I like you."

"We're friends," she repeated. Her hand had dropped to his chest. He was uncomfortably aware of her body under the light pair of shorts and strappy top she had on. She was so tiny, but her weight was coming back up. She looked al-

174

most like a normal girl. But one of her eyes was tearing and red.

"What happened to you?" he asked, pointing to her eye.

"I tried to put on lashes. . . ." she said, and stopped. "Mascara. I almost poked out my eye." They both began to laugh, and then they were kissing. He didn't know which one of them started it. He was longing for Bridget so much, or else Maureen; he lay down beside her on the bed and pulled her on top of him. His mouth trembled when he gently touched her small breasts.

"We need to stop," he said. But Maureen took his hand and began moving it in small circles, lower and lower on her belly.

"No," she said. "I'm not . . . a baby. I'm not retarded."

"We're friends."

"Yes," she said. "But I love you."

"I love you, too," Danny answered, remembering that whatever she thought would drop from her brain to her mouth like a gum ball down the slot.

"You can love me," she said. "I mean, this way."

"I can't, Maury."

"Why, am I ugly?"

"You're beautiful."

"Because I walk in that? Stupid? Crash? Stupid head? I'm not stupid, Danny. I'm not the same, but not stupid."

"Don't be nuts," Danny said. "It's not that! I just don't think it's right for us!"

"Because of Bridge?"

"Because of everything!"

"You almost thought before!"

"That was a long time ago, Maureen, and we both agreed it wasn't right."

"Then someone else will!" she told him angrily. "I almost died. I came back to life. I don't want to wait forever."

"You're only sixteen. That is hardly forever," Danny said, kissing her again, running his hands along her warm back. Then he said, "I'm confused, Maury."

"You were with Bridget."

"We were together for three years first."

"So?"

"So, you have to know it's right. I know I want to be with you, but not like that. At least not yet."

"I know I do. I know that my whole life could go by."

"You just trust me because I'm Danny Carmody, good ol' Danny. And you have that confused with a bigger feeling. If I did this, it would be like taking advantage of a kid. . . ."

She slapped him across the face.

"Don't! I'm not a kid!"

"I take it this means you don't want to go to the prom," Danny said, standing up.

"Yes, I do," Maureen said. "I am just so . . . um, haunted. No."

"I'll wait."

"Hungry for life."

"I know. I am, too. I feel like a part of me was buried."

"Bridget is dead," she pleaded with him. "We're . . . alive."

"I know. I have to think. You do, too."

"Will you be ashamed of me?" she asked. "At the prom?"

"That's stupid, too."

"I have the body of a little kid. I know it."

*But not the mind or the heart*, he thought. "You have weeks to eat nothing but chocolate and ice cream."

"Danny, I'm sorry I slapped you. I'm sorry I . . . what would you call it?"

"Tried to rape me?" he asked lightly.

"Yes. I will not rape you again."

"You sound like English is your second language. Do you mind my saying that?"

"It is not my first language."

"What's your first?"

"Martian," she said, and all of the tension drifted out of the air.

"You are my friend, Maureen. It's not like I'm not attracted to you."

"Thank you, Rag . . . Danny!"

"You were going to call me the dog's name!"

"Look." She pointed to her head. "Swedish cheese."

"Swiss cheese, you mean."

"Shut up," Maureen said. "I can punch you."

When Jeannie got back from Mass and they told her

about the prom, she was worried. What if all that stimulus was too much for Maureen? What if she started to cry? Got hysterical? Had a seizure? She didn't have . . . bathroom accidents anymore, but she could say something.

"Mrs. O., people at dances don't stand around and have long conversations. The girls just squeal and go to the bathroom, and the guys just wait for it to all be over," Danny told her. "I'll look out for her. It's got to be terrible not to be a normal kid."

"She's getting better. Since being home, her speech is a lot better. A LOT. But she's never going to be the same," Jeannie said. They were deliberately making tons of noise with the bags and the cabinet doors to make sure Maureen didn't hear them.

"Then they're immature idiots if they don't get it. She is who she is now."

Jeannie patted Danny's arm. "Okay," she said. "I'll go try to find something she can wear, in a size two."

"Don't make it a baby dress, Mrs. O. Let her look like the other girls."

In the end, Leland came, sobbing, apologizing for being so rude to Henry, and asked to help do Maureen's hair.

Everyone knew Leland had a gift for this, so it was great that she had the big regret at the right time. Molly, Taylor, and Britney B. came, too.

Leland tied a satin band around Maureen's head, gelled her short hair around it, letting the ends of the band trail, and then sprinkled everything with a fine dust of hair glitter to match the strapless silver dress. The dress had a wide band and pleats that fell straight, disguising Maureen's little-boy hips. The hem dipped below Maury's knee on one side and rose way too far above on the other side—according to Bill. Britney swept dark gray eye shadow with silver highlights on Maureen's brows. She applied eyeliner and colored mascara. Heels were out of the question, so Maury wore black ballet slippers.

By seven o'clock, Maureen looked like any other girl.

The others departed, like a swarm of butterflies.

Molly and Taylor were the last to leave. The only one of the four who was a junior, Taylor had made prom court—Bridget would have been the sophomore representative. Taylor was the first cheerleader to be on court since Eddy went to Bigelow. She needed to take extra care with her prep, even though she was absolutely sure no one would let her be queen. Her dress was cream, floor length with berry-colored off-the-shoulder ruffles. She would wear a berry-tinted ribbon with a cameo around her neck and shoes to match. Very *Gone With the Wind*.

Everyone else was wearing strapless sheaths.

Taylor didn't want to look like anyone else.

"I have to go, but we'll see you there!" Taylor told Maureen.

"I'll never forget you guys did this," Maureen said slowly.

"We're just happy you'll be with us again," Molly said with an air kiss, as she jumped into her car. She didn't put on her seat belt, and Maureen felt her stomach fold and tighten. But she dragged that out of her mind.

Taylor stopped for a moment.

"I have to tell you something, Maury," she said. "When I do the Liberty or when I tumble, I feel like you're with me, every time."

Maureen threw her head back. "After all that, if my makeup drips . . . runs . . . I'm sunk. I don't want to cry." She and Taylor hugged each other hard.

Holding Danny's arm, she smiled widely for the hundred pictures her parents insisted on taking. Then she revealed her surprise, an aluminum cane. Tommy had brought it; and Maureen had practiced, marching across the room when everyone else was in bed.

"You need to bring the walker just in case," Jeannie said, hovering.

"Mom, I've practiced for a week," Maureen said. "If I get tired. I can sit down. The theme is Paris in Springtime. They have little tables. Britney said. Don't you think that anyone would give his chair to a crip?"

"Stop that," Jeannie said. She looked at Maureen thoughtfully. Then she went upstairs and came down with her mother's cane, which had a rubber tip but was made of dark wood with a silver lion's head at the end of the long handle. "You might as well do it in style."

Maureen tried out the old cane to see if the length was right. Grandma Forbes had been small, like Maureen, so it fit her like a hand in a glove.

Finally, they were in the car.

Danny had planned to take Maury to dinner. But she confided that she had enough stamina for the dance but not for two huge new events in one night.

"I don't have a memory of going to a restaurant," she confessed.

So they drove through Culver's. Danny got a double Butter Burger and Maureen fried shrimp with onion rings.

"Oh," she cried a moment after biting into the first onion ring. "Bad breath! I just love onion rings!"

"I've got two full packs of strawberry bubblegum."

"Never thought I would be happy for that!"

"And baby wipes in the glove box if you get your hands dirty! I use them all the time, because my hands look like feet after I plow with my dad."

"I picked the right date," Maureen said.

"As I recall, I picked you," Danny told her.

"Fair enough."

"Let's go someplace quiet to eat," Danny suggested. He wanted to calm himself before they walked in. His parents were not in favor of it. His mother had gone so far as to call it "sick," and for the first time in his life, Danny told her to shut up. His father, in a towering rant, would have grounded him on the spot if it were not for the fact that this would disappoint Coach—Danny noticed that his father didn't mind disappointing Maureen. He was more interested in Danny's berth on varsity at 163 pounds than in Maureen's feelings, or Danny's for that matter.

"Do you want to drive to the creek?" he asked Maureen, who had delicately covered herself with napkins in case one of her hands shook when she tried to eat her fried shrimp.

"I want to go to the cemetery," she said. "I have never been. I would like Bug to see me." She said suddenly, "Onions!" and then apologized. "That happens sometimes. If I think really hard about something, I say it without knowing. I want to go see Bridget."

Tears burned at the back of Danny's eyes. But he drove to the cemetery—there was plenty of light to see by—and spread a blanket on the grass near Bridget's grave so they could sit down to eat.

"It's not exactly a white tablecloth and candles, but it's clean," he said.

"I'm fine," Maureen said. "I love it outside."

*Now I've done it all,* Danny thought. *I'm having my dinner on prom night at my dead girlfriend's grave with her best friend.* But Maureen didn't seem depressed or even over-emotional.

"Bridgie Bug," she said softly, touching the pink granite. "Look, I'm all new. I'll never be you. But I'm going for both of us."

They ate in silence, enjoying the warm but not yet oppressive evening air. In a few weeks only idiots would sit outside at the mosquito witching hour.

"Are you nervous?" Danny asked.

"Not so much," Maureen said. "Remember, I was dead. Not much scares you after."

She did falter a moment when Danny pulled up in front of the school. She threw back her head so that no tears would ruin her eye makeup. "Do you recognize it?"

"I don't remember how it looks. But I know I was happy here," she said.

Couples were scurrying toward the entrance, but Coach had given Danny his faculty permit so they could go in at the side door. There was a long breath of silence when they walked slowly into the gym together. Then, slowly, everyone began to approach them, gently touching Maureen's arm, saying how beautiful she looked. Brittany W. even said she wished she could be that thin. They sat at a table and drank ginger ale punch, and gradually Maureen's heart slowed down. With Molly seated beside her, looking like a costume doll in her hoop skirt, Danny slipped away and drank a shot of vodka with Ev outside the gym. A wad of bubblegum to cover the smell and he felt entirely at ease.

At nine, the court did the grand march down the white satin carpet with their dates.

As they waited in a row—Taylor, Sheila Braden, Maria Brent, Abbey Jewell, Francie Castellucci, and Lisanne Colawitz, the odds-on favorite—Mr. Beckwith got up to read the name.

There was a drum roll, and then he opened the envelope handed to him by the president of the faculty senate.

"Well," he said. "Well. By vote of the student body, this year's king of the junior prom is Mark Shessel. And this year's queen is . . . Lisanne Colawitz."

Lisanne took a deep breath and smiled as last year's queen placed the tiara on her long, blond hair. She didn't act surprised. She acted as if it were her due. Everyone cheered and whistled. Danny had to admit Lisanne had a body that wouldn't quit. She took Mark Shessel's arm and licked her teeth to pose for pictures—when everyone noticed that Mr. Beckwith was still standing on the stage at the mike.

"Before the traditional dance, I, um, have a second announcement to make," he said. "This is untraditional. The faculty senate and Key Club have unanimously agreed to bestow a second honor at this event. They have chosen a prom princess from the sophomore class. And that girl is . . . Maureen O'Malley." He looked out over the lights. "Maureen, are you here tonight?"

Maureen was so stunned that she couldn't answer or even get out of the chair. Assuming that she felt weak, Danny helped her to her feet. Maureen glimpsed the look of shock and rage that passed over Lisanne Colawitz's face before she smiled widely and began to clap. Sheila recovered in a second, and Taylor jumped up and down.

The rest of the kids stomped and clapped, with far more gusto than they'd shown for Lisanne.

Slowly, Maureen made her way to the stage, leaning heavily on Danny's arm, and waited while the vice principal, Joan Karls, brought out a bouquet of white roses, a tiara, and a sash with PROM PRINCESS etched in blue lettering.

Mark Shessel's comment was pure Mark. As quarterback for three years, he was used to untoward attention. The red velvet crown on his head made him look like someone out of a cookie commercial.

"I want to thank everybody out there for having such good taste—in me," he said. When the giggles died down, he added, "What I really want to say is that Lisanne is the queen of queens and everybody knows it. But I would give this crown back to see Maureen's face again when Mr. Beckwith said her name."

People applauded wildly.

Lisanne said, "I want to thank everyone in Bigelow, and especially the student senate and Bigelow, for this honor. I really feel I represent Bigelow and hope that I can be the best we have to offer in my year as queen." She stopped, then added, "And we all know what Maureen has gone through, so this is a nice surprise for her."

"They expect you to say something," Danny whispered.

"I can not say," Maureen told him urgently. "No one knows I talk like this."

"You'll do fine. Go slow and look right at me." He lifted her onto the stage as Coach and Mrs. O'Malley, summoned by a frantic cell phone call, tore in through the door.

Maureen smiled and leaned on her cane.

"I know," she said, and drew a deep breath. "I know that this is not me. I mean, for me. Not really. I know it's because this thing happened to me. But I am." She paused again. "Happy that all of you let this happen. It might not be fair to Lissy and Mark because this is their night. So many things aren't fair, though. Bridget would be here if things were fair. I am happy because this and everything else made me feel not like an old lady tonight. I feel like a happy kid. And I did not . . ." Maureen looked down at Danny. "I haven't felt like a happy kid for a very long time. Thank you."

As she left the stage, Maureen was engulfed by a sea of teachers and kids who kissed her and congratulated her. After Lisanne and Mark, she and Danny posed under the phony rose arbor for a prom photo; and the *Bigelow Beacon* took a picture that would be on front pages all over America by Sunday morning—even before Thursday's *Beacon* was published in town. The picture in the *Beacon*, under the headline "Our People's Princess!," would be twice the size of the rightful king and queen's.

When the photos were over, Maureen and Danny left. Maureen was visibly drooping, her eyes hardly open. It was only ten o'clock. In the car, she relaxed, took off her satin headband and the band across her chest. She ruffled her hair with her fingers.

"Do I get to keep this?" she asked.

"I think there's never going to be another one. So I guess it's yours."

"Maybe I'll do two in a row," Maureen said with a laugh.

Danny asked, "Are you happy?"

She asked, "Were you in on this?"

"No way. I swear. I was as surprised as you."

"Promise? Real?"

"I promise. Did you feel happy, though?"

"Yes," she said. "I am feeling happy."

"You don't sound happy."

"I am."

"What would make you happy?"

"If I knew it. Was. Real."

"They all sounded like it was real," Danny said.

"I don't mean that," Maureen answered. She turned in her seat and looked at him in the way he remembered, that open-flower face that invited anyone to hurt her or to love her.

An hour later, they drove to a Kwick Stop far out in the country, where no one knew either of them, and Danny made a purchase. Then he and Maureen slipped into a ski resort that was closed for the summer. As he spread out his blanket, Danny reminded himself that he had spent part of almost every day with this girl for the past five months—and before that he'd known her for most of his life. So it wasn't really their first date.

On Danny's picnic blanket, in a cove of small pine trees, they made love.

Afterward, they held each other tight and cried.

Neither of them knew if this was right, or if it was the beginning or the end. It was impossible not to think of Bridget. But Maury was right.

They were the ones who were alive.

. . .

A week later, when she heard the doorbell ring, Maureen opened the door to receive a package. It was only when she saw the horror on the man's face that she remembered she was wearing only her underwear. She simply hadn't remembered to get dressed. A doorbell rang, so she answered. By the time Jeannie got downstairs, Maureen was huddled in the laundry room with her face in her hands. Her father had come running, but too late. Why had she opened the door?

The mailman lived on Sweeney Street, near Taylor's house, and it was his wife who told Taylor's mother. Taylor told Maria and made her swear not to tell anyone else. And by that night, fifty kids were texting each other about Maureen the Queen and her nudie act.

Evan Brock was afraid to tell Danny, afraid someone else would first. As it turned out, he was at bat when the catcher murmured, "I wish my prom date answered the door naked." Danny ignored him, popped up a high fly, and jogged back to the bench, where he asked Evan what the hell the guy from Ludding was talking about. Evan had no choice but to tell him. Then Danny had no choice, at the end of the game, but to ask the guy to take a walk. The catcher was on his ass in the dust, rubbing his jaw, when Danny turned on his heel to get on the bus.

But before he could, the catcher said, "Is it better with a gimp?"

In an instant, Evan Brock jumped the catcher, the first baseman was all over Danny, and both teams stormed off the bus to get in on the rumble. Danny ended up with a three-day suspension and had to sit out the playoffs. The catcher had to miss the next game.

But that would have been the end of it if someone hadn't posted a photo of Maureen, smiling shyly in her tiara, on top of a gross topless photo on MyPlace.

No one knew who sent the picture to Maureen.

PART III

*maureen and danny*

# long winter

"I said no," Dave Carmody repeated. "It's bad for you, it's bad for her, and it's bad for business. That's not why it matters, but it's true." Danny and Dave were loading slabs of sod onto the big garden truck outside Dave's greenhouse. The truck was new and the name of his dad's business, Green With Envy, was stenciled on both sides.

It was June 10; and despite Danny's efforts to keep everything low-key, the word about him and Maureen was out.

It was way out. Parents knew.

"Dad, it has nothing to do with you," Danny said evenly.

"Everything that has to do with you has to do with me. It's already gotten you suspended, which would have been

193

on your record permanently if I hadn't been able to convince Old Beckwith there were special circumstances. You're only seventeen. While you live under my roof . . ." Dave Carmody stopped and rubbed the back of his neck. When he started again, his tone was down in the lower registers, gentler. "Danny, you're a great kid. You've got a big heart. I know you want this poor girl to feel accepted. I know Coach is grateful to you. But enough is enough. Sympathy only goes so far."

"Why do you think she's with me out of sympathy?" Danny asked, knowing it would piss off his dad.

"Listen, smart ass. I told you what my feeling is on this, and I expect you to pay attention. You have state the year after next, and a good chance for a full ride if you pay attention to your work and your sport. You don't have time to be the white knight and handicapped driver to Bill's messed-up daughter."

"She's not messed up."

"Danny," said his father, sitting down on the truck's tailgate. "I know what goes on. Steve Collins's wife told me about the chances of her ever being normal, back when they thought she was Bridget. I don't mean she would gossip about Steve's patient. I doubt if he ever told her the specifics. But she used to be a nurse herself. And she said she felt so bad for you because it would be awful if Bridget died and awful if she lived. I know. I do their plantings. And I know why you got into that fight. It's a terrible thing. I don't fault you there. But you've done your best. You've

194

fulfilled your obligation to Bridget."

"We don't think of it that way," Danny said, hefting more sod onto the truck. He got his gloves out of his pockets. Maureen cringed at dirt under his nails, and during June he could scrub them with a brush all day and not get it off.

"'We'?" his father shouted. "So it's 'we' now? Listen, as long as you're in high school, the only 'we' in your life is your mother and brothers and me. Do you get that? Am I clear? I don't know if you're doing this just to get to your mother and me or not. You've never given us a day of trouble. Let's keep it that way."

"I'm not going to stop seeing Maury."

"This discussion is over."

"That's fine. But I'm still going to see Maury."

Suddenly, Danny was spun around by his father's two powerful hands gripping his shoulders. Danny was strong for his size, but no match for Dave, who had five inches and forty pounds on him. "Son. Look at me. What in the name of all that's holy do you see in a girl who can't even take care of her own . . . personal needs?" Danny looked away, but Dave cornered him. "That girl is going to be a burden on her parents all her life, Danny. You heard what Dr. Collins told the Flannerys. The brain does not get better!"

"You have no idea what she's like! Do you think she wears diapers or something? You're wrong. If Mom would let me ask her over here, you wouldn't think she was any different from anyone else unless she got nervous and started forgetting her words. She's practicing driving. . . ."

"That's great," said Dave. "Maybe someone else can get killed."

"Cut it out, Dad! Listen to yourself! Maureen has a brain injury. She uses a cane. She limps. Maybe she's never going to take pre-calc the way she could have before. But she's taking piano lessons. She's learning to read music, learning fast! She's as smart as she ever was in some ways. She's smarter than me! You're a Jaycee, Dad. Isn't that all about helping kids like Maureen live full lives? Or is that just bull? What if she had cancer? Would you want me to drop her because she had to have chemo to be cured and lost her hair?"

"It's not the same thing at all," said Dave. "But yes, to be absolutely honest, I wouldn't want you to tie yourself down to anything, especially when you're not even eighteen yet, that will ruin your future. What if you keep on with this? What if she gets pregnant, Danny? Do you think of that? I hope to God you're not thinking of getting really involved with her."

"If I was, it wouldn't be any of your business, Dad."

"You're in high school, Dan."

"You met Mom in high school."

"That was a different time."

"You hate it when I say that. You hate it when I ask how it was back in the day."

"You need to tell her, in a nice way, that you want to be friends."

"I don't, though. I'd be lying. I don't want to be just her friend. I don't know if it'll last over the summer. I don't know what will happen when we go back to school. But I

196

want to be with her now."

"It's your funeral, Danny," Dave finally said. He swung into the truck and, before Danny could hop into the cab beside him, drove off alone.

"You asshole," Danny said quietly, shoving his hands into his jeans pockets.

He wanted to punch someone. He wanted to cry. He wanted to throw his stuff in his car and move to his brother's house. He loved his dad. His dad hadn't missed a match since Danny was ten. And he wasn't a beast, like other wrestling dads, giving their kids diuretics and urging them to kill. The only thing he had done to redshirt Danny was keeping him out of kindergarten until he was six so he'd have a power advantage. Danny loved his mom. His mom still treated him like he was ten; but if he was sick or in need of something for school, she'd come on cross-country skis if she had to to make sure he had it. Mom worked days baking for the Art House Café and weekends mending things for the dry cleaner to make sure Danny, Dennis, and David Jr. had iPods and at least a small college fund. She loved telling her bad jokes and always told them wrong, getting all flustered and saying, "Wait! I forgot to tell you! The famous genetics guy was eating a stork!"

Making him choose between Maury and his family was something nobody should ever do to a kid. The shoe would be on the other foot if he were the one who was sick or . . . dented.

If he thought of Maury's disability at all, that was how

he thought of it—a dent that couldn't be pounded out. A flaw that wasn't her fault. Otherwise she was perfect. It was almost sweet the way she couldn't keep her mouth shut. When they got into the car, she'd say, "Let's go make out! I have thought of this all day!" He knew she didn't have a gatekeeper on her mouth, but it also was pretty wonderful to be loved that way.

He was damned if he was going to trade all the sweetness she gave him because of his parents' prejudice.

They didn't know how hard she cried when she saw the picture from MyPlace. When she was out, unless it was with him alone, she barely spoke. If she did, it was so slowly that people got impatient, so Maureen usually faked a giggle and said, "Never mind. Brain blooey!"

It wasn't like they were together 24/7, the way he had been with Bridge. He couldn't be with her every minute of the day. He was starting practice for American Legion ball, playing shortstop on a team that could really make a dent in the Cities' dynasty if they learned to get over being individual hot dogs. He had practice three nights a week and a game on Saturday. Maureen went to therapy at Anne Morrow Lindbergh on the days he didn't have practice.

There was the business of the Flannerys' whole take on this, too.

He'd seen Kitt twice—but the time that scared him was when he was helping Maureen into the car one Friday night.

Kids were still outside playing double-dutch and basketball in the cul-de-sac. Bridget's little sister Eliza had a new tetherball. He spotted Kitt sitting on the front porch, smoking. When her eyes met his, they were like lasers, boring a hole through him. He flinched; and Maureen glanced up, puzzled. She caught on right away.

"Stares. She doesn't like seeing," she said. "Kitt."

No one said a thing, but Kitt's eyes followed him down the street. She looked like a skeleton. She was always thin, but now it seemed as if she didn't eat at all. Miss Bliss, the lunch lady at school, who was friends with Danny's mom, said Kitt was a big drinker now. Danny got that. Who wouldn't be?

To be honest, he also got why they were mad about him and Maureen. And Maureen got it, too.

They talked it over one night in a way that they never had before.

"I guess I ask myself how I could feel this way about you if I felt that way about Bridget," Danny said. They were fishing in the creek—Maureen was hysterical every time she caught a blue gill.

"You don't know if you and Bridget would last. Have lasted," Maureen said. "You don't know if she would have stayed."

"I felt like it was expected. I expected it, too. I just worried about when we went to different colleges."

Maureen shrugged. "Maybe then. People change. Fish. Wish. Wish. I knew. Us."

"I wish I knew about us, too," Danny said, thinking that

it was going to be hard for him next fall, when she was in school dragging her foot and repeating her thoughts.

Maureen read his mind.

"You want to stop now? It's okay. Okay, I mean," she said. "I care. I always cared. But next fall, will you feel shame of me? Be ashamed of me?"

"Not ashamed."

"But something."

"Something. I don't like to be on display."

"I don't have a choice," Maureen said. He was so proud of her then. She didn't have a choice. She had to go back to school knowing everyone would watch her every move, knowing she would have a private aide with her at all times, knowing someone would have to take notes for her, help her in an adaptive PE class at the Y twice a week, knowing all that. Danny thought, *I am keeping her going. I am helping her face that. But what do I feel?*

"We can be friends. We were friends."

"Would you date another guy?" he asked.

She looked stung. "So, if I would, you'll stay with me. Just so I don't give it away?"

"No!"

"Be true, Danny. Be honest, I mean. That was what you were thinking."

"Actually, I was thinking we could try being friends, but I couldn't do it if I thought you were with another guy."

"You have to have me as a girlfriend not a friend."

"I guess. I think I'd be jealous if I tried to be just a

200

friend after what we did."

"We aren't engaged!"

"I know."

"You don't ever have to go out with me again."

"That's not what I want! But people are going to say things."

"So you are ashame. I mean ashamed."

"Look, Maureen, if I have problems with that in the fall at school, I have to get over it. If I'm here with you now, I have to be okay with being there with you then. Should I say, absolutely not, it will never have any effect on me? You're right. We don't lie to each other. It will have an effect on me. It already has an effect on me. My parents give me a lot of garbage."

"And so do mine," Maureen said.

"Why?" Danny asked, incredulous.

"They think you forced me because I have no impulse control. See it. Do it."

"How do they even know what we did?" Maureen examined her hands. "Maury? How do they know?"

"Well, I was never good at lying. Now I can't lie at all. And I have to take the pill. I'm seventeen. My mother knows."

"Pardon me while I drown myself!" Danny said. "I can feel Coach's hands tightening around my neck."

"He does not know."

"Oh. Thank God for that. So Mrs. O. thinks I'm this psycho sex fiend."

"No. She knows that I did this to feel alive. She was glad

it was you. She trusts you. She is worried about me. But you, too. She thinks you feel sorry for me."

"Oh, God."

"I told her it was my idea."

"Oh, that helps," Danny said with heavy sarcasm.

Maureen said, "She is worried just because, cause, claws, claws, pause. Stop. Because she thinks you still love Bridget, and you're just going on loving Bridget in your mind. She thinks this because you came to see Bridget in the coma and you loved her and prayed she would wake up and then, whoops, I was the one who did. So I was like the booty . . ." Maureen blushed. "The bobby . . ."

"The booby prize," Danny finished for her. "That's the longest speech you've made since you moved here from Uzbekistan."

"No, Mars. Yes."

"Well, I don't love Bridget now. I mean, I'm not dying from love of Bridget. I don't think of Bridget when I'm with you."

"Mom feels sorry for you."

"You said that."

"Okay, well. Of course you still do love Bridget."

"I don't love her that way."

"Duh. She's dead."

"What scares me is, I don't know if I ever did. Maybe I liked you all along. Maybe I was really looking for a girl I could talk to and joke with and feel the way I do with you, but I was worried about my image. I mean, who wouldn't

202

want to be going out with Bridget Flannery?"

"Thanks. That makes me feel better," Maureen said, struggling to get to her feet, throwing down her pole. "I am the booby prize."

"Maury, no! She was just the girl everyone wanted! You know that. I was in eighth grade when I started going with Bridget. I was thirteen years old. All you think then is, If I go out with the best girl, then I must be this big manly man. I mean, maybe I loved you all along. I know I felt something. But I denied it."

"Me, too. I always loved you. And too bad you have to find out when I a freak. When I am a freak."

"You're not a freak."

"I am a feet!" Maureen screamed. She stamped her feet. "Wait!" she said. "I stamped both my feet! I'm a freak who just stamped both her feet!"

Danny picked her up and twirled her around.

"You're getting better and better. Why wouldn't I love you as much for coming back from this? Maybe I like you better as a feet. I admire it." They began to laugh, tried to hold it back, and gave in. Danny kissed her and sank down with her in the grass, and in moments her legs were finding their way around his.

"Well, feet, I don't have anything with me. It's a long walk back to the car. Are you sure you want to take advantage of a poor dumb jock?"

"Start walking," said Maureen. "You've got two good legs."

# *joy in the morning*

She woke sweating at four AM.

School.

Danny would drive her, but still.

School.

She couldn't get it out of her mind.

The aide would help her, but she would have to find the rooms. Eventually, some teacher would call on her in class. Eventually, people would hear her talk. And they would make fun of her. It was supposed to give her character. That was BS. Nobody got "character" from being put down. That was just therapy happy talk. She was not a better person for having this happen. She had been a good person before.

It sucked.

She and her parents made the choice. She was starting over as a sophomore, at least technically, to give her more time to catch up. It meant her friends, now juniors, would graduate before her. But at least this way, Maureen thought, she might actually graduate.

At least she was tan. Her hair looked cute. Her lion cane was like her good-luck charm.

By the time the sun came up, she had dressed carefully in her brown leggings and pink miniskirt and double tanks. She didn't dare wear flip-flops, because her right leg got tangled up when she got tired. So she had five pairs of ballet shoes her mother had dyed in every color. Today was pink. Through the soles, she could feel the floor. She concentrated on that. During PT Shannon had told her, "Reach for the floor like it's your anchor. Hold on to the earth." Maureen did that.

She went down the stairs, slowly.

Since the beginning of August she'd been back in her own room—a room that Tommy had totally redone for her as a late birthday gift. The pink paint was dark now, almost coral. There were no curtains. Everything else was white, from the blinds to the furniture. Her mother had surprised her by making her a new quilt, just like the one buried with Bridget.

*Oh Bridge*, she thought. *Be with me*.

In her dad's office was the piano. Maureen began to play the *Moonlight Sonata*. Slowly, carefully, so no one would hear. She used both hands fairly easily now. It was still more difficult to use her right hand. It always would be. But she could do it. If she could play this without getting tangled up, her first day would be okay. She was almost three-quarters of the way through it when she felt a presence at the door. There stood her father.

"How did you do that?" he asked. He was dressed for his run.

"How you get to Carnegie Hall," she said. "Practice."

"You were using your right hand."

"I have been."

"I never thought you would use it again, especially . . . Can you really read the notes, Maury?"

"I really can, Daddy."

"So, you made something new of yourself."

"What choice was?"

"Was there."

"What choice was there?" she asked. "I practiced. Practice. Perfect. Practice."

"Don't get nervous."

Maureen slammed the cover down over the keys. "Don't get nervous! Everyone there is going to star, star. Stare. Stare at me! Don't tell me not to be nervous!"

"Settle down!" Jeannie told them. "Pat's still asleep." Pat would be heading back to school at the local junior college in a few weeks. He was studying to be an air traffic controller. "What the heck is all the ruckus?"

"He says don't be nervous!" Maureen sneered.

"Don't call your father 'he,' Maureen O'Malley," Jeannie snapped.

"Don't let him tell me I'll be jus fine. Just fine! I won't ever be fine! Deal!" She grabbed her cane and stomped into the kitchen.

"I just worry because kids are so cruel," Bill said.

"We can't protect her," Jeannie said. "She knew this was coming. The state would have let us homeschool her. This is what she wanted. She should have worn her seat belt."

"I heard that!" Maureen shrieked. They heard a plate hit the floor with a sharp clang, like a bell breaking. Then another. And before they could grab her hands, another.

"Stop it!" Jeannie told Maureen. "That's my only full set. We'll have to replace that!"

"Too bad can't replace me!"

"Maury," her father began.

"I didn't wear my seat belt because it was broken! It was broken and I didn't want to tell! Why did you get me no car with an air bag? Too cheap? Not too cheap for Tom and Henry and Pat and Jack! Every soccer camp! Out in California! All for your athletics! Your athletes! What about me? You send me out in a cheap, busted, rusted. Broken car with a broken belt!"

"I didn't know," Jeannie said.

"Don't you think we've thought about that a million times? And suffered about that? Don't you think we know we were idiots for thinking, Well, she's just driving to school and back; we don't have to get her a car until she's in college? Don't you know we feel responsible?" Bill asked.

"You think I'm respondable! Responsible! I heard you, Mom! You said I should have worn my seat belt! I always wear my seat belt! Always!" Tears were running down Maureen's face and her nose was leaking.

"Go run," Jeannie told Bill, and he literally ran for the door.

"Maury, if you keep this up, you're going to have to miss the first day. Do you want that?"

"You blame me?"

"No! I blame us, so I say stupid things," Jeannie told her. "Listen. I didn't know until now that the seat belt was broken. And if I didn't think I would cut my feet to shreds on the broken dishes, I would puke in that sink. As it is, I'll go in the bathroom."

Maureen sat down. Then she got up, and, using the broom as a cane, began awkwardly sweeping up the pieces of smashed crockery. When her mother emerged from the hall bathroom, Maureen said, "I'm sorry."

"Well, you shouldn't be. Yes, we were cheap. On the other hand, you should have told us. Don't shake your head. Do you think we wouldn't have done something about it? Do you think we really care more about the boys than you?"

"No," Maureen said.

"Go fix your makeup."

"Okay. Will you get it?"

"It's upstairs. Go up and put it on!"

"You suck," Maureen said, and then slapped her hands over her mouth. "Mom, I'm sorry." Fresh tears erupted. "I didn't meant that."

"Just go upstairs and put on your makeup. I know you didn't mean it. I'll make your breakfast, Maureen. And when you get your adaptive license, we'll find a way to get you a car that is as safe as . . . We'll buy it new if we have to. We were wrong." Jeannie began to cry, quietly, intensely. "We were wrong."

"Mom," Maureen whispered.

"Go put on your makeup and let's try to save this day."

But it didn't need saving.

Maureen learned to find her classes. She learned to read the aide's clear, bold handwriting. Everyone she met, even if she didn't recognize him or her, was kind. Her locker was decorated with black-and-gold streamers and a poster that read WELCOME PRINCESSA! Danny was waiting for her at the end of the day and slapped five with her as soon as she got into the car.

But that was only the first day.

# *corridors*

The aide didn't follow her into the bathroom. But someone was smoking in there, and not a cig.

Potheads usually crossed the street to toke up. What was the matter with whoever this was?

"Is that weed?" Maureen asked Molly.

"Don't talk about it," Molly told Maureen quickly.

The girl who came barreling out of the stall was huge and dripping in black and chains. "Who said that?" she asked. "Oh. Gimpo. I don't punch out the handicapped. I just tell them to keep their mouths shut."

"Fat Butt," Maureen said.

"Maury, no!" Molly whispered.

"She is. She called me Gimp," Maureen said. "Don't you

call me Gimp, Fat Butt."

"You asked for it now, Mental Girl."

"I'm not metal. I mean, mental," Maureen said. Her bad leg was quivering, shaking like Elvis's. She leaned on the sink.

Molly took her arm. "Maury, let's go," she said quietly. "Let's go to lunch."

"I . . . will not let her call me that."

"What are you going to do?" The huge girl leered at her. She put her face up close to Maureen's, bending over, fat rolling over her too-tight waistband. She reeked of weed and cheesy perfume. "Drool on me? Hit me with your stick?"

"Yeah," Maureen said softly; and when the girl wheeled away, Maury put out her cane and tripped her.

"She's gonna kill us now," Molly said with a resigned sigh. The huge girl started to get up, her black nails clenched. But just as she did, another girl all in black burst through the bathroom door.

"Anna! What the hell are you doing down there?"

"Uh, Lily, I'm looking at my twenty-dollar stockings ruined by the Killer Gimp here!"

"I'm not fall. I'm didn't fall on the floor," Maureen said.

Anna's friend glanced back and forth between them.

"Uh, what? Oh, I know you. You're the crash girl. Don't pay attention to Anna. She's pissed off because she got dumped by her boyfriend. Did she get on your case? Anna, don't you know who she is? How could you pick on a girl

211

that's handicapped?" Lily had piercings in every available flap of skin and wore combat boots with fishnets. But she somehow managed to maintain a sense of sweetness.

Anna howled. "She's the one who tripped *me*. Look, my leg is swelling up. I'm not going to be able to walk. Look at that bruise!" Molly was astonished that a faculty member hadn't stormed into the bathroom and handed out detentions all around by now.

"Now you know how it feels," Maureen said quietly. Anna stood up and glared down at her. Her voice suddenly went as soft as a child's. Maureen could hear the child Anna had been.

"Does it hurt? I thought it was your brain that was screwed up. You don't have brain pain."

"It hurts all the time," Maureen said. "It hurts every day."

"I was going to put a joint in your locker. And I still might, if you piss me off again. But it must suck to have it hurt all the time. And it sucks you lost your friend."

"It sucks big-time," Maureen said.

"I'm gonna starve," Molly put in.

"We can go. Will you let us. Let. Get. Let. No. Will you let us pass?" Maureen asked.

Anna moved her bulk aside. "I never had anybody talk back to me."

"She served you," said Lily.

As they made their way into the steaming sea of the commons, Molly said, "You are my new hero."

. . .

Maureen got through September on the compassion of her teachers, who were amazed she was there at all. But as weeks passed, the academic part of school was more daunting than the social part. That was not what Maureen had expected. School had always come easily to her. She once did Bridget's English papers and her own in an hour. Math was her best subject.

Now, math looked to her the way musical notes used to look. They had signed her up for Algebra I, but she spent hours on the homework with her tutor, Lauren, and got a D on the first quiz.

"It's passing," Lauren told her that night at the O'Malley house.

"What am I going to do on the ACT?" Maureen asked.

"That's not until a year from now," said Lauren. "And you haven't lost any of your language stuff. What about the paper you did on *Monster?* I wrote it down, and it's good."

"That's because I had already read the novel last year," Maureen told her. "How am I going to write about some book about guys carrying stuff in Vietnam? Or a lady who had a kidnapped kid? I still had a whole brain then, and apparently this novel got stuck in the part that's left. And what if I do okay, I get an eleven or twelve on my ACT? Where am I going to go? Cupcake State? What am I going to plagiarize? Major? Pledge? Major in?"

"Probably not math," Lauren admitted.

"But what?"

"English. Maybe . . . music."

"Oh please."

"I didn't say you were going to be a performance major. But theory. Teaching. The history of music. It's what you love. There'll be someone like me there to scribe for you. You're getting better at using the keyboard."

"I only email Molly and Danny. And Zoe, the girl from the hospital. Otherwise nobody could read it. I don't even use punctuation."

"Clue up. Nobody your age does."

"Still."

"You could get a scholarship for people who are handicapped."

"Yeah. I could have got a scholarship for people who weren't."

"Let's do some algebra, kid. I could have been a national-type skier, but I blew out my knee. You're not the only one in the world who has stuff they regret," Lauren said.

"I'd rather blow out my knee than my brain," Maury murmured.

"So would I," said Lauren.

"Why don't you just get out?"

"Your parents are paying me," Lauren said.

They both laughed.

By November, math was harder, murderously complicated; and Maureen begged to drop it.

"No," Bill said.

"Don't tell me no, Dad," Maureen said.

"You have to do it."

"Why? Do I have to be like one of your mat rats? Do I have to prove I can go through the pain for the gain? Well, screw that! I'm quitting and that's it. In fact, I'm going to get my GED."

"Go ahead," Bill said. "You'll always know you could have made it. You'll face life like a loser!"

"No!" Maureen screamed.

"You will," Bill said quietly. "I'm not saying every kid who drops out is a loser. There are a lot of reasons to drop out. You don't get the help you need. Your parents don't give you support. Your home life is violent or abusive. But what's your excuse?"

"Uh, holes in my brain?"

"Maureen, I have students in my PE classes who have bigger holes in their brains, and they were born with them. I have students who get by on sheer guts. You're smart and you're pretty. Okay, so you drag your foot. But I know my daughter. Or I knew my daughter. And she wasn't a quitter."

"That was your ex-daughter."

"Okay," said Bill. "Quit."

"Okay," Maureen said, "I will." She swept her folder and both of their teacups off the table to the floor. "Fine." She marched toward the stairs.

"Don't forget your cane, poor little crippled girl!" Bill called. "You don't use it half the time, you know. You only remember to use it when you get upset. You use it like a security blanket."

"I hate you," Maureen shouted.

"Shut it, Maury!" Patrick yelled from upstairs. "Some of us have to study!"

"I hate you, too!" she yelled, making her way up the stairs, again forgetting her cane.

When she got into her room, she threw herself on the bed. Bill followed her.

"Did I hear you, you know? Knock?"

"I didn't knock." Maureen's door no longer had a lock, because her parents feared that if she used it—consciously or without realizing it—they might not be able to get to her if she were hurt. "I came to tell you that you aren't dropping math. And you aren't dropping out. And the next time you tell me you hate me, I'm going to ground your butt to this room until you forget what it looks like outside. No more watching your precious Danny wrestle. No more walking around like you're a character out of an opera. Time to shape up."

"Get out!" Maureen yelled, throwing her lamp at the door.

"When you're done cleaning that up, you can go down and clean up the kitchen floor," her father said. "Good night."

And in the morning, Maureen did pick up the shards. The cane went into her locker until after lunch, when she got tired. And though Maureen threw her binders against the wall or sat staring at the ceiling and refusing to do anything that required lifting a pencil, Lauren the tutor refused to give up either.

During midterms, Maureen sweated through two layers as she took her exams in a quiet room with her aide. She passed algebra with a C. She got an A in English and Bs in history and biology.

One night Steve Collins knocked, unannounced, at the door. After making sure she was dressed and didn't have spaghetti sauce on her face, Maureen answered. The doctor leaned against the door frame. "Maureen?" he gasped. "They told me, but I had to see for myself."

"What?" she asked. She remembered this voice but had never seen this face.

"I'm Dr. Collins. I worked on you that night in the ED."

"Well, hi. I guess I owe you thanks," Maureen said. "So, thanks. I'm semifreezing. Cold. Mold. Cold. Chills. Sorry. You can come in. My mom is just upstairs folding laundry."

"This is amazing," Dr. Collins said, stomping the dusting of new snow off his shoes.

"What?"

"You're like it never happened."

Maureen said, "Uh, no. You'd have to look inside. I got a mercy C in algebra."

"Maureen," said Dr. Collins. "No one as sick as you ever comes back this far. Lots of kids don't even pass algebra with all their cognitive faculties intact." He paused. "Can I see your mom?"

Maureen called; and Jeannie came tripping downstairs,

217

trying to poke her flat hair into some sort of order.

"Hi," she said. "Long time no see. We go to the hospital once a week still, but they're telling us she's on her own after the first of the year. . . ."

"She's amazing," Dr. Collins said.

"We think she is."

"Lots of luck here."

"Lots of hard work," Jeannie told him. "She fought."

"Would you mind . . . do you have a job?" Dr. Collins asked Maureen.

"Yes, I am a ballerina," Maureen joked. "No. It takes all I have just to keep up with my school and piano. I go out one night a week."

"You play piano?"

"A lot of people play piano," said Maureen. "I didn't. I don't. I didn't. Don't. I don't play very well."

"Actually, she does," her mother put in.

"We have a series at the hospital, of inspirational speakers. I don't know what they pay. Maybe two thousand? Three thousand? Would you be interested in speaking for us sometime?"

"No," Maureen said. "No thank you."

"Yes, she would," Jeannie said.

"When you guys decide, call me," Dr. Collins told them, holding out a card. "I am so pleased and happy to see you, Maureen." He glanced across the street. "How are they doing?"

"Well, better," said Jeannie, her chin lifting as she lied.

"It's taking Kitt a while. But I see them going out now, more often. The girls are doing well. Bill and Mike talk."

"Please give them my regards," Dr. Collins said.

"I will," said Jeannie. In fact, each time she spoke to Kitt, Kitt seemed frightened of her, as though she wanted to run back into the closed, dark confines of her beautiful tomb.

Later, as they were doing her exercises, Maureen slammed her leg down and said, "I am not giving a speech."

Jeannie pushed the leg back up and said, "Yes you are. It's time you did something."

Maureen said, "Something? What do you think every day is like for me, Mom? I'm not doing a speech! It could be for a million dollars and I wouldn't do it."

"You're scared then," Jeannine said, helping Maureen stretch her other leg. "I get it."

"You think? Wouldn't you be?"

"You don't think you owe it to Bridget and Danny and yourself, and Lorelei and Shannon and Dr. Park and other kids like you."

"Good grief. Goody. Good guilt, Mom. But that would still be a no."

That day, puzzling over whether or not to take Dr. Collins up on his offer, Maureen walked away from the toaster oven. The kitchen cabinets were scorched by the time she turned back, the smoke alarm screaming.

But nobody got mad at her.

Nobody got mad at her when the dog walked through the open paint she left on the floor when she tried to paint over the scorched places on the cabinets.

Everyone understood. She did owe them something.

On January 30, with her parents, brothers, Danny, Molly, Britney, Leland, and Lily-the-Goth in the hospital auditorium, Maureen told her story simply and sweetly. She had written everything on cards and rehearsed in front of the mirror until the words were like low fences she could clear easily. She described her outbursts of temper, her shame at wetting herself in church, her tantrums, her baby steps toward normality, her agonized loneliness for Bridget. She told the truth. She didn't leave out the ugliness and the pain, the endless hours of squeezing the slingshot until the night—just two months previously—she felt the two handles click together for the first time.

"I stand here because I was loved," she said. "I am not a hero. The doctors are heroes. The nurses are more heroes." A ripple of laughter widened in the room. Lorelei felt her eyes well up. "But I owed it to my parents to be as good as I could be. I left this place thinking I would never walk unaided again, or live alone or go to school. And I will do those things. I wanted to give up. I can't tell you the times I told my parents I hated them for pushing me. But they never felt sorry for me or themselves. My boyfriend and my friends didn't feel sorry for me. And so how could I?"

After she finished, Maureen sat down at the grand piano

on the stage.

She had never touched such a beautiful instrument. But she was able to play "Clair de Lune," the simple version, as she'd practiced, with only two mistakes.

The check was for four thousand dollars.

After she hugged Lorelei and Dr. Park and Dr. Daater—she remembered nothing of any of them except Lorelei's red hair—she handed the check to Bill, sure he would give it back. Instead, her father smiled and thanked her. Miffed, Maureen kept Danny out past one that night and got both of them grounded for the weekend.

The next morning Bill and Jeannie walked her to the door, each holding one of her elbows, insisting she keep her eyes squeezed shut.

It was a Honda, a cute little silver box with four-wheel drive and an upgraded stereo that Tommy had installed. Maureen's jaw dropped.

"And you just paid it off," Bill told her, "with your speech. Now I guess you've got to get your adaptive license and learn how to use those hand controls. The seat belts work great."

She hugged them, trying to disregard the voices in her head that told her, *No, no, no, never, never drive again!*

But it wasn't until *This Story, This Week* called and asked to do a documentary on her recovery that Maureen realized how bad life could really be for a girl with a cute boyfriend and a new car.

The story aired on the first anniversary of the day Maureen awakened, February 23.

The next morning Maureen found the tires on her car slashed and all the windows smashed.

No one on the street had heard a thing.

# stone tears

At Bill's request there was no investigation, except the one required for the insurance. Kitt Flannery hinted—to almost anyone who would listen—that she had done the damage herself. When friends mentioned it to Bill, he simply shook his head and said he was sure it had been kids from another town.

The little silver car was repaired. It looked pristine. But privately, Bill was angry that it wasn't "new" anymore—even when Maureen joked that it was now a repair job, as she was.

Jeannie had other fears.

When Maureen triumphantly passed her adaptive driver's test, which included a grueling interview and a long written exam, on the second try, Jeannie refused to let her drive alone. Maureen threw a fit, this time impulsively throwing all her shoes down the stairs like a seven-year-old. The display only sealed Jeannie's resolve. Maury was better, but her judgment was to be trusted even less than that of most seventeen-year-olds. Maureen had no memory of ever having driven. She might take chances, despite her history. She might miss cues from other drivers or panic if she saw snow. Finally, grudgingly, Maury had to hand over her keys to Jeannie.

"Indulge me," Jeannie said. "I'm a poor old mom who almost lost her baby chick."

"Now that I want to do it, you won't let me!" Maureen snapped.

It wasn't just fear of other drivers and road conditions, or even Maureen's perforated consciousness, that plucked at Jeannie's nerves.

To Jeannie's shock, it became clear to her at church that the Flannerys weren't the only people in town who thought it was in poor taste to let the story about Maury's recovery be aired on the anniversary of the day they learned that it was Bridget who had died in the accident. But she and Bill hadn't chosen the date. It was the anniversary of Maureen's rebirth as well!

"Let's just say that some people think it wasn't really fair to put the Flannerys through that," Kathy Bohack told Jeannie one day during coffee hour.

"Through that! We . . . we're just proud of Maureen, and

we didn't go to the show! They came to us! She's worked hard, Kathy," Jeannie objected. "I thought her speech was sweet and inspiring to other kids who suffer losses in their lives." Part of a video recording of Maureen's speech had been played on the show.

"I wasn't the one who said it was wrong," Kathy answered. "I know how hard she has worked. But, Jeannie, I do see the Flannerys' point. That was the anniversary of their learning of their child's death, and you let it be a celebration of Maury instead. I don't know that I wouldn't have been hurt. The whole town saw that show."

Jeannie relented. She spent fifteen minutes the next afternoon knocking on the Flannerys' door and finally left a note of apology, explaining their ignorance of the show's air date, and saying how much they still wished that Kitt and Mike would see them, how much they still missed Bridget.

The next day Jeannie found the card, trampled and torn, on her welcome mat. Farther down in the yard, someone had dumped bags of garbage and slit them open. Sauce and bones and crusts of bread splashed over the previously unblemished snow.

Jeannie didn't try to approach the Flannerys again.

But she did notice the looks, and heard the comments that might have seemed complimentary if not for the thorn in them: "Quite a star, your girl, eh?" "Nothing but the best for Maureen, hey . . . Hard to imagine it was just a year ago, must seem like yesterday to Kitt and Mike." "I think it was wonderful you let her go on that show. I just wouldn't want to put my child out there in front of so many people that way."

It was in March, during a thaw, that Maureen finally begged and teased enough that her parents allowed her to take her first solo drive.

In fact, Jeannie wasn't the only one who was afraid. Maureen had begged to drive alone only because she felt she needed to get out there now or she never would. But she was terrified. After repeated nightmares, she spoke over the phone to the hospital therapist. She told him that she dreamed of driving off a bridge and drowning, of forgetting where the hand-operated controls were on the car, of being stuck on tracks with the lights of a train bearing down on her, of spinning around and around on ice until she careened off a cliff.

Understandable, the therapist told her. Perfectly appropriate anxiety dreams. After all, she was setting sail in the very ship that almost destroyed her. Getting back on the horse. Getting back on a ship after having sailed on the *Titanic.* If she was anything but anxious, she'd be insane. If the dreams didn't taper off after driving became second nature, she would need more sessions. He advised Maureen to keep her first forays predictable, well planned, and brief.

And so Maureen did that.

She printed out MapGo directions that would take her

to two places: Apple Creek Mall, where she was to meet Danny after morning practice on Saturday to help him buy a new suit for the wrestling banquet.

And Bridget's grave.

The flowers she bought were daisies. But she tied them with one of the silver wires from her prom corsage—extracting it carefully from her memory book. At the cemetery, Maureen knelt to pray. It wasn't a formal prayer; it was more a conversation with Bridget about Danny and about how she hoped that Bridget was happy for them and not jealous.

Then she heard something behind her.

A voice, almost a growl, asked, "What are you doing here, Miss Goody-Goody?"

Maureen didn't open her eyes.

"Kitt," she said. "Please don't hurt me. I'm here because I loved Bridget."

"That's crap," Kitt said.

What she actually said sounded like what Maureen used to hear on tape recordings of her own voice when she was learning to talk again: "Thassss crap."

Maureen could smell her now—a hot tang of cigarette smoke and something else, overlaid with way too much cologne.

"I'll go. I'm sorry."

"Why haven't you come over to see us?"

"I didn't think you wanted me to."

"No, you were scared to. Scared!"

"I didn't think you wanted me to." Maureen opened her eyes. In a white tracksuit that dragged in the mud, Kitt stood with her legs planted, behind the headstone.

"Did you think we didn't want you to because you got hold of Danny Carmody? Because Bridget died and he had to settle for second best? Do you think he really cares about you? Or that it's just easy for him, and everyone thinks he's a big hero for taking you out in public?"

Holding on to the edge of the monument for support, Maureen began to pull herself to her feet. Kitt slapped her hands.

"Don't you touch that!"

Maureen dropped back onto her knees.

"Are you supposed to get some kind of award just for living? A new car? Maybe a scholarship? You and your Holy Roller parents? Do you know what people say about you, Maureen? Do you really want to know?"

"No," Maureen said, reaching for her cane and standing up. Kitt's face was terrifying. Her skin hung over bones that jutted out beneath her enormous, wild eyes. She looked not just old, but like a victim of a fire. Her tan was grotesque, unhealthy. Maureen began slowly to back toward her car. It was only ten feet to the gravel road. Her cell phone was in the pocket of her jeans. Should she call 911? "I don't want to know. I just want to leave."

"They say that you're a pig for sleeping with Danny. Oh, everybody knows. Don't you think he tells everyone? He jokes about it. They say you tried to have sex with the mailman. They say you lied about Bridget in your big speech at the hospital and made yourself sound like a big hero. And they hate you for it. Why were you so weak? Why didn't you drive your own car? Why didn't you just stay dead?"

"I'm so sorry," said Maureen. She tried to run for her car but stumbled and fell. Kitt loomed over her, quick as a cat, grabbing the back of her hair.

"You stay here and listen to me! You should be dead. You shouldn't be in school. You disgust people. The sight of you disgusts me. You couldn't be Bridget in a million years! The sight of Danny coming to your house disgusts me!"

"So move!" Maureen shouted. Finally angry, she struggled to her feet again. "Move! We haven't done anything wrong. You trashed my car! You threw garbage on our lawn. You're the one who's craze. Daisy. Daisy. Crazy!"

"Blub blib blug blig blah blah. Bridget put up with you because you always did what she wanted. Do you know that? You were the only one who always, always did what she wanted. You're not fit to stand in the same room."

Maureen reached out and pushed, firmly but gently, to get Kitt out of the way. Kitt stumbled, and Maureen made a last desperate push to reach the car.

She clicked the button on her car door and got in before Kitt could catch her. She locked the door; and when Kitt spat on the windshield, she turned on the washers. When Kitt stood in front of the car, she started the engine, then, using the hand brakes, she drove carefully around her.

When Maureen got out to the main road, she was crying

so hard that she needed to pull over. She thought of calling her father, but she didn't want trouble with Mr. Flannery. So she called Danny instead. He told her to wait for him, that he would come to get her. Maureen told him no: She couldn't wait for him. Kitt might come out of the cemetery and try to do something really nuts, like push her off the road. Slowly, so slowly that she got stopped by a county police officer for driving thirty miles per hour in a fifty-mile-per-hour zone, Maureen made her way home.

Danny was in the driveway.

Maureen crumpled in his arms.

"I have to get out of her. Hear. Here," she said.

"Don't let her scare you. It's depression or whatever. She's out of her mind."

"If half of what she said is true, if people think that . . . you feel sorry for me . . ." Maureen hiccupped and gasped. "And that I tried to sex. Sex. Have sex with the Martian. The mailman . . . and that you laugh at me behind my back . . ."

"No one thinks that. How could you believe that?" Danny said, but he couldn't help but wonder how many people laughed at him.

"But they are mad about you and me."

"Some are," said Danny, and he shrugged. "Do you care?"

"Sort of. Everyone thought you and Bridget were the perfect couple. Danny, there's a . . . I'm never going to think of the word . . . that goes with going out with a girl people think is retarded."

"Stigma," he said. "It's their problem."

"Not if it lasts forever!" Maureen cried. "Not if people think it as long as you're together!"

Neither of them noticed the squad car that slid silently up to the curb. Henry Colette got out, rubbed his hands together as if to wash them, and approached Danny and Maureen.

"Hi Dan," he said. "Good morning, honey."

"Hi," said Maureen, quickly using the heels of her palms to wipe away her tears and streaks of makeup. "My dad's inside, Mr. Colette."

"Okay." But Colette stood there. "Let's go inside and talk to him. Dan, this concerns Maureen."

"What's wrong?"

"Maybe nothing," said Colette. "Maybe nothing at all."

"Maury, do you want me to come in?"

"Is it okay if he comes in, Mr. Colette?"

"Ah, I'd rather he stay outside, or come back a little later."

Defiantly, Danny kissed Maureen and said, "I'll pick you up in an hour. We'll still go to the mall." As he got into his car and slammed the door, Colette smiled.

"He's a good boy."

"Yes. He's a nice boy," Maureen agreed. "Why? What? What are? What do you are want? I'm sorry. I'm all upset."

"I see that. Let's get your pop."

Bill and Jeannie were sitting down to lunch with Patrick when Maureen opened the door. Henry Colette stepped in behind her.

231

"Henry?" Bill said, half rising from his chair.

"She's not hurt. Even a little," said Colette. "A little dirty maybe."

"What happened?" Jeannie asked, automatically starting a pot of coffee, as if her hands required her to offer something. "Did you fall, Maury?"

"I tripped in the cemetery," Maureen told them.

"Your neighbor across the way has filed a complaint against Maureen, saying she tried to strike her with her cane at the cemetery," Colette said. He pulled up one of the side chairs and sat down. Maury sat on the bench near the telephone. Her parents had one of the only wall telephones still in existence.

"What happened, Maureen?"

"I was putting flowers at Bridges. On Bridges. At. At. At," Maureen said helplessly.

"Slow down," Patrick told her.

"Kitt pulled my hair. She called me names. She slapped my hands, and she tried to stop me from getting in my car."

"Did you hit her with the cane?" asked Colette.

"No! I tried to push her aside. Gently," said Maureen. "So I could get to my car. She was screen. She was scream. She was screaming at me. About Danny and Bridget and saying I was a . . . pit. A pin. Pin. Pig."

"Huh," said Henry. "Do you think you could just talk about this with them, Bill?"

"Hank, we've tried. Jeannie and I. Kitt's not herself," Bill said politely.

232

"Well, how are we going to deal with this?"

"My daughter isn't violent, Hank."

Colette said, "I heard her myself tell a whole crowd when she gave that speech that she threw her books and broke plates and yelled at her parents. Heard her on TV, too."

"That's because of her brain injury. You don't think . . ."

"Mrs. Flannery said she was knocked down. Hurt her arm and her back."

"She's a drunk, Hank," Bill said. "She drinks all day long. Not that I blame her. There were times when I thought Maureen was gone that I could have gone that way myself, if I were a drinking man. The truth is, that woman hates Maureen because she is alive and Bridget isn't. Maureen spent more than half her life in that house, Hank. You can see why Maureen just living drives her out of her mind. Kitt doesn't come outside now except to get a new bottle or go to the grave. You ask anyone. My daughter's a child. You're saying she assaulted a grown woman and beat her with a cane?"

"No, I don't think that, Bill. But I have a problem. People have seen Maury lose her temper. Kitt says all she did was ask her not to leave metal on the grave . . ."

"Metal?" Maureen asked.

"She said you had metal . . ."

"A silver wire from my prom corsage. I wrapped flowers in it! For Bridget! You can look. . ."

Colette continued, "Then she said you took a swing at her. She has a big bruise on her arm."

233

"She fell! She was drunk! You could smell it!" Maureen told him. "She tried to hurt me! Why don't you believe me? My blood? Blame? Brain? My brain?"

"Hank, please keep this out of the papers," Jeannie pleaded.

"Too late. They'll be calling," Colette said. "She's already called up Jerry Russo at the *Beacon* and raised a big stink about Maury being dangerous. Now, I've told him that he dare not write a word about a minor like Maureen when no charges have been filed. But she's only seventeen, Bill. Eventually she'll be an adult under the law. She is now, for most purposes. I got Jerry to back off for now, but I don't know that he'll back off for good unless we figure out a way to handle this. I'm sure I don't want it to turn into a 'she said, she said' thing and neither do you. I want to go fishing next month, Bill, not mess with this. But Mike Flannery is all up in arms. Says Maury's a danger to his children."

"Damn it, Hank. That woman took a bat to Maureen's car the day after she got it. You know she did. I didn't say a thing. She left a letter Jeannie wrote her torn up with mud all over it on our mat. Our steps were deliberately iced back at Christmas." Bill got up and threw down his sandwich. "I'll go talk to Mike myself."

Colette said, "Well, it can't hurt. But I'll go with you."

When they returned an hour later, Danny had joined Jeannie and Patrick at the table, but no one had eaten another bite.

"Well," Bill told them. "She agreed not to press charges if you stay a hundred yards away from Sarah and Eliza at all times and if . . . and if . . . if you don't drive."

"Let her press charges then," Patrick said. "She has no right to take Maury's life away."

"It will be her word against Maureen's. If this gets into the papers . . . I told her you . . . I said you wouldn't drive until next summer."

"Daddy!" Maureen shouted. "That's wrong!"

"It's all wrong, but it's better than you being examined by a court-appointed psychologist, Maureen! Maybe getting your license taken away! Kitt told me to my face, 'That girl is promiscuous. That girl is dangerous. That girl shouldn't be out alone.' If she's told me, she's told others. When I went over there, she didn't smell of booze. She was all dressed up in a pink skirt and blouse with her arm in a sling!"

"I'll drive you around," Danny said helplessly.

"That's not the point," Maureen told him. "It's my car! I earned it! I love my car! I want to be like everyone else!" Maureen cried. But the downcast eyes around the table told her she had lost this battle. She scampered up the stairs. Danny got no answer when he knocked at her bedroom door. In the end, he went to buy his suit alone.

That night Danny's father asked him into his den for a closed-door talk. Surrounded by Danny's, Dave Jr.'s, and Dennis's sports trophies, he laid down the law. This was enough. Danny was not going to forfeit his future for some foolish small-town scandal. If his feelings for the girl were strong, they would survive.

"Survive what?" Danny asked, terrified that his father had found a way to send him to military school or something.

His mother came into the room. She nodded as his father told him he was going to Sky, Montana, for the rest of second semester. He would live with his uncle, his father's brother, who had two boys, one a year older than Danny, one a year younger. He'd work on his uncle and aunt's ranch; and if he wanted to play baseball in the spring out there, he could play.

"What about Maureen?" Danny asked.

"She has plenty on her plate," his mother said. "Kitt Flannery is saying terrible things about Maureen. Now, I'm not saying that they are true; but I'm not having you be part of a huge scandal, Danny. I'm not having our family made to look foolish. I agree with your father. It's a break; that's all. You've done your season. And if it's real, it will last."

"The semester is half over!" Danny said.

"Your uncle talked to a counselor in Sky. The credits will transfer back."

His father told Danny he was leaving in three days. His mother had already started packing.

"This is ridiculous. It's bogus and you know it," Danny told both of them. They didn't blink an eye.

The next night when he told Maureen, she began to cry and, of course, blamed herself. Exhausted, Danny tried to bolster her confidence. He suddenly felt as though he'd done nothing else for his whole life.

"Now I've lost my car and you, and everything," she said. "People in town think I'm crazy and a slut . . . and practically everyone wants you to stop seeking me," Maureen told him as they lay in the basement at Evan's house. She sighed. "I mean they want you to stop seeing me. I'm so sick and tired of correcting myself. I've probably said twice the number of words I intended to ever say in my entire life."

"I told them nothing would do that. But they want me to look at the college out there, which I do want to do. Or the college wants to look at me. In Montana. My uncle's going to make sure I go over to look at Colorado at spring break. So it's not all a loss."

"Just for me," Maureen said. "You're not even coming back for spring break?"

"They say they can't afford it," Danny said murderously.

"You could drive," Maureen said.

"But if I did, I'd have, like, two days here."

"I know," Maureen said, resigned.

"Well, at least you have your music, and you could get a job," Danny suggested. "You have Molly and school."

"You don't even care!"

"I do," Danny said, and kissed her nose and eyes. "It's only three months till summer."

But in fact, he was weary, tired of fighting his parents day and night over something he could not explain and they could not understand. It was so much worse since the underwear and TV show incidents. He was sick of gossip. He almost looked forward to being away from the constant tension, from Maureen's fragility. He thought of riding his uncle's horses and skiing his uncle's hills, and it didn't sound all bad. A break, that was all. Like his mom said. He didn't think Maureen would go out on him. With a guilty gulp, he realized that he didn't think anyone would ask her.

But when he tried to look at her with unfamiliar eyes, he saw that she was beautiful. She was desirable again, even if she was still too skinny. And if he could get past those things about her that bothered other people, so could another guy.

Ev, for one, said that once you knew Maureen, you didn't even notice them anymore.

"I have something for you," Maury said.

"What?"

"Music," she said, handing him a CD.

"What's this?"

"Music to your song, that you wrote back then. I got a mike for my computer. Or, I'm sorry, there's a microphone in my computer."

"My one song. I was going to be the new Vince Gill. You remember that?"

"Funny, huh? I didn't remember. Didn't. Mine. Mine. My own. My father, but I remembered this."

. . .

All the way out to Montana on the plane, he listened to Maury's CD, to her pure, high voice singing, "I won't be the one who goes. You will. / Your hand will crush the sweetest rose. You will. / Your heart is restless and it shows, and everybody knows. / You will, you know you will."

And Danny thought, *This makes no sense.*

# parting

After the one-two punch of Kitt's attack in the cemetery and the abrupt loss of Danny, Maury would gladly have spent the rest of the school year in bed.

As much as she wanted to deny it, Kitt's words in the cemetery sounded a cruel, hollow gong of unwelcome truth. She knew that what Kitt said about her was only what other people thought.

Maureen would always be an object of pity and suspicion.

A weirdo.

On display.

The killer crip, who should have driven her own car and killed her own stupid self instead of her best friend.

Why would Danny's parents want him to be with her? Whose parents ever would?

If she got married, she'd forget to turn off the gas and blow up at her husband, or go off on him for getting the wrong kind of bagels. She'd done it to her mother! How could she be sure if she had a baby that she wouldn't forget and leave it outside in the rain? Danny understood. No one else ever would.

Who knew how long he would be gone? What if he had to stay for the summer? How many girls would he meet—girls who didn't need a cane and didn't show up at school wearing one blue shoe and one black shoe? Sure, he had turned to her in the terrible days after Bridget died. But out there? With new people to meet who might think Minnesota was actually interesting because they'd never been there? Who wouldn't start over?

But she soldiered her way through the days until spring break. "It's like some horrible Romeo-and-Juliet thing," Molly said one night when she and Britney dropped over to play the cheer squad's new dance music for Maureen. A big competition was coming up, and Eddy had hopes that Taylor had improved enough as a tumbler that Bigelow could at least place in the top three. The girls were only trying to make her feel part of them. Maureen knew that, and clapped and smiled when they showed her pieces of the complex dance. It was torture, though. She could still feel the dance moves in her legs, legs too watery and weak to obey her. "It's not like you won't wait for him. You

241

totally love him. But why do the Carmodys have to be such idiots?"

"It's not just him. We're seventeen. We're just kids," Maureen said. "We thought it was love because we went through so much together. But I don't know if it really was. And his parents obviously don't want him to be around a . . . well, a handicapped girl."

"You're not handicapped!" Britney squeaked. "You're only a little different! No one who didn't know you could tell!"

"Same distance," Maureen said.

"You mean, 'same difference,'" Britney went on.

"See?" Maureen asked with a shrug.

"Danny doesn't think like that. Danny thinks you're a goddess," Molly added.

"I'm so snot," Maureen said, and burst out laughing despite herself. "I mean, I'm so sure. My words have been mixing up much . . . much . . . mix much again more . . . again since he's been gone."

"It's so romantic," Britney said. "You're totally falling apart. He's probably up on a mountaintop right now, on his horse, thinking of you."

In fact, at that moment Danny was at the trail opening of the road to Wolf Face Mountain. But he was in the steamed-up cab of his cousin's truck with Lindy Lassiter, a leggy, red-haired senior. In Sky, the whole senior class was only twice as big as one of the English classes back home. Bigelow was a small town. But there were at least fifteen kids in a class. In Sky, kids came from eight ranches and two streets of houses plus the apartment where the Carson kids lived over the grocery store, there were only fifty seniors. Danny, a junior, was flattered. A senior with guys running after her from all over the county, Lindy played basketball. She was fully as tall as Danny and could beat him when they went running. Her hair fell to her waist in natural corkscrews like some rock singer, making her as hot as any girl he'd ever seen anywhere, including the Twin Cities. She had a complete crush on him, too. They worked out every day, and he went to see her in the play-offs when Sky's team won. They rode up to Grave Creek Ridge and hung out in a hunting cabin up there, drank beer, and danced to somebody's million-year-old CD player. Lindy was as wild as the Montana wind. And she was eighteen, almost nineteen. He could do whatever he wanted.

In the coyote-wild darkness with Lindy—his shirt off and Lindy's bra unhooked—it was hard to hold back. But Danny did. The thought of Maureen, so trusting, so completely his, held him back when he was with Lindy.

Until he could tell Maureen that they had to stop seeing each other—and he didn't know if he would ever want to do that—he couldn't hook up with anyone else.

They went out for two months. Eventually, Lindy sent him a note saying she was going to start seeing a guy Danny knew slightly, a senior who was going to Texas on a basketball ride. "Life's short," she wrote. "You're one sexy guy, Dan. But I'm moving on, because I can tell when a guy doesn't have his mind on me."

Danny didn't know whether to be angry or relieved.

When Maureen didn't hear from Danny, she didn't know if she'd been dumped or was being mourned.

She was being mourned.

Danny tried hard not to think about her. Everything was easier when he didn't. Lindy had been a major distraction. He could have fun, goof around, stare at girls, flirt, play ball, and play cowboy. When he was alone at night in his bed, though, he remembered Maureen's sweet, pale body on the night of the prom, and those few other times when they'd really been together. It made him sick to think of her with someone else, now that he was over thinking no one else would want her. Evan was right. . . . It wasn't a turnoff if you knew her.

Maureen lay awake and tried to picture Danny's face just before he kissed her. She thought she would go out of what little mind she had left.

Jeannie could see that the progress Maury made was withering. The pain of continued loss was too much.

"It's like I am being punished for living," Maureen told Jeannie.

Jeannie held Maury against her shoulder. "I'm going to tell you something you don't want to hear. This is the price you pay for living, Maury. Bridget got away easily. I don't mean that her parents did. But you went on living with the suffering and loss; and she went on to our Lord, where there are no problems and memories of grief. Life is much harder. You have to pray for the strength, because no one is going to give it to you on a plate."

"I wish they would," said Maury.

Jeannie didn't answer. But she knew she had to get Maury out, back into the community so she could see that she wasn't universally despised. She had to get her back into life without Danny's arm to shield her. Jeannie and the rest of the O'Malleys weren't about to give up Maureen's progress to a depression. Without her, the O'Malleys held a family meeting when the boys were home from spring break.

It was Patrick who first drove Maureen to the community pool. Though she swam weekly against the current at the therapy pool, Maureen hadn't been to the town pool, with its big roll-back top, since the summer before last. Patrick had to threaten to carry her into the building. The Bigelow swim team was practicing, and Maureen did not want them to see her.

"I am not walking out onto that deck with that cane," Maureen told him. "I look like Queen Elizabeth. I'd rather crawl."

"Then crawl," he said. "You're never going to build up that right leg unless you use it hard, Maury. I'm not saying you'll be a ballerina. But you could lose that cane and just have a limp. And lots of people have a little limp."

"I'm not going," Maureen said. Patrick pulled open the passenger-side door before she could lock it and took hold of her wrist. Finally, he picked her up and brought her inside.

Maureen didn't use her cane. Slowly, she all but slithered out onto the deck, step after tentative step. And when she was no more than a foot from the protective support of the pool ladder, she slipped and fell flat on her rear end. The glare she sent Patrick was tipped with a thousand poison arrows. He felt tears tickle his eyes as he looked away, determined, while Maury, in front of a dozen members of the boys' swim team—one of whom had the class to actually snicker—slowly got up to her knees and slipped into the warm pool. It was all Patrick could do not to rush to her and pick her up. But he made her drag herself into the water and use the paddleboard for a full half hour that night, until she was exhausted.

Within a few weeks she was doing the breaststroke—crookedly, but with all her might—and by the end of April, the sidestroke.

Soon Maury had real muscles—maybe not the rugged muscles of cheerleading, but real muscles, visible muscles.

One night when Patrick had to pick up a few things at the grocery and had dropped her off at the pool, Maureen pulled herself out after her laps and met Miss Bliss, the chubby lunch lady she and Bridge had conned out of Girl Scout cookies so long ago.

Miss Bliss was just about to get into the pool.

"I work here nights now, Maureen," Miss Bliss said. "I work in the back office. But a couple times a week, I come out here and do water aerobics to get rid of some of this fat." She slapped her big thigh. "The first time I had to

246

put on a bathing suit in front of Catherine Castellucci and some of my other neighbors, the lap swimmers, I wanted to die. But I had to, or die. You know, really die. Die young. Well, not young. But too young. And with a bad-looking body, too."

Not understanding, Maureen smiled. "Did you lose weight?" she asked.

"Twenty-six pounds so far," said Miss Bliss. "The thing is, I've been watching you, and here's the thing, I thought I was brave. But you put me to shame." She put her arms around Maureen and held her close. "Don't think that there aren't a lot of us in town just cheering for you."

"Thank you," Maureen said. "Miss Bliss, I feel like all everyone does is stare."

"They stare because they can't believe how much you can do. I promise. Not all of them are staring because they think you're weird. And the ones who are, well, to heck with them, right?"

Maureen couldn't really believe what Miss Bliss said, but she tried to.

Jeannie's next task was to get Maureen a job.

What could it be?

Maureen worked hours each night on homework she once breezed through. All she had time for afterward was piano practice and a round of phone calls before she crawled into bed exhausted. The things that had come easily to her brought her to tears when she simply could not remember how to do them—because she could remember the feeling of knowing how to do them. All the adaptations in the world would never make Maureen the math student she had been. Nothing would ever let her hope to study it in college—if she ever got to college.

Jeannie and Bill talked it over.

"Why doesn't she work at the country club on weekends?" Bill asked. "So many girls from the high school do."

"She can't stand that long, Bill. And she'd have them out of dinner plates after one sitting . . . wouldn't she? We've replaced six sets of dishes since last year."

Jeannie pondered.

Maureen needed something to do when she would otherwise be thinking about Danny. Or cheerleading. When she would be thinking about what was lost for now, or what was lost forever. Molly still came; but as spring days grew longer, she came less often. Maureen's friends were going to be seniors next year. They were all taking their ACTs. Those who had their eyes on the world outside Bigelow were starting to think about what they would do when they got there.

Jeannie worried that Maureen might never have such a life. Her daughter would certainly live on her own. She wasn't stupid. But could she go to college? Her memory had come as far as the rehab specialists believed that it would. Only with her tutor was she pulling Bs and Cs. Unless she found a specialized field, or gave up the love she had for math and science for art, design, or something else she could do with computers (because computers would func-

248

tion as her memory) she wouldn't be able to hack it at UM or even the community college. Jeannie wanted her daughter to start focusing more on what was possible instead of dwelling on what was not.

Finally, when decorating the altar at Holy Mother of Sorrows for Easter, removing the dark altar clothes and solemn draperies of Lent and banking the sanctuary with decks of vanilla-colored lilies and pale irises, Jeannie spoke with Janet English, her old school friend, and Betsy Lemon, another member of the Altar Society.

Betsy offered to line up a summer job for Maureen working with the older kids at Toddle Town, the preschool and summer day care. Jeannie didn't think that Maury had the patience or the strength to run after the babies. But then Janet English suggested that Maury might work at her sister Ruth's new bakery and craft shop, Crafty Crumpets. The grand opening was the Sunday after Easter.

"What if she spills something on somebody?" Jeannie asked Janet.

"We'll put her behind the counter making the drinks and getting the bakery goods frosted," Janet said. "It'll be good for her hands, and she can sit on a stool when she gets tired."

So, within weeks, Maury was spending all day Saturday and every other Friday night making quad, half-decaf, extra-tall, part-soy, no-foam gingerbread lattes with an extra cardboard sleeve. What her mother had hoped would help with her hand-eye coordination did even more: It taught Maureen to use memory tricks, such as matching the drinks that the "regulars" ordered to their appearance. For example, the extra-tall, no-foam gingerbread man was extra tall himself. Soon she no longer came home with drink orders scribbled on her forearms like temporary tattoos.

On some Friday nights, there were musicians, whom Maureen loved. That night, Crumpets had what they called a coffeehouse.

Evan and his friends, among others, came in on those nights to watch and flirted mildly with Maureen in her red pants and polo with her red-striped apron. Maureen bit back the urge to ask how much Evan had heard from Danny. All she got were one-line emails, signed with love but telling her that writing more would make it worse because he missed her too much already. There'd been one awkward phone call on the night of his birthday.

Then one night Evan and Slade Dinerson came in with a portable keyboard and a guitar case. It was open mike night; and Evan and Slade came on next to last, before Mrs. Rottier sang some horrible song about vegetables from *The Fantasticks*. The guys sang a couple of old Woody Guthrie songs, including one about California nights and stars that Maureen loved. And then they played an Ian Tyson song that Judy Collins sang—one Maureen's mother liked—about a young man who rode the rodeo. She caught herself singing along, "Someday soon, going with him . . ."

And she remembered how much she loved to sing, and about how silent her months had been since she and Danny had sung along with the radio through the long summer nights with the stars dancing above them like fireflies on strings.

She remembered that there was a boy somewhere riding a horse, and that she still loved him. She was being true to him, too, not that anyone else had broken down the door to ask her out. Someday soon, going with him . . .

The next time there was an open mike, Maureen shocked Evan by slipping off her apron and joining him and Slade for the old Stevie Nicks song "Landslide."

"I forgot that Danny told me you had pipes," Evan said with a really sweet smile. He told her that they ought to be a trio. She could get a couple of black nightgowns and be the Stevie Nicks of Bigelow, Minnesota.

But Maureen reminded him that she was the "coffee" in "coffeehouse" at the Crumpet.

In Sky, Montana, Danny was seeing a lot of sky.

Naturally, as the new kid in a small school, he had been an object of considerable interest to girls after Lindy went her own way. He thought he was ripped from wrestling, but he found out what sore really was working nights and weekends on his uncle's ranch. More and more, he was trying his best not to think of Lindy or Maureen or girls in general, not in that way. He was trying to be content to hang with groups of kids, and the occasional date he had was casual. One night as he was getting ready to meet a girl his cousin had fixed him up with, a text from Maury popped up on his phone, about singing at some café in town with

Slade Dinerson and Ev. Danny wanted to run every mile back to Bigelow. Then he thought that maybe he should grab this girl he was seeing tonight and send pictures to Maury of them making out.

She sounded so normal and breezy. She was so over him.

How could she be over him?

Danny rode. He cleaned tack and mucked the stalls and fed the freshening heifers. One night, he was with his uncle when twin calves were born—it was a miracle that both survived. That night Danny started to think his cousins had it made. They lived wild and free. Every corner of the ranch looked like some calendar picture, and it was all going to be theirs someday: His uncle had a good job down in Missoula, but he wanted to move his life to Sky forever once he got enough money. Year by year, he bought more land for the heifers. He had other plans, too. He wanted to raise horses, beautiful quarter horses like his big bay stallion, Turk. Pictures of the house that his uncle and aunt were going to build on the south ridge, just under the brow, looked like some massive hotel for skiers.

And a lodge, his uncle said, might come next.

If it did, he might want a guy like Danny around.

Danny started to think that hotel management might be something to study. Music might be just a hobby, like his dad always said. In Sky he got grades like he never got back home—he guessed it was because there were no distractions—and slept hard every night. Some nights when the sky was a riot of stars, he dreamed he might never go back. His cousins' tales of fly-fishing in the canyons at sunset made him wonder if staying through the summer wouldn't be so bad. Having his own horse, Soda Pop, to ride and herding the calves up to the spring pasture sure beat hauling sod for his dad and sucking up to the richies in The Corners while he planted their annuals and pulled their weeds. He missed his mom and Den and Dave; but he figured he would be leaving home in another year or so anyway, and this was what college would be like. He told his parents he'd like to spend the summer in Sky. To his surprise—he knew his dad relied on him to work at the business—they agreed.

Finally, it was June. The term ended in Montana before it did in Minnesota. It was time to go home to see his senior teammates graduate.

He'd see Maureen.

He'd be home for three full weeks.

For two days before he left Sky, Danny couldn't sleep. He played out in his mind what he'd say when he saw her. He'd play it cool. He'd pick her up and swing her around. He'd call when he knew she was at school and leave a message.

But when Danny got home, even his parents weren't there. His brother picked him up from the airport, and he found a note saying that they couldn't wait to see him. There were sandwiches and cake in the refrigerator; but his aunt Laura, his dad's sister, had picked this Saturday of all days to up and marry the guy she'd been dating for years. She'd given them exactly one day's notice. Even Dave Jr. and Den weren't invited. His parents would be home by nine at the latest. They were so sorry . . . blah blah.

Danny was in the house, alone.

Could he bring Maureen here?

Why did he think she'd even want to come?

He could barely remember her cell number, but he pushed the buttons. It went right over to voice mail.

Danny tried to lie down on his own soft bed. It felt like a veritable cloud after the thin mattress in the bunkhouse, but it might have been a gravel road for how comfortable he could get. Danny tossed and turned and finally gave up on a nap. He got in his car, which Den had started religiously every week while Danny was away, and drove past the O'Malleys'; but no one was home. He saw the curtains twitch at the Flannerys'; but everything was quiet over there, too. He drove on to the school and walked in through the gym entrance. Decorations were already up for graduation. But he could hear the cheerleaders in the side gym.

It would be fun to surprise Brit and Molly.

When he walked in, though, it was Maureen he saw, Maureen without her cane, clapping out the rhythms of "Hey, hey, hey, talk that ball away. Go, go, go, Bulldogs from Bigelow . . ." Her hair was longer, pulled back in a band; and she was wearing khaki shorts and a couple of those strappy things girls wore one over the other. She'd put on weight. She looked beautiful, already cocoa dipped by the sun. Danny didn't recognize the girls learning the cheer until he spotted the youngest Hillier girl. These must be eighth graders, getting ready to try out for junior varsity.

He thought of Bridget at the top of a cheer pyramid, suspended high on the Smith sisters' shoulders, her beautiful leg extended alongside her head, her toe a perfect point. For a moment his head shimmered with all he had lost. In the vision, the faces of the two girls he loved slid back and forth, morphing into and out of each other—Bridget and Maureen, Maureen and Bridget.

But this was now. This was his Maureen.

What was Maureen doing?

"Come on now!" she told the younger girls. "Let's practice some jumps! What's more important? Enthusiasm or perfection?"

"Enthusiasm!" the little girls called. They looked so very little and young.

"That's right!" Maureen called. "It's spirit! It's the big give-it-all-you've-got! Perfection comes after you do something a hundred times. Let's start with some stretches. Down for three sets of leg lifts in a straddle. Hands behind you on the floor. Now lift, lift, lift! Yeah, I know it hurts! Point your toes, Corey! That's it. Stretch! Legs straight! You can't throw a jump if you're going to pull a muscle. . . . I used to do it all the time. "

Moments passed before each of the girls, one by one, noticed him and, self-consciously, stopped what they were doing. Maureen whirled.

Then she was in his arms and his mouth was on her

mouth; and for both of them, it was like a cold drink after a long hike.

Hours later, as they left Danny's darkened house, after he'd scribbled a note for his parents telling them he was going out with some friends for a pizza, she put her hand on his arm.

"I've had a good time since you were gone," she said. "I worked hard."

Danny could still smell her cologne, the Irish cologne he had given her before he left, on his skin. He stepped back.

"I . . . I had a good time, too. Sky is great. My uncle's great," he said.

"But this is what I want to tell you. I don't care if you love me," she said. "I love you. And if it's not going to last, that doesn't mean I don't love you now."

Danny could breathe again. He said, "I was going to say it if you didn't."

And they had a whole week until his dad found out that he was with Maury again.

Danny had to admit to Maureen that he'd agreed to go back to Montana for the summer.

"How could you?" she asked him, through tears.

"I didn't know I'd feel the same," he said. "I didn't think you'd feel the same, to tell you the truth."

"Can't you get out of it?"

Danny argued with his father. He offered to work six days instead of his usual four at Green with Envy.

His dad was unmoved. "It was your idea, son," he said. "Your uncle created a job for you. That's how it is."

Danny had no arguments left. He held Maureen close the following night, as they lay on a blanket at the ski lodge.

"I can't ask you to wait all summer," he said. "I'll understand if you don't want to."

"And you'll want me to understand if you don't," Maury said bitterly.

"I love you, Maury," Danny said.

"I love you, but what does that mean?" she answered.

When Danny left the second time, Maureen thought that if she didn't give him up—really give him up, with all her heart—she would go out of her mind.

And so she wrote him a letter.

> *Dear Danny,*
>
> *If someone can break up with someone by saying she loves him too much to stay together, that's what I'm doing. I care too much about you to make you wait for me, or for me to wait for you. If I do, it's going to be all I think about. It's going to be no life for me except wondering when the next time you'll call me will be, or if they'll ever let you come home. You're going to college out west after next year anyhow. We'd be apart no matter what we felt. And so, I'm going to tell you that it's never going to be over in my heart, but it has to be over for now. You'll be my*

*friend. You'll be my first love. I'll never forget.*
*But all our loving each other has brought you is*
*trouble. And I have to face school and the world*
*on my own, without Danny Carmody to stick*
*up for me. When you come back, I don't know*
*how you'll feel, or how I will. But you'll always*
*be my Danny.*

    *Love,*
    *Maureen*

She waited until she was sure, and then sent it.

June slipped away. Maureen checked the mail every day, and no answer came. Then she began to count the days until school began.

# *two again*

To be safe, Maureen took the bus to school the last week in August.

She felt like a complete fool, with middle-schoolers whacking one another on the head with their binders and mooshing their faces flat against the back windows. Tucking in the ear buds of her iPod—purchased with her earnings at the Crumpet over the summer—she stretched out her legs and tried to doze. Inevitably, she thought of Danny, although she tried to pay attention to the lyrics of the songs.

Danny had come home two weeks before. He didn't call the first day. The next day he did, and was eager to see her. But when they'd finally hugged, they both felt awkward and broke away. They ended up going to a funny movie and studying each other secretly. The letter Maureen had written back in June sat between them like an open question neither of them wanted to answer.

Danny didn't know if she wanted him back, or if he wanted to go through what getting back with her would mean.

Maury didn't know if she wanted him back for nine months, just to lose him later.

Danny was taller and leaner and tanned. But he also had a changed spirit. He seemed to approach things in general more casually, as if content to let life unfold slowly.

Maureen looked different too. And the change was more than physical. Maureen's mother once told her that a month in the life of a teenager is a year in the life of an adult. It was true.

She'd spent the summer serving lattes and muffins at the Crumpet and occasionally visiting the lake cabin up north that Molly's parents owned, flirting with boys at the music camp across the bay. She'd swum every day and had felt herself getting stronger and more coordinated. The pool sessions had definitely made a big difference; and she had written Pat to tell him so and to thank him. She had made tapes of herself talking and played them back, and learned that if she simply spoke more slowly, she didn't have so much trouble with the words. She'd let her hair grow. With her mother, she'd sewn new clothes that didn't scream "handmade."

Danny had spent the same time chasing calves and

sleeping in a barnlike bunkhouse with his two cousins and the rest of the men at his uncle's hobby ranch. After several days of soaking his legs in a stream because of the sores he'd gotten sitting five hours at a stretch in a saddle, he got used to riding and loved it. He drank beer and smoked cigars with the cowboys, who came from Missouri and New England and Mexico. After he had gotten Maureen's letter, Danny had nearly fallen for a dark-haired girl—Marianna, the daughter of the rancher down the road. She was strong and curvy, as strapping as Maureen was tiny, and rode up to the house on her big Morgan, never bothering with a saddle. They had come close to it one night, high up in a mountain meadow.

But Danny had drawn back, again thinking that he and Maureen deserved another chance.

And anyhow, if he got a scholarship to Missoula, Marianna would still be there.

Danny had sent Maury one card.

She had sent him a card, too—a funny one—for his birthday.

When he came home, he knew he was changed; and though Bigelow was not, Maureen seemed changed, too.

She didn't use her cane anymore, except for long walks. And her arms were buff with muscle, her shoulders wider from daily lap swimming.

She was no longer Danny's broken angel.

He was no longer her devoted protector and constant companion.

And so they circled each other for the early weeks of school.

Their first dates were with groups of friends, and Maureen apparently was happy with that. Keeping it light seemed to be what she wanted. That was fine with him . . . well, actually it wasn't, but Danny was too proud to say.

October came, and homecoming.

They went together, but in a group. Danny brought Maureen flowers; but after a huge pizza meal, they didn't pair off to be alone. Maureen went home with Molly for a sleepover.

Neither brought up the fact that they'd done no more than kiss since school started.

Although Danny wanted to be with her—no candle had winked out, in his mind or his belly—he wasn't sure he could handle such an intense bond. He wasn't sure anymore what he meant by "love." The more he thought about it, that past closeness seemed like something they had needed then but not something they could easily resume now.

And Maureen was so busy it wouldn't have been possible to spend much time together anyway.

She was taking piano, and now voice lessons twice a week, and working Saturdays at the Crumpet; so their times together were few. Ev had dated Britney Broussard for about two weeks, until he realized that if they hung out, he would never be allowed to speak a full sentence again. So he went back to being the all-around flirt. Molly had been with Brandon Hillier since the middle of the summer. Maureen and Danny were absorbed into the usual rumble-tumble of a loud gang of couple-friends—no longer the intense and isolated pair they were before. Part of it was due to Maureen's recovery. Now she could go easily with Danny to watch Evan play fall soccer, and to the homecoming bonfire. With what probably had been a massive effort on her part, she'd overcome her naturally shy nature and the compound effects of her brain injury. Once withdrawn and clinging to his arm, she now drifted among the others, joking and teasing. No one in their group brought up the accident. No one treated her as if she were breakable. He noticed that she'd grown adept at turning attention away from that.

One night, lying in his bed with the warm October breeze stirring, Danny took stock: Maureen was just a girl again—a girl who struggled in math and needed help writing and organizing her English essays—but where she once had been Bridget's little water carrier, now she and Molly were equals in their growing friendship. When she went to the Apple Creek Mall, it was with Molly; and Maureen drove. Molly stayed over; and, now, Maureen often slept over with Molly or Britney. She went to cheerleading practice sometimes and watched, a sweet, ironic smile on her face. She continued to help train the junior varsity squad and had learned to enjoy working with the younger girls. It was almost like cheering herself. Sometimes when Danny called, she wasn't home; and Jeannie didn't know when she'd be back.

Most nights she texted Danny before she went to bed, but sometimes she didn't. She still grinned so that her whole face bloomed whenever she saw him, but that eager grin no longer was for him alone. He saw other guys looking at her, and he minded, but did he mind enough to make a stand?

Did she need him anymore?

Was that what he wanted, for her to need him?

Had he rushed into his thing with Maureen without ever having finished grieving for Bridget? Obviously. But was being with Maureen his way of grieving for Bridget? And why did Bridge seem such a distant, distant part of his past?

He didn't have ready answers.

A mile away, Maureen was sifting through the same sort of thoughts.

There was no doubt about how much she had missed Danny.

But why?

She had helped Danny through the most difficult part of his life to this point, helped him face a grief he would always remember.

He had helped her, literally, to come back to life.

There would always be a bond between them, but she honestly did not want her first love to be the only love she ever knew.

She honestly didn't want that.

She was sure.

What they'd done was crazy—now that she looked back at it. They'd had—what? Over a year together? A long time, but how much of it was just him helping her?

On top of that, both sets of parents seemed so happy with the new tone in Maureen and Danny's relationship. Why kick over the gates and start up what would be a touch-and-go relationship at best if they weren't sure how much they loved each other?

No one in the O'Malley household talked about the last, awful incident in the cemetery with Kitt. But Bill still thought about it; and when he did, he boiled.

Apparently, Kitt Flannery had been hospitalized during the summer. She emerged looking much like her old self—refreshed, stronger, active in the business. She and Mike had taken up golf; and their friends from The Corners, where Dr. Collins and his wife lived, came to their house for dinner parties. Beyond the Colettes, the Carmodys, and a few other scattered families in the parish whom Kitt had told, no one had any idea of what had happened the previous winter. Kitt had become an active church member. Though she did not speak to the O'Malleys, she smiled at their house in a distracted way and raised a hand when she pulled out of her driveway—in her new BMW that matched Mike's in every way except that Kitt's was crystal blue.

Bill snarled every time he saw Kitt's car, thinking of Maury's silver Honda, slashed and broken.

He thought of both of Maury's cars.

And then he repented. Kitt and Mike had lost a daughter. What was the ache of a neighborhood range war that would fade with time compared with the lifelong agony of that grief?

"Forget it, Daddy," Maureen told him when she saw him staring at Kitt's Euro taillights disappearing around the corner.

And Maureen tried to follow her own advice. But when she woke from dreams that left her sweating and panting, they weren't about her accident but about that day in the cemetery. It was then that Maureen hardened her resolve to make her way back into the sweet anonymity of her town's life. She saw that the passage was clear but fragile. She walked it carefully.

Maureen was grateful that her disability no longer was the hub of her family's life, or the first thing people thought of when they saw her. She was glad to see her brothers and parents easing back into taking her for granted. As wrestling season approached, Bill grew more and more excited. Some of his best wrestlers, his hand-reared boys, were seniors this year. Amber Kresky's young husband, Mitch, who had finished his degree and now taught social studies at the middle school, was Bill's new assistant. Coach had a state champion for his team to model.

When Sarah and Eliza Flannery sang the national anthem at the first football game, with Kitt and Mike beaming in the stands, Mr. Calabretti, the choirmaster, was all over Sarah in minutes. Although freshmen usually didn't sing in the concert choir, Sarah was recruited. Her strong alto would make a lovely counterpoint to what Mr. Calabretti considered a squeaking nest of sopranos. Sarah, everyone admitted, had an exceptional voice.

Maury hadn't planned on going back to choir. She had planned to take art, to improve her hand-eye coordination, but missed choir too much. Before the two-week drop period was up, she dropped art and Mr. Calabretti enthusiastically welcomed Maury back.

She was tentative, but her lessons had helped her get rid of some Minnesota nasality and had actually broadened and deepened her range. There was the added power of knowing she could read music now too. But beyond that, singing had helped her measure and modulate her speaking. Danny walked her to the choir room the first day because she had an eleventh-hour fit of nerves. It wasn't until she'd taken her customary place in the first row with the first sopranos that Maureen spotted Sarah.

She almost ducked out of the room.

She almost smiled and waved.

She did neither. She stood flat-footed while Sarah stared at her.

Mr. Calabretti, in his doltish way, said, "Well, you two are neighbors, so you must already know each other . . . ," and then proudly introduced the choir's only freshman member to the rest of the group. Everyone clapped politely, although from high above in the risers with the guy tenors, Evan kept shooting Maureen worried looks.

That first week the teacher assigned solos for the Christmas concert—which was still called exactly that, instead of the "winter" concert, because no one in Bigelow celebrated Hanukkah, the solstice, or Kwanzaa. One selection was the ancient "Coventry Carol." Sarah was assigned the first solo. And because the song, in Mr. Calabretti's arrangement, proceeded into higher ranges, Maureen was assigned the third.

She almost refused.

But she stopped when she heard Sarah's muffled snicker.

"Thanks," Maureen said loudly. "I'd like that."

And then she wanted to run to Danny. But she'd heard Danny was spending time with Emily Hay, a fellow senior, who'd come back from vacation with physical attributes she seemed to have purchased from a hot-girl shop in Southern California. So Maureen cried into her pillow one night until she fell asleep and told herself that this was all in the nature of growing up.

Which was, in her case especially, better than the alternative.

That Saturday she drove to Danny's house. Sitting in the car, she planned carefully what she wanted to say. Her feelings for him were probably more complex than the feelings she had for anyone else. And yet, perhaps because of that, she thought it must be right that she see other people for a while. She had no idea what she'd answer if he said they were already doing that.

They would part when he went to college anyhow. Molly would be gone, too. Silently Maury cursed the time she'd lost to her recovery that left her only a junior now, when her former classmates were seniors.

When Danny stuck his head in at the passenger-side window, she was concentrating so hard that she gave out a sharp little scream.

"Hey, since when am I that scary?" he said. He sat down in the car, smelling oniony from his five-mile weight-cutting run, and turned up the high beams on his smile. "To what do I owe the honor? You've been avoiding me lately."

"You're seeing Emily Hay."

"Get to the point, why don't you? And I am not," Danny said, but he blushed. He wasn't seeing Emily Hay. He had kept her crushed against the side of the greenhouse for a half-hour makeout session just two nights ago. Since then he had been able to think about no one but Maureen. Seeing her car parked in front of his house, exhausted as he was, he had broken into a sprint. "We just hung around."

"Hung around or got together?"

"I kissed her," Danny admitted.

"And that's why I came," Maureen told him, biting her lip so hard that she tasted blood. "I was thinking, we shouldn't feel like we can't see other people. We had a time when we needed each other. . . ."

Danny felt as though the seat were sinking, but he nodded and said, "Makes sense."

"And it ended up causing everybody to go crazy. I mean our parents and stuff. So, I was thinking, Danny; you know I'll always be there if you want to talk or you need me. But as for the rest of it . . ."

"You'd like to try to be with somebody else."

"No!" Maureen said. The tears at the corners of her eyes spilled over. "Actually, I thought I'd go back to thinking of myself as not ready for that. I want to start thinking that . . . that's for when I'm older. I'd never do that with anyone . . . with anyone I didn't . . ."

"What?" Danny pressed her.

"With anyone but you. Okay? No, I didn't meant that. I don't know what I mean. Now, please, get out of my car and let's end this as friends."

"That works for me," Danny told her, giving her a quick peck.

It didn't work for him.

Now that it was real, it completely didn't work for him.

What the hell was he saying?

All he wanted was to feel her heart beating, fluttering against his chest; for her to marvel at his biceps; for her to guess the tune while he strummed the guitar and start to sing the words.

He was getting out of the car. She was starting the engine.

"Have a good one!" he called.

She gave him a cheerful wave.

He went into the house, got into the shower, and turned it on so hot that he wanted to scream.

She went for a swim at the indoor pool. Her face was wet and nobody noticed. It would have been wet anyway.

Neither of them slept that night until the moon set.

The Christmas concert was on Bridget's birthday, December 10. When Mr. Calabretti introduced the "Coventry Carol," he said it was a lullaby and that Sarah Flannery had asked that it be dedicated to the memory of her sister Bridget.

Maury felt her throat close.

The song was short.

By the time Sarah had sung the first few measures, Carolyn Tiske was up. Maureen was walking down the risers to the mike. At the last moment, she looked up at Evan and gave her head the slightest shake. As if it were planned, Ev stepped down and stood beside her. When she began to sing, he improvised the harmony so that instead of a hideous botch, they ended sounding bittersweet and perfect.

Before Mr. Calabretti led them into "Sleigh Ride," he said, "For Bridget. We all miss you."

And at last they were filing off the stage to their parents's applause. Maureen took a deep breath—another disaster averted. Then a low voice at her shoulder said, "Killer."

She turned slightly to see Sarah, her hazel eyes pits of pure hatred.

"What?" Maureen asked. Little Sarah. Sarah who had played with her and Bridget's pom-poms and said she wanted to be a cheerleader when she grew up. The first time Maureen had seen Sarah was in a baby pack on Kitt's shoulders.

"You heard me," said this new, grown Sarah. "Why did you let her drive your wreck of a car? My mother's right. You should be dead, not my sister."

"Your mother doesn't really think that. It was when she had problems, Sarah. Stop," Maureen begged. The rest of the choir members had drifted away, pulling off their robes to return them to the massive closets, rushing out for cookies and hugs. Maureen was uncomfortably aware that she and Sarah were alone in the long hall. This could not be happening. "Sarah, she offered. Sarah, she offered to drive because my leg was hurt. It was nobody's fault."

"It was your fault, Muh . . . muh . . . muh . . . Maureen," Sarah said. "You think someone's always going to rescue you, the way Evan did just now. But it's not like that. You know, I think about my sister every day. . . . I miss my big sister every day."

"And so do I."

"Oh, sure! I'm sure you thought about her when you were on your personal TV special!"

"That's so over, Sarah. This is over. It was nobody's fault." Maureen said, but her mind prodded: Say it. Bridget crossed over the line. You can't pretend forever that it didn't happen.

"It will never be over for us."

"You have to go on living."

"You did. You got her boyfriend. You got her friends.

Molly and Bridget were this close, Muh-muh . . . Maureen."

"Don't do that. Don't make fun of me. You're just a kid."

"What? Was? Where? What?" Sarah mocked her.

"Girls, stop chattering! Time to put the robes away," Mr. Calabretti called.

Maureen slipped her robe over her head, arranging the cowl in back the way Mr. Calabretti insisted they do. She said, "Stop this. We both have to go to school here. And Danny and I aren't together anymore."

"Are you surprised about that? Did you think he would stay with you? Did you think he wanted skanky-girl germs?"

"She used to say that," Maureen said softly.

"What?"

"She used to say, 'Skanky-girl alarm!' Your sister. She could be one of the sweetest and one of the meanest people I ever knew. Except she was never mean to me. She was so brave and tough and beautiful, and she picked me when she could have had anybody else for a friend. And I wanted to keep it that way. I would do anything she said just so she didn't turn on me. . . . She wanted to get home that night. Home to Danny. They were going to be apart for a week. Your family was going to Disney World. Remember? Bridget had no patience. She said that I'd drive like an old grandma, especially with a pulled muscle. She wanted to drive faster."

"Stop it! How can you say that!"

"She thought she was so much better than everyone else, and that's because she *was* so much better than anyone else. No one wanted to cross her. She lived in the nicest house in town. She had clothes the rest of us only saw in magazines. Everyone wanted to be with Bridget. Your mother is like that. She shines like a diamond. But she cuts like one, too, Sarah. Don't you be that way."

"Thanks for the advice. I'm so sure I'm going to take it. Maybe I can end up living with my mama and dada for the rest of my life in my teeny-weeny little poor people's house. . . ."

"Bridget crossed the yellow line, Sarah." Sarah stopped in the act of zipping up her robe. *Oh please, no. What had she said? She had said it.*

"Say that again."

"No, I won't," Maureen answered, rushing now, dropping her robe on its hanger, struggling to pick it up.

"Say it again!"

"No!"

"You said it was her fault! You said my sister drove over the line, and that's why she got killed. You don't know that."

"I've always known it. I never wanted to remember it or say . . . even say it." Maureen intended to say, *But I didn't mean that. I got angry and it slipped out.* Instead, she said, "It's true. You can't blame me forever. It was probably my fault for goofing around with her when she should have been paying attention to her driving. But Bridge drove over

274

the line and the truck hit us. I know because people saw the marks. The police report says it. I read it after I woke up. You know it, too. You have to stop looking for someone to blame. It was bad luck. I'm sure she couldn't even see the line in the snow. . . ."

Sarah reached up and clawed a line of welts along Maureen's cheek.

"That's from Bridget," she said. "I hope she haunts you."

Maureen was so shaken, she nearly wrapped her errant right foot around a pole making her way into the washroom. She ran brown paper towels under cold water and then pressed them to her face until the bleeding stopped.

Then she looked in the mirror. Her hair had grown back. Her scars didn't show on the outside.

She had survived, and dared to thrive.

And because of that she would always be a target as long as she lived in Bigelow.

At home, Maureen rummaged through her desk until she found the number of the Iowa Liberal Arts Academy in Fall Creek, Iowa, sent to her by Rosemary Bishop, the director of admissions. The following morning, from school, she phoned Miss Bishop—who was delighted to send Maureen forms for possible admission as a scholarship student. And would Maureen travel to ILAA or send a disc? A disc? They would need her to sing a traditional ballad, an up-tempo song but nothing from the pop charts; and she would also need to include a piano piece.

Maureen asked Evan if he would accompany her on a couple of songs she was recording. She told him it was for a joke gift. He agreed gladly, if he could take her out afterward to Tintoretti's in St. Paul. It was, he reminded her, their one-month anniversary of hanging out together.

Maureen began practicing Mozart.

# *far and away*

Evan and Maury had finished the recording in a booth Maureen rented for a half hour with her savings. She sang a song she'd found in an old book of solos, about a town called Mira, so small that everyone knew her name. And then she sang the song she knew from her mother's music box: "Love Makes the World Go Round." Maureen loved the way Jeannie used to sing along whenever she wound up the box. It was in the same old song book as the one about Mira.

"Should I do them again?" she asked Evan, who was folding up his portable keyboard.

"You didn't flub anything," he told her. "Why bother?"

He listened as Maureen played the *Moonlight Sonata*.

She played it twice, deleting the second attempt.

"I feel like I should use up the whole half hour," she said. "Anything you want to record?"

"Maury, what happened to your face?" Evan asked.

So her carefully applied cover-up did nothing to conceal Sarah's scratch marks. Maureen laughed and said she'd scraped her face on the sandpaper walls in the choir room—legendary for the number of girls' tights they'd ruined.

"Ouch," he said, reaching up to touch the scratches.

"Yeah, you know my right leg has a mind of its own sometimes," Maureen told him.

"Do you want to do something together for the school coffeehouse?" Evan asked, abruptly switching gears. "Because I was wondering. We sounded pretty good together up there . . . at the concert."

"I am your slave forever. You saved me."

"Then let's put together an act. Just two songs. We have two weeks. All kinds of people come. Not just trumpeters from the marching band."

Maureen looked up at Evan. He, too, had changed. He was no longer Danny's chubby, cuddly sidekick but a tall, slender, really kind of cute guy. No hard-core jock like Danny, though Evan golfed for fun and played wing on the soccer team—not well enough to be a star, but well enough. His family had recently moved to The Corners, where, he told people, he would walk downstairs to breakfast in his underwear and find golfers staring in the patio windows at him from the seventeenth green. He was funny and gentle. His aviators only made him look smart.

"Well, sure," she said. "What'll we sing?"

"So you know any Emmylou Harris? There's this old song my mom taught me about that old loving-you feeling. . . . You ever hear it?"

"I love her voice, but I don't know that one."

"I'll play you the CD."

They practiced together at Maureen's house the following night and then at Evan's on Saturday.

When he drove her home, Evan turned to face her and slipped off his glasses, hanging them over the rearview mirror. When he kissed her, she thought, *How nice, how nice to kiss a boy whose first touch doesn't tie you all up in knots.* She softened her lips and kissed him back.

"You're not my best friend's girl anymore," he said. It wasn't a question. "I don't want you to drop into someone else's lap before I get my chance."

"Cut it out."

"Maureen, I've been looking at you since middle school."

Maureen flipped her hair, which now hung below her chin, from side to side. She knew the effect it had.

"Cut it out. No one ever saw me. It was always Bridge."

"Some of us did," he said, and kissed her again, flicking the latch at the front of her seat so that it reclined. "We'll have to practice again tomorrow."

. . .

A crowd of guys from the team helped Danny lift the three bench seats into the smaller of his dad's two landscaping vans to head over to the basement of the Lutheran church for The Bulldog Café—somebody's adorable name for the annual coffeehouse, a talent show that was literally underground. The coffee was lousy; but the hot chocolate was decent, and welcome. Since no self-respecting guy from Minnesota would wear a parka unless it was below zero, all of them had on light denim jackets without gloves or hats and were freezing after jogging three blocks from the closest parking space.

Danny thought there must be a hundred kids crammed into the room.

There were a couple of acts that were hysterical unintentionally: Three girls in pink cowgirl hats sang a Tracy Huson song about having their hearts tied to the fence post like a runaway horse, and a guy with a blond beard who wore a black Rasta wig plunked out an old Bob Marley song. There were two that were hysterical intentionally: The Three Stooges doo-wop band and two guys who sang traditional surfing songs of Northern Minnesota ("If everybody had a gun rack / across the U.S.A., / then everybody'd be surfin' / the Minnesota way. / You'd see them wearin' their blaze orange, / through the woods all day. / Everybody'd be surfin' / the Minnesota way.").

And then Ev came out and sat down at the bench of the old grand piano. Evan's older sister Kate asked for the lights to be doused and turned on a spot they'd brought from home.

Danny didn't recognize Maureen. She wore a floor-length red dress slit up the side, and her hair was swept over one eye. Evan lifted her onto the top of the piano in a way that made Danny's stomach flip. She smiled at Evan. Then each sang longingly of how that old loving feeling came back every time the two of them saw each other again and then, together, how this was why it had taken "such a long time to say good-bye."

The audience clapped like they were bonkers. Guys whistled. Maury tossed back her hair. There was something calculated about that toss.

"We're going to sing one more thing," Maury said into the cordless mike. "And actually, we wrote this. It's called 'But Not That Way.'"

"You called me just to say good-bye," she began. "But I knew you'd already gone. / We just had nothing left to say. / You love me, but not that way. . . ."

Danny had a hard time finding her among the people crowded around her and Evan.

"That was really good," Danny said. To Evan, he nodded. "Bro."

"I didn't know you were here," Maureen said. "I thought you had a meet."

"This morning."

"Did you win?" she asked.

That was Maury. It was never about her.

"Yes, ma'am, with a pin in twelve seconds. And on points in the second match. A few fine gentlemen from a college or two wanted to have a chat!"

"Oh, Danny, good! You can major in prelaw or music and have your sport! Good!" She patted his arm.

She patted his arm.

She loved him . . . but not that way.

"We'll have cut our CD by then," Evan said, putting his arm around Maureen and nearly lifting her off her feet. "My little songbird."

"I have to get on out," Danny said. "Some guys came with me."

She had already turned back to the group around the piano.

At home, Danny lay staring at the clock. It was ten forty-five. A Saturday night. If he had to guess, Maureen and Evan were tangled up on Ev's basement sofa, the same one next to the heating pipe on which he and Evan used to eavesdrop on Kate making out with her boyfriends. What were they, in sixth grade then? Evan used to say, "I don't know what love is, but I know what it sounds like."

Danny threw himself out of bed and drove to Maureen's house. Patrick had put up so many chasing lights for Christmas that staring at them could give someone a migraine. On the roof was Coach's Santa Claus about to climb down the chimney. The light was on in the kitchen. Although he knew that Coach might be annoyed, he knocked on the door. Maureen answered, wearing a robe so white and spiky that it looked like a Hostess Sno-Ball.

"Hi," she said. "You want a grilled cheese?"

"Is Ev here?"

"You want Evan?"

"No."

"Because he had to go to his grandmother's at the crack of dawn. His parents made him come home early. He almost refused, because of our magnificent debut. . . ." She struck a pose, with one arm on her hip, the other holding an imaginary cigarette holder. "But Kate told him their dad would go savage. They're having a big family reunion before Christmas."

"Who's down there? I'm not trying to heat the great outdoors," Coach yelled.

"It's Danny, Dad," Maureen called back.

"Hi, Dan," Coach called.

"Coach," Danny called.

"Either come in or out. I'm freezing up here," Bill called back.

They smelled burning.

"My grilled cheese!" Maureen shrieked, running to pull the smoking pan from the stove and throw it out the front door, where it quickly melted a ring of snow.

"People are trying to sleep!" Bill called again. "What, are you moving furniture now?"

"Close your door, Daddy," Maureen called back.

But Bill came downstairs. "She tell you about her news?" he asked with a broad smile.

Danny couldn't help but smile back. Coach had on the most bizarre set of flannels Danny had ever seen:

red devils and candy hearts that said KISS ME. Tops and bottoms.

Too late to retreat and put on a robe, Bill realized the error of his apparel and hid as much of his pajamas as possible by seating himself at the kitchen table.

"This girl has been invited to go to the Iowa Liberal Arts Academy, on a full ride," Bill said. "They want her to study vocal performance and music theory. How about that, Dan? It's one of the best boarding schools in the country. You ever think that that poor little busted-up thing in the hospital not so long ago would be asked to leave her old mom and dad and go to *prep* school? We're sure going to miss her though, huh?" He hugged Maureen tight against him. "I'll leave you two guys to talk. Night, Dan."

"See you, Coach," Danny said.

He thought he might fall down if he didn't sit.

"Is this true?" he whispered.

"It's true!" Maureen told him, twinkling. "I sent my application in a couple of weeks ago. I start January twelfth! They won . . . they waived the regular time period for acceptance because of my special circumstances." Maury made quote marks in the air with her fingers. "I got the scholarship for academics and, uh, because . . . I'm, well, handicapped."

"That's great," Danny said. A great hollow pit opened under his breastbone. He looked down. Maureen's Uggs sat next to the door, on the mat. "Let's take a ride. I'll buy you a grilled cheese."

"I'm in my pajamas! People will think I have a brain injury or something!"

"I'll buy it to go."

She shoved her feet into her boots, and they made their way down the steps to his car.

"Start it! I'm freezing!" she cried.

Danny reached in the backseat and gave her his blanket. "It's not a white tablecloth and candles, but it's clean." Maureen stroked the frayed ribbon edging.

"How could I ever forget?" she said softly. "Oh, Danny."

"So you're leaving us for the big city."

"Fall Creek, Iowa. Hardly. The nearest city is Dubuque! But it's a great school, and I'll never get another chance like this. You know they're never going to let me . . . live it down . . . here. In two days, it'll be the anniversary again, Danny. Sarah . . . Sarah Flannery practically jumped me in the hall after the Christmas concert. I guess I finally know the meaning of the old saying, Excuse me for living."

Her voice was soft and low, and she spoke clearly, measuring each word. Danny backed out of the driveway, glancing at the Flannerys' house, decked from eave to eave in lights like white chandeliers.

At Eva's Diner, Danny waited at the counter while someone whipped up a grilled cheese soaked in butter. Without any of the mannerisms food usually brought out in girls, Maureen devoured it to the last crumb.

"Yum," she said. "Thank you. What did you want anyhow?"

He kissed her salty mouth and pulled her to him so hard he thought he might crush something under her fuzzy robe. When he undid the tie, she let him, tugging his shirt loose and touching his chest. And then she breathed in sharply and sat back.

"We are . . . in the parking lot of a diner."

"There are places we can . . ."

"We're not together, Danny."

"That's just crap. You're my girl."

"Danny, it's not . . ."

"What, like your song? You want to be friends?"

"No. The opposite. I want this too much. Way too much. That's partly why I decided to go."

"Why?"

"Because we fell into this too soon! And we did it because we were both trying to replace something and somebody in our lives! That's not a way to make something work!" Maureen wrapped her robe around her and tied it tightly.

"It's not that way now," Danny argued. "It's not about Bridget!"

"When you came home before, it was all different. You were different. And now you just think you want me because you know I won't be here. I have to see if the rest of the world treats me the way Bigelow treats me. Sure, it's fine when I'm with Molly and Evan . . ."

"How much are you with Evan?"

"That's not the issue, and . . . not at all like us," she said firmly. "It's fine when I'm with people I know, but for everyone else I'm always going to be that girl. That girl who was supposed to be dead but wasn't. I want to be my own self! I want my parents to go on with their lives! I even want Bridget's parents to go on with their lives. Every day I remind them of what they lost!"

"You're going to let them run you out of your own home? You're going to leave me?"

"Danny, I don't want to leave you. But you're going to Montana! You're going to Colorado!"

"Not necessarily," he said. But he realized that what he had planned was to do just that—try out life in another place, counting on the fact that Maureen would be here, or at UM, waiting for him to come home for Christmas, for the summer, waiting for him unless he was drawn to someone new. She'd turned the tables on him. It was she who was leaving him before he ever got a chance to decide . . . if he wanted her.

He had believed she was his for the asking.

"So this is, like, it," he said.

"No. Maybe. I don't know," Maureen said. "If you want to know if I'll miss you, I'll miss you every day. I'll come home at spring break and in the summer. . . ."

"Big deal."

"You're right. Those things never work out," Maureen agreed. "Take me home now, Danny."

He did, getting out with her to make sure she negotiated the steps safely.

And when he turned to leave, it was Maureen who pulled

him to her, holding his face between her hands as if learning it by heart. "It was you who helped me get here, Danny. You told me that I could do this."

"I guess I dug my own hole," he said. "I hope you love it, Maury. I hope you knock 'em dead."

"I think my health issues were mostly why I got in," she said. "I don't think they expect me to be the next Julie Andrews. And don't act like it's the last time you'll see me. I'll come to see you wrestle at state. I'll be cheering for you."

"Will you write to me?"

"Do you think that's a good idea?" she asked.

"Probably not. It will just make it harder."

"Danny," she said. "I love you. I just wish it had always been me."

"Me, too. I hope I don't figure out it always was," he said. "Merry Christmas, Maury."

She stood in the doorway and watched until his car rounded the corner and disappeared.

# after life

The workload at Iowa Liberal Arts Academy made home-work at Bigelow look like making cupcakes in the sandbox.

Miss Bishop had made it clear right away that ILAA was not a "performing arts" school. It was a good college prep boarding school with opportunities to develop fine arts talent. But it wasn't a conservatory. Maury would be held to the highest standards of performance in her classes—even more so than in her singing. Singing was only an enrich-ment. Many of the kids at ILAA were planning careers as doctors or teachers or athletes. They simply also had a love of drawing or creative writing or music.

Maureen had lessons the first week with two different sopranos and then was assigned to one of them, a beautiful woman called—oddly enough—Melody. She studied with Melody for an hour twice a week. She was expected to practice voice for at least a half hour each night.

And then there were the academics.

History, math, HONORS English, ASL as a language, and her elective, Basic Acting.

She had two free tutors, both students from the college in Ames, to work with every night in the study center. She was never assigned exercises in acting that required her to run or leap. But nobody made concessions outside her special needs. They weren't that special. There were three kids at the school in wheelchairs who were doing fantastically—one majoring in violin performance.

So Maureen had to keep up somehow.

Biting the bullet, she realized that if she could play the piano, even with many mistakes, she could learn to touch-type properly. She did it with a little program her mother sent her in the mail, typing for hours on weekends with a towel over her hands on the keyboard so she couldn't see the letters.

After two weeks, she didn't need the towel anymore.

But she was still studying four hours a night, and sometimes just grabbed a sandwich in the cafeteria and went back to her dorm to work through dinner.

Her first exercises in typing had been emails to her folks—a line or two—and longer letters to Molly and Evan, and to Danny.

She missed him so much she thought it would make

her physically sick. Every night she allowed herself to take out and relive one of their moments together, turning the memories this way and that until, if they had been garments, they would have been soiled with fingerprints and tears. She could imagine the shape of Danny's hands, the smell of his hair.

> *Hi Champ*, she wrote. *Well, I am really being put in my place here. Obviously the teachers at B. were giving me pity grades, but no one is here. I'm so scared of the first-quarter exams. I know I'll flunk everything. Then I'll be back, ha ha, and you will get caught with Emily Hay. Seriously, I hope you are having fun with her and with everybody. I wrote to Molly, but she does not write back for days. I guess everyone's busy. It's beautiful here. The campus is right down by a little lake, and people go ice skating. Not me! Dad told me you finished with a first in state in our division! Danny! Why didn't you tell me? The scholarships must be lining up!*
> *Love,*
> *Maury*

She waited for a day, then two, then three, before she wrote again.

> *Did my email get to you? Because you didn't*

answer. It turns out that I'm really a cruddy singer. My coach, Melody, says we have to rip me apart and put me back together. I told her, Been there, done that. But she says I have so many bad habits, like puffing my lips out when I sing, that I have to learn all over again. Well, I'm good at that. The food is pretty basic here, so tell your mom any goodies will be greatly appreciated. My mom sent me some gingersnaps the other day. Hard as hockey pucks. She never was much of a baker, but your mom is a pro.

Love,

Maury

A day later she got an answer.

Great that you're having so much fun. Same old, same old here. I'll tell my mom to send you some cookies. Everybody says hi.

Your friend,

Danny Carmody

Your friend? Danny CARMODY?

Well, what had she expected?

He was either still mad at her for leaving or never cared at all.

When the brownies came, she gorged on a few, then shared the rest with her suite-mates. Four girls shared a common bathroom, and her roomies were merciless. When she took too long, they pounded on the door and told her to get her slow butt moving. All in all, that was good for her.

Just before the Valentine's Day dance, one of her suite-mates, a girl named Ali who'd become a friend, told her that Josh Jancy had a crush on her but didn't know if she had a heavy hometown honey. Of course, they all knew who she was, but no one made a big deal about it.

Aching for Danny, Maureen made it clear that she would happily accept Josh's invitation.

Josh Jancy stopped the next day after history and asked, "If I'm willing to wear a suit for you, will you forgive me for stepping on your feet?"

"I'm not much of a dancer," she told him nervously when he picked her up at her dorm, just across from the Great Hall.

"Most people just stand there and shuffle from foot to foot," he said. "When they start the fast songs, I sit down. So you're safe with me."

A week later, on Saturday night, Maury was surprised her gossamer prom dress still fit. Josh picked her up at eight at her dorm across from the Great Hall. "You can walk over, right?" he asked.

"You have to carry me, "Maureen answered.

They talked more than they danced. Josh was study-ing piano but didn't want to concertize—not that he was good enough. He wanted to get into a good school, such as Northwestern, and become some kind of interpreter. He was basically fluent in Spanish. Maureen began to wonder if she might be able to make a living signing, not singing. She had learned to sign in rehab, to help her communicate when she had trouble retrieving a word. There were all kinds of places that used people who could do simultaneous translation for the deaf—from churches to the theater. "I've always loved watching the interpreters," she said.

"I don't know," Josh said. "I've heard you sing. You might be able to do that if you could write songs."

"I have written a couple," she said, as he put his arms around her and they moved out onto the dance floor. Josh was so big and tall, much taller than Danny, that she practically felt lifted as they danced. They raced for the tables when the deejay began to spin R and B. "I can sing it, but I haven't got the moves," Maureen told Josh.

"Not everybody has to be able to dance," Josh told her. "Half the girls here just dance with their arms anyway. It's like they were cheerleaders."

"I was a cheerleader," Maureen said. "Before I got in a bad car accident."

Josh gave her a turned-down smile. "I know," he said. "We all know. You're some woman."

"Not so much," Maureen told him. "Anyhow, I didn't have a choice."

"Most people would have just curled up in a ball."

"I tried!" Maureen said. "They wouldn't let me."

But she still tired sooner than the others did. Josh walked her back to her dorm room before the event ended.

"Sorry," she told him. "I'm just not used to the grind here yet. It's a hard school!"

"Can I come in and talk for a while?" he asked. She knew he didn't mean talking, really, and felt a little thrill in her chest.

Both of them were flushed and sweating after half an hour of making out on her bed.

Finally she said, "You better get going before my room-mates come back. And, this is really as far as we should go."

"I didn't think you'd even let me kiss you. I know you're still all over your guy back home."

"He's not my guy," Maureen said. "We broke up before I left. Mutual."

"So I wasn't out of line," Josh said with a smile.

"Not at all."

"So if we go to brunch tomorrow, it'll be okay."

"Sure," Maureen said. At the door, she stood on her tip-toes—her right foot cooperating for the second it took—and gave him a kiss.

Then, without even bothering to take off her silver dress, she threw herself on the rumpled bed and thought, *At last. I'm over Danny.*

But she couldn't sleep. She tried drinking a glass of milk and eating a few saltines, then finishing her paper on Emerson. Still, she couldn't sleep. By the time Josh showed up tomorrow, she'd look as if she were forty. At last, she flipped open her laptop and scanned her emails. The usual greetings from Mom, who warned her to wear her boots with the treads on icy walks. A cheerful hello from Dad and a note from Jack, saying he was traveling to Spain with the soccer team at spring break. *Fabulous,* she wrote back. *We're all hitting the road!*

There was no word from Molly or Danny.

Although it was past one AM, Maureen tapped out a note to Molly, describing the dance and Josh, telling Molly she had become the biggest grind in the history of the world and that she was sure she'd be back in Bigelow by spring, having flunked out of this place.

To her shock, a message from Molly popped back up almost instantly.

> *Hey baby!* Molly wrote. *I'm so glad you're settling in. We miss you so much! We just got you back and you took off. But really, I am so happy for you. I'm trying to get my parents to let me drive there and pick you up for spring break—you would think it was France instead of one state south! It's really neat about the guy. I'm dating someone new, too. It's weird. Everybody in a small school seems to end up dating everyone else. Well, I got my acceptance letter back from UM! I'll be Nurse Molly in a few years! Got to crash now. . . . LUV U MOST!*

Before Molly could go off-line, Maureen typed, *A new guy? Tell, tell, tell! Now I know why you're so slow answering me!*

She thought Molly must have shut down and was about to do the same herself when a reply popped up.

*Actually, I'm dating Danny, Maury. I'm surprised he didn't tell you. It's totally nothing serious . . .*

Maureen couldn't bring herself to read the rest. She looked down at her dress, the dress she had worn on the night she and Danny . . . on the night she came back to life. Carefully, sure she would rip it to shreds if she let herself and then regret it later, Maureen got her dress into its garment bag and slipped into her pajama bottoms. In the drawer, she found Danny's old Bulldogs wrestling T-shirt and tenderly pulled it over her head. *I'm glad I loved him*, she thought. But suddenly her world seemed to have shrunk to the size of the room. Molly! How could Molly do this? But she was the one who'd left. Maybe Molly made Danny think of her—as she had once made him think of Bridget.

She was better off out of it.

But she messaged Josh, telling him that she had realized too late that she was too backed up on studying to go to brunch—how about next Sunday? When Ali knocked, Maureen said she had a stomachache and was going to sleep it off. After writing to Molly that she was happy for her and for Danny, Maureen lay down carefully on the bed.

This was as bad as it got, she thought.

It didn't get worse than this.

What her parents went through when they thought she was dead was worse; but for someone her age, this was major. If she could get through this, she would be fine. She would be fine.

Maureen slept for hours, then hopped into the shower and joined everyone for dinner.

A note from Danny was waiting for her when she got back to her room. A real, printed note, not an email. Her hands tingling, she opened it. A valentine.

On the front was a small boy offering half his candy bar to a little girl. On the inside, Danny had written, *"I said you'd be the one who goes. I guess you did. But there isn't a day goes by I don't think of you, and how proud I am of you. Maury, you were my first real love. Don't expect me to forget."*

Maureen almost tore the card in two—he would have written this days before Molly told her the truth. Then, instead, she placed it in her top drawer, beneath a stack of clean and folded shirts.

And she didn't hear from Molly again for a month.

The annual concert was to be held a day before the school closed for spring break. Molly wrote that her parents were being total idiots and would not let her come; but Maureen's parents surprised her by telling her they were coming to bring her home and to attend the concert, with Pat and Henry and even Rag Mop. The drive was not that long.

They would stop to see Grandma on the way.

So it was with longing and excitement that Maureen passed the week, taking her midterms, getting respectable Bs in everything but math, still passing that with a low C. She began practicing her solo. It was no honor. Every voice performance student had one. But her song was in Latin and not an easy one to learn, despite the many times she had heard it. Over and over, Melody told her, "Stop rushing! I want to hear reverence in your voice. This is a song of praise. Everyone knows it. So slow down and form each word."

Maury listened to the tapes of herself and then, with a backing tape Melody made for her, sang the song so many times that her suite-mates complained that it felt as if they were taking Communion.

She retreated then, tromping through a wet and unexpected snow, to the basement of the arts building, where it was possible to reserve one of the ten soundproof practice rooms.

Two days before the concert, on Melody's orders, she stopped singing altogether and simply spoke softly and drank cup after cup of tea.

She thought she would go mad with joy when she heard the plop of a snowball against her window and saw her brother Henry standing outside. As close as she could come to running, Maureen made it down the stairs and threw herself into four pairs of waiting arms. Rag Mop wiggled out of her mother's purse and, after polishing Maury's face, jumped down and raced around and around them in the snow. That night she stayed with her parents at a cozy bed-and-breakfast, sleeping on a roll-out sofa, sitting up late to talk to Jeannie—outlasting even her brothers.

"Mom, I know Danny is dating Molly," she said once Bill had turned in and they were alone.

"I thought you would. How do you feel?"

"I felt horrible at first. I couldn't eat. I never thought that Molly would betray me that way."

Jeannine asked, "Do you really feel that she betrayed you by dating a boy you broke up with? And is Molly really the one you should be angry with?"

"No," Maureen said honestly. "I don't think that. But I feel it. I'm not going to let it ruin my summer at home, though."

"So you've decided against the summer term? I'm so glad. That house is too quiet," Jeannie said.

Maureen fell silent. If she took a full load in summer term, she could go home for a few weeks but make up most of a whole semester and graduate only one semester behind her Bigelow classmates. She could start at the University of Wisconsin, her first choice, in the spring of next year.

"I'm not sure, Mom," she said. "It might be too painful for me back in Bigelow. Especially now. Speaking of that, are the Flannerys doing better?"

"Honey, a for sale sign went up in front of their house last week. They're not leaving Bigelow, but I gather the business is doing great and they're building a super mansion out at The Corners."

"Wow. Is that a relief for you?"

Jeannie sighed and nodded. "I'd like to look across at a friendly face, I have to admit it."

"So much has changed."

"That's the one constant of life," Jeannie told Maureen, stroking her daughter's hair.

It was nine at night when Danny Carmody turned to Evan Brock at Overture Cinema and said, "Road trip."

"Now?"

"Why not?"

"Where?"

"Iowa. Five hours by my calculations."

"You're nuts, brother. She doesn't want to see you . . . or me. And what's Miss Molly going to think?"

"All I want is to hear her sing. Coach says she has a solo at this rinky-dink school with a hundred students. I don't want her back. I don't even know if I want to talk to her. We'll stay one night and turn around. I'll drive most of the way."

"Gee, I always wanted to see Iowa in March," Evan said with a groan.

"I'll go myself then. I'm a free man, pushing eighteen. I can cross a state line."

"No way. Let's get some subs and clean drawers though."

They pulled into the Holiday Inn Express outside Fall Creek at three in the morning. The only room left had a single king-sized bed.

"I never thought of you this way," Evan told Danny as they sat down on opposite sides and chucked their shoes.

"Life's full of surprises," Danny told him, slapping Evan across the head with a pillow. He fell asleep as soon as he lay down, but not before thinking, *She's a mile away from me.*

The auditorium was already filled by the time he and Evan showed up. An irritated woman with the biggest boobs Danny had ever seen on anyone in real life shone a flash-light on their tickets and pointed them to seats in the first row of what she called "the loge" but which was a big cliff of seats that jutted out above the main floor. They could see Coach and the family in the third row down there.

"How'd you get these seats?" Evan asked.

"Called two weeks ago."

"So this wasn't really just on the spur of the moment."

"Kind of," Danny said. "I didn't think I'd have the nerve."

"So you bought twenty-five-dollar tickets. Two, no less. I think you take me for granted."

"Shut up. It's starting," Danny said.

They had to listen to people squall for what seemed liked years before Maureen, dressed in a long blue velvet dress, walked out onto the stage.

The music began, low and tender. A harp. A single flute. Maureen waited. Then she raised her face.

*"Ave Maria,"* Maureen sang. *"Gratia plena, / Maria, gratia plena . . ."*

How her voice had changed.

302

It had grown from a single-stemmed flower into a young tree.

Danny could still hear the voice he knew, but something richer and finer now trembled in its depths. He caught himself holding his breath for Maureen, willing her to reach for the higher notes. *"Ave Maria,"* she sang, *"Ave Maria . . ."* And then it was over. Maureen dropped her shining blond head and gently dipped one knee. He heard Jeannie's trademark whistle, but he was too stunned even to applaud. Another girl sang a song from *West Side Story*.

At the end, all of them joined hands onstage while the families stood and clapped for them. Maury was shorter than anyone else by six inches. She looked up as the lights came on, and he saw the smile drain away from her face. She had seen him.

Danny began to jostle his way to the exit.

Evan yelled after him, "Wait up! Idiot!"

"I'll get the car," Danny called back.

But when he emerged into the lobby, there she stood, at the foot of the staircase.

He had no choice.

When Jeannie and Bill, with the boys and Josh—whom they'd met that day at lunch—slipped past the other parents into the lobby, they saw Maureen in Danny's arms, kissing him as though his mouth held her own breath.

# a place for us

And then they were lost.

There was only waiting—for her visits on the weekends, for his visits to her, the hundreds of phone calls with bills that made the veins stand out in Bill's neck. He'd chosen the family plan.

After a week of sulking, Molly blogged on MyPlace that true love was a force too great for anything to overcome. She enjoyed a certain celebrity at school, being a part of the most romantic story any of them knew firsthand. Molly thought it was easily as good as a Nicholas Sparks book. Leland thought the crash added a lot to it. Molly thought Leland was morbid by nature.

Maureen announced that she had decided to come home

for the summer after all.

Jeannie announced that Maureen had already applied for and been granted her summer scholarship, and she was going to use it or answer to her father. One day in May Danny drove Maureen home for the confrontation. He had barely closed the door behind him when he heard Coach roar, "And I am telling you no, Missy! I will not have you end up pregnant! No! You've come too far for that."

"Dad, all it means is that it'll take me a year instead of a semester," Maureen pleaded. "I should work for the summer and pay you back for some of those phone bills. . . ."

"Don't hand me that, Maureen. I know exactly why you want to come back here. And it's fine. If it lasts for you two, it's fine. But no daughter of mine is going to get married out of high school."

"Like you did!"

Danny fled.

The next morning a chastened Maureen was sitting on her front porch when he pulled into the driveway.

"Does your dad have a shotgun in there?" Danny asked.

"No, it's the other way around. He'll shoot you if you want to marry me! I lost this round."

Danny took a short breath and sat down. Marriage? He loved Maureen. He knew he did. But marriage . . . that was a long way off.

"Not that I want to get married," Maureen said hurriedly. "I'm not saying that! God, Danny! You didn't think . . ." She began to laugh. "I might meet a millionaire! You might meet a senorita in Colorado. It's just that I'll miss you so much, honey. Eight weeks of summer term and then just two weeks and back at school."

"I'll have to really train, anyhow," Danny said. "I'm not exactly the top guy in my weight class in America. They're giving me a chance, not a promise."

"But we'll have holidays. We'll . . . I wish we could just promise to meet right here after graduation."

"I wish that, too, but you have to take your chances," Danny told her.

They drove downtown to the new café that had replaced the bacon-and-eggs joint where Danny had bought Maureen her grilled cheese sandwich. The lunch lady, Miss Bliss, was the manager of the new place. She enfolded Maureen in a huge hug and asked, "So, how's this new school? I heard from one of the ladies at church that it's all set up for kids like you."

"It's not just for kids who sing. It's a regular high school, just with dorms and that. . . ."

"I meant with special helpers and such," Miss Bliss said. "Kathy said it was the kind of place where a kid could get an education without having to compete so much."

Danny watched Maureen's face crumple and saw her chin begin to quiver. But she stood up straight and smiled at Miss Bliss. She said, "It's not a school for brain-injured kids. I'm the only one there who's brain injured. There are some kids who are disabled in different ways, and I have tutors to help me. And when I go to college . . ."

"College?" Miss Bliss asked.

"I'll always have to have special help . . . and adapting . . . adaptions . . . and . . ."

"I think that's wonderful!" Miss Bliss said. "Colleges are sure different now!"

"They have to be," Maureen said. "It's a law."

"We want to have lunch," Danny said.

But both of them only played with the club sandwiches they ordered, and finally they had them wrapped. Without speaking, they drove out County G and turned on Bellwether Road. Danny spread out the blanket.

"It's not exactly a white tablecloth and candles," he said.

Maureen looked down on Bridget's grave. The grass had grown in thickly, and someone had planted two pink rosebushes—at the head and foot of where Bridget lay.

"One for her and one for me," Maureen said. "Does Kitt still come every day?"

"I don't know," Danny told her. "I don't see them anymore. Sarah's fine. She's really grown up a lot. She actually told me to tell you that she was sorry."

"You know, I believe that. And I was scared to death of Kitt, but I don't really even blame her. Losing your child, especially that way . . . You'd lose your mind." She sat down awkwardly on the blanket. "I'm never going to be able to sit down right. And I'm never going to be able to live in my hometown, Danny."

"You mean Miss Bliss."

"It's going to shock people that I can have a job. It's going to shock people that I can have a baby."

Danny shrugged. He knew she was right.

"It's not the only town on Earth," he said.

"But it was mine," Maury answered.

He dropped her off early, planning to have dinner with his folks—who were tight-lipped about the whole Maureen matter—before he drove Maureen back to school. It was ten hours round trip, and he had school Monday. He would pick her up at nine the next morning and be home by nine Sunday night.


Just before he left, Danny opened his folder of college mail and extracted an envelope. He sat down at his desk and read the letter. Then he dialed a number.

In his home office, Ryan Ebberly, who coached varsity wrestling at the University of Wisconsin in Madison, just under a two-hour drive from Dubuque, sat back in his chair. He pushed up the brim of his cap with satisfaction. He called his assistant.

"Dan Carmody," he said. "The kid from Minnesota. Changed his mind. Got a full ride to Colorado, but he didn't sign yet."

"We knew he was going to Colorado. We filled that space," his assistant said.

"He's a good kid. A good student. He can wrestle for it. He's a tough kid. I want him here. Let's give him money."

"Dan Carmody. That's the kid . . . Remember that,

Coach? The little girl who was supposed to be alive except she really died? A few years ago? That was his girlfriend."

"Huh. So you're saying he might be screwed up," Ebberly said. "Well, I know Bill O'Malley coached him. I'll call Bill."

"That was the other girl," his assistant went on. "I remember it now. Bill O'Malley's daughter. She was mistaken for her friend. It was all over the TV. You remember that."

"Well, yeah, I do. How long ago was that?"

"Got me. Years."

Ebberly dialed Bill O'Malley. Was Bill at home? It was Sunday. Was it too early?

The phone rang just as Danny pressed the doorbell and beckoned Maureen out onto the porch. Bill watched them through the porch window. Yes, he told Ebberly. He couldn't recommend a boy more. Maureen threw her arms around Danny's neck. He lifted her off her feet. Yes, a solid wrestler, even-tempered, a team player, never a whine out of him.

"Congratulations," Bill told Ebberly. "He'll make you proud."

Bill shook his head. Well, there were worse things than finding the one you loved before you knew who you were. There were worse things than losing that love, too. All of it went into the folder labeled EXPERIENCE. They had raised Maury under their wing, but it was under their wing that she'd almost slipped away. If this was time for Maureen to find her true love, or her first heartbreak, Bill was fine in either case with that being Danny. Bill had lost her, and gotten her back.

Now he had to let her go.

Sarah Flannery waited on the steps for Shane Baker to pick her up. Shane was going to drive her to the cemetery. They'd just starting dating—even though she just turned fifteen. It was a special privilege because her parents knew the Bakers so well. When she saw Danny and Maury on the porch, she glanced away and then back.

She thought of how many times Maury talked Bridget into playing just one game of Monopoly Junior with her before they went out.

On an impulse, she waved.

Danny waved back. And after a moment, so did Maureen.

At the grave, Sarah tended the rosebushes she had planted this spring—an act of contrition—one for Bridget, one for Maureen. She snapped the blown blooms off above the three-leaf as her mother had taught her, then checked to see if the little scrap of silver wire was still tied around the branch of one of the bushes. It was.

Sarah had never removed it. As she had since the day that she'd planted the roses, she wondered what it was and who had put it there.

# acknowledgments

This is a work of fiction. Although at least two separate and heart-wrenching cases of mistaken identity after a motor vehicle accident have really happened over the past decade, there is no intentional similarity to the experiences of any actual family or individual.

Understanding the recovery process after brain injury is difficult even for researchers and clinicians. Although I know personally of only three cases in which individual progress after a significant brain injury was as rapid as it is for the survivor in this story, accounts similar to this one are uncommon in the literature of brain injury but by no means unknown. The way the brain responds to trauma and rehabilitation is intensely individual.

For their generous help in giving me the information that would help me even generally re-create the heroic efforts of men and women to save lives in a single hour, I must thank the physicians, social workers, chaplains, and rehabilitation specialists at the University of Wisconsin—Madison Hospital and Clinics in Madison and the Riley Hospital for Children and Methodist Hospital of Indianapolis—especially my friends and superlative physicians Dr. Bob Collins and Dr. Ann Collins. Thank you to my pals Holly, Maureen, Jane, Karen, Pamela, Sara, Joyce, and Mary, and to my husband and children, especially Martin and Dan, for their valuable suggestions. Lastly, but very importantly, I thank "my" cheerleaders, the cheerleaders of Oregon High School, who give their absolute best, always, as the status of their difficult sport changes over the generations. They and their supervisor shared openly with me their triumphs and sadnesses, making Maureen and Bridget real. As always, I am indebted to the staff and friends of the Ragdale Foundation in Lake Forest, Illinois, where this book was written in November 2006 and January 2007.